I0670085

CHAPTER 1

THE INITIAL ENCOUNTER

"You're in my city!" The notification from Sophisticated Beauty on Instagram flashed on Kunle's iPhone 11 Pro, as he checks for the location of his Uber while raising a hand for the check from his breakfast at The Oaklander Hotel, part of Autograph collection from Marriott.

First a frown, then a smile that lasted a little too long as Kunle opens his Instagram application. Before opening the message from Sophisticated Beauty, who's real name is Maria, he viewed his Instagram stories to see what he had posted the night before when he went out and had a few drinks with his colleagues and clients, a total of seven people. One post revealed that Kunle's night started off with drinks at a local watering hole where he had a glass of Jameson Black Barrel, but did not depict the diversity of the patrons which included a few engineers, consultants, lawyers, some enigmatic characters, graduate students (MBA, Law, and a couple of medical school students), and this group of kids in their early twenties who just twerked along to every song. Kunle remembered thinking, "I didn't know you can twerk to My Way by Aloe Blacc" and being genuinely intrigued. He also remembered his African American colleague, Travis, asking, "not your scene?" and Kunle responding, this is exactly my scene, with a perverted smile.

The next post showed him at dinner where he had the salmon with Brussel sprouts, but just him and only two other colleagues were present. The next post showed him and Travis at the hotel bar having a nightcap. Every single post included either the name of the bar, restaurant, or hotel. "Ready for the bill? Breakfast is included with your stay sir, thank you for being a platinum elite customer." Kunle looks up with a sense of pride and entitlement and says "thank you Sandy," as he slips her a $5 tip.

Travis came out of the elevator and saw Kunle waiting at the lobby and said "my bad man, my girl wouldn't get off the phone." All good bro, Uber is here." Kunle responded. They got in the Uber and after some chit chat, Kunle went back on Instagram and looked at his DM. He finally is caught up and can now respond to Maria.

"You're from Pittsburgh? How neat!" Kunle typed. "Where are some of the places I have to checkout?" Kunle, with a smile on his face, locks his phone and starts to discuss the details and agenda of their first client meeting of the day on the 30 minutes Uber ride.

Kunle: "We still don't have the final valuation from PwC, but I sent you the draft. Put it in the model as soon as it's available; knowing you, I don't think I'll have that many comments, if any. Send it and we can finalize the calculations. I completed the first draft of the memo, it's lit.

Travis: Got it boss. Weren't you a little tipsy last night? How did you finish the memo?

Kunle: Alex woke me up at 6 this morning and after she left, I wrapped it up.

Travis: Alex who?

Kunle: Oh my bad, the light skinned girl at the bar last night, she came over after you left and we had a couple of drinks, in my room.

Travis: My man, that's why I formally requested that you be my coach!

Kunle: Haha, let us just get past this 2 hour meeting first.

The Uber pulled up to the offices of Secongrada, Inc. and Kunle and Travis walked into the building. Kunle wearing a grey pinstripe suit from Hugo Boss, sky blue button up shirt, and tan shoes to match his tan belt; and Travis spotting a clean pair of black slacks, white shirt, and a grey sport coat; they both put their game faces on and disappeared into the lobby. The Uber driver, a retired engineer, looked on as he received a notification on his phone that Kunle tipped him 25% and thought to himself, "my man."

During lunch, Kunle looked at his phone and realized that Maria had responded to his message almost immediately.

Maria: There are a few hidden gems that you can't find on google, let me buy you a drink and I'll show you.

Kunle: I'd love that, but only if you wouldn't judge me for being boogie.

Maria: Haha, deal. I'm free after 7pm tonight. How long are you in town for?

Kunle: I'm free after 7pm too actually and I'm here till Friday; but I'm due back next week. However, if Pittsburgh proves to not be boring, I might just stay through the weekend.

Maria: You're staying at the Oaklander, correct? It's kinda all over your IG stories haha.

Kunle: Oh right, I love it there lol.

Maria: Perfect, I can pick you up at 7:10.

Kunle: Okay. Dress code?

Maria: I should be asking you, Mr. "boogie."

Kunle: Haha, I deserved that. Hmm, comfortable and relaxed. Think Saturday morning farmer's market run for someone who lives in the South.

Maria: You want me to dress like Meryl Streep in It's Complicated?

Kunle: No, more like Insecure Issa Rae, although It's Complicated is one of my favorite movies of all time.

Maria: Haha, I can definitely do that.

Kunle: Cool, I'll see you at 7:10.

After lunch, Kunle got off a call with his manager, Kevin, a cool 42 year old caucasian man from middle America; he made partner at the firm in his mid 30s. Sharp, witty, and a charming man. He was thanking Kunle for turning around the 200 page memo two weeks ahead of schedule. Kunle told him how he worked the past few weekends to get it done because he wanted to focus on his other client's disaster in the making that's slowly coming to light. He has a solution, but needs to do extensive research. All of this was BS because Kunle already figured it out and just wanted time to explore Pittsburgh on the client's expense account.

Back at his hotel, Kunle danced to sweet Soca music as he applied a little perfume to the inside of his wrists and behind each ear. He put on a red short sleeve shirt, a denim jeans, a navy blue sport jacket, and black Italian leather loafers. By 6:45 pm, he was in the bar upstairs having a glass of whiskey. Travis was already there, plugging away at the model, with a bottle of Voss water keeping him hydrated.

Travis: Heading out?

Kunle: Yea, meeting up with a friend that lives here (even though Kunle had never met Maria).

Travis: Nice.

Kunle: How's the model coming?

Travis: Bro, I'm frustrated man, my VLOOKUPs are not picking the right data.

Kunle: Try index and match.

Travis: I'm not 100% solid on that yet.

Kunle: Let me see (puts down his glass to write a formula; later glanced at his gold apple watch at the message that read, "I'm 5 mins out."). Here.

Travis: Holy crap, that's it?

Kunle: Something like that. Replicate that formula on the other tabs and you should be good!

Travis: You're the man. I've been trying to figure this out for the past 4 hours.

Kunle: It's okay bro, we've all been there haha. It took me a few times using it to get it down, so if you need additional tutorial, just send message me.

Travis: My girl is gonna call me in 2 minutes, I'm gonna take the call in my room, it's loud here.

Kunle: Cool, see you at 8 in the lobby tomorrow morning (as he responds to Maria and told her to valet park and come up to the bar for a drink).

Kunle sat outside on the blue couch on the balcony looking at the sunset, as Sweetest Taboo by Sade started to played in the background, and wishing he had a cigar to complete the moment. He looked inside through the glass wall and noticed Maria standing there looking lost. Kunle was shocked at her beauty. She was wearing denim jeans that she rolled up to her ankle revealing her 6" heels, that looked like they might not be comfortable, but she seems extremely relaxed and graceful. A light blue button up collared shirt to match her jeans, and her big curly hair looked like she has her own attitude and requires perfection. Kunle looked on as she reached for her phone to send him a "where are you?" text. She looked up and saw Kunle looking like a deer about to be run over by a Lexus Rx truck.

Kunle waved at her as he flashes a smile. She smiled back and blushed a little. The sunset behind Kunle, his choice of outfit, red shirt, blue blazer, denim jeans, and his stance (left hand in his pocket, right hand holding his whiskey with no ice, his locs [dreadlocks] neatly disorganized). Maria kept her eyes on him and his on her as she walked towards him, taking 3 left turns, to get to the balcony where he was holding the door for her. He reached out and gave her a firm but respectful hug; firm so she could feel his presence and leave an impression, she smelled his perfume and loved it, and he smelled her perfume and thought she smelled like daisies.

Kunle: You look lovely. Nah, you look fucking amazing!

Maria: (Blushing and smiling uncontrollably) Thank you.

Kunle: (Cutting her off) I meant to curse, but in a respectful way.

Maria: (Still blushing uncontrollably) It's okay, I'll allow it, this time.

Kunle: Drink? I'm drinking Jameson Black Barrel!

Maria: Already? Are you going to get all trashed on me?

Kunle: If I had a cigar, it'll take me 1 hour to finish this double shot.

Maria: I've always liked your style and how you just seem to enjoy your own company. I feel like you don't even need me, you're fine with your memories and Sade in the background. Not like I stalk you on Instagram or anything, you just seem...

Kunle: Are you kidding me? Your presence is going to elevate my experience here, probably redefine it. Did you see how I was looking at you like a puppy that's been missing his owner for months?

Maria: Haha, well I'll take that as a compliment, but you looked more like a deer in a headlight. (Both laughed at the comment and were interrupted by the waiter).

Sandy: Can I get you a drink ma'am?

Kunle: Sandy, you're still here? Can I please see the menu?

Maria: I'll have what his having, but with a splash of tonic water and some ice!

Kunle: Forget the menu (he says sarcastically).

Sandy: I left after my 4 hour breakfast shift but came back for the evening shift. I'll be right back with your drink. She walks off and closed the door.

Kunle: Ma'am? Lol!
Maria: I get that a lot actually!
Kunle: Must be all that boss energy that radiates out of you!

Sandy returned with Maria's drink and Maria and Kunle toasted as they sat on the navy blue sofa, comfortable but not too close to each other, and gazed into the light show after the sunset as I Want

You Around by Snoh Aalegra played in the background.

Maria: (Observing Kunle vibe to the song in awe) what do you know about this?

Kunle: Haha. So, what's on the agenda.
Maria: It's a surprise. (thinking to herself, I love this vibe, where can I bring him?)

They finished their drinks and headed down to the lobby where the valet guy, Tony, enthusiastically greeted Kunle. "Good evening Mr. Olu; keys are in your car ma'am, he says to Maria." I'll see you when I get back, Kunle responded as they got into Maria's Model S Tesla.

Kunle: Okay, now I definitely see why they call you ma'am!

Maria: Haha, it's not that serious.

She drove him to Burn, a cigar lounge, bar, and restaurant in Northshore. Upon arrival, Kunle was impressed. She ordered Pierogis, Nachos, and Caesar Salad for them to share and Kunle ordered two Jameson Black Barrel with a tonic water on rocks. The waiter was quick with the drinks and Kunle proposed a toast.

Maria: What are we drinking to?

Kunle: Chanced encounters!!!

Maria: Mm, I'll drink to that!

Kunle: Do you mind if I smoke a cigar?

Maria: I brought you to a cigar lounge for a reason (she said with a smile).

Kunle: I had to make sure. Do you want something?

Maria: I'll share with you!

Kunle disappeared into the cigar room (a separate humidity controlled room that's at the back of the establishment). He chose the Churchill Double Chateau by Arturo Fuente for himself, and chose a Petit Davidoff with the Connecticut wrapper for her.

While away, Maria was still mesmerized by how charming Kunle is, how well he carries himself, his sense of style, and how great he smelled. She especially loved how he seems to see her. She felt heard, he was witty, and she felt they hit it off right away. She noticed a middle aged Caucasian man approaching. He was wearing an oversized suit, a shirt that is hanging on for dear life because the buttons looked like they could pop any minute now, and worn out black shoes that needed some polish. She thought to herself, I wonder what

Kunle's shoes looks like, I haven't noticed. "Need some company sweetie?" The man asked. No thank you, I'm waiting on my husband, she responded. "Well, he's one lucky man" the man responded. "I'll be sure to let him know, says Maria."

As the Caucasian man walked off, another Caucasian man approached her. He was younger, better dressed, and less obese. As he said "hey, how are you?" Kunle emerged with a cigar between his lips, light smoke escaping from his mouth; as he ran his left hands through his locs, and an extra button undone because he thought he looked too serious, but Maria thought it was to give her a peep of his chest chest and his small gold chain.

Maria: (Looking aesthetically at Kunle) Honey, what took you so long?
Kunle: (Playing along) Sorry babe, I wanted to choose the perfect cigar for my lady.

Hi, is there a problem? Kunle asked the curious dude, let's call him Brandon, looking on.

Brandon: "No problem, I assumed your lady was by herself but she clearly is not.

Kunle: Yea, that's why I left my drink, so people can see that there are two glasses.

Brandon: My bad, enjoy your evening.

Maria: That's clever.

Kunle: What is?

Maria: Leaving the glass.

Kunle: Apparently it didn't work.

Maria: It probably did, to an extent. (They both laughed and Kunle presented her with the petit cigar he had picked out for her). You don't like to share, do you?

Kunle: I actually love to share, just not my cigars!
Maria: Fair enough. What did you get me?
Kunle: Something mild, Davidoff. And I got myself a mild cigar as well, Arturo Fuente!

Maria: Nice. So where are you from...

Kunle and Maria exchanged background stories, she did most of the talking. He learned that she was born into a catholic family where both parents were advanced degree holders (mother PhD and father MBA). She's from Georgia, went to University of Pennsylvania for her undergraduate and MBA and works for a tech company as a Chief Operating Officer. She loves sunsets, sunflower dresses in the summers, long walks on the beach, and travel. Kunle told her about his job as an international tax consultant, briefly about his travels, and about his passion for writing.

They were both fascinated with each other, but often had to remind each other that this was just the first meeting. Maria finished her 2nd drink, Kunle his first and took the last drag from his cigar and asked what's next?

Maria: Wanna go somewhere with music? I can dance a little!

Kunle: Oh okay, on a work night?
Maria: I'll work remotely tomorrow.
Kunle: Let's do it!

Maria: Don't you have work tomorrow too?

Kunle: It's supposed to be half a day because I was scheduled to fly out tomorrow.

Maria: Was scheduled to fly out?

Kunle: Haha, I'm hoping the next destination wows me and I stay for the weekend.

Maria: I think your mind is already made up and my job is to not mess it up, haha.

Kunle: Mm, you may be right. I'll stay if you've got the moves.

Maria: Haha, you may want to check-in to your flight now.

Both laughed as Kunle paid the tab and they walked out. Maria was okay to drive, despite having two drinks. They drove to The Shady Side neighborhood in Pittsburg, where they went into a lounge/club with no name. It was only 9 pm and there were college students everywhere. They walked into the lounge after their IDs were examined and they were both searched. Kunle thought to himself, the music must be good here to warrant all this search.

They got upstairs and Kunle ordered drinks. Maria hung out close to the DJ booth and when Kunle returned with their drinks, he remembered how amazingly breathtaking she was. He handed her a drink and whispered in her ears, you're incredibly beautiful. Maria gazed at him and said, "dance with me." She stood up clumsily and grabbed Kunle by the hand and led him to the dance floor. They both started dancing as the DJ played R&B and hip hop songs from the late 2000s, Neyo, Drake, Rhianna, Sean Paul, etc. The DJ switched to dancehall and Kunle couldn't compose himself anymore. Like Glue by Sean Paul made Kunle want to get a little closer to Maria, so he did. He grabbed her by the waist, pulled her a lot closer as they rocked left to right in harmony. "What are you up to this weekend, Kunle asked." Maria couldn't hear him because she was on a different plane.

Maria couldn't remember the last time she was this close to, felt such a connection with, or was this attracted to anyone. The faint smell of the cigar, mixed with his perfume, and his natural odor gave her this intoxicating smell that she couldn't resist. She was lost. She felt his hands on her hip and his other hand locked in hers as they danced cheek to cheek. Maria couldn't believe she was already horny and that she was entertaining the thoughts in her head. Snap out of it she thought to herself, but it was already late, she was already gone. She had to fight the urge to not guide his hands to private places.

Kunle realizing that his voice was too low decided to not ruin the moment and didn't ask again. Still holding on to her hand, he raised it up and used his other hand to gently guide Maria to turn around and they started to bump and grind. After she was turned around, Kunle released her hand and she still stood straight with her butt rubbing against his groin. She stayed on beat and they started to dance like a pair of college kids that went to school in the late 2000s. When the DJ played She Drives Me Crazy by Kevin Little, Kunle felt like he was having an out of body experience. He watched himself glued to this gorgeous woman while he used his finger tips to trace her arm, almost like he was looking for a secret passage. There was no pressure at all from his touches, but she felt every single nerve he touched. It tickled her a bit sometimes and other times it made her even more aroused. She grabbed his hands and placed them on her breasts 30 seconds into I'm Still In Love With You by Sean Paul and Sasha. Kunle accepted the invitation and gently caressed her breasts, she pushed up against his groin and noticed he was getting aroused. When she applied more pressure, Kunle squeezed her breast a little tighter.

Maria turned around when the DJ started playing Busy Signal's version of One More Night. She put her arms around his neck and Kunle had both hands on her butt. She looked straight into his eyes and he stared back, as if he was a nine years old boy gazing lustfully at the stars. He leaned over and kissed her soft moist lips. She kissed him back as she ran her hands through his hair, gently pulling his head closer. "Oh my fucking god he's an amazing kisser that tastes so good," Maria thought to herself. Kunle couldn't believe how good of a kisser she was and how amazingly comfortable he felt in her arms as they kissed.

Maria pulls back slowly and said "it's 11:30, want to start heading out?"

Kunle: Yes gorgeous, after you.

Maria: Gorgeous? Is it because I let you kiss me?

Kunle: It's especially because of that. If I said it sooner, you might have thought I was only trying to get in your pants and you wouldn't have believed me!

Maria: You just always seem to know what to say, don't you?

Kunle: Only when in the presence of an angel.

They walked back to the car and Kunle opened the door for her, even though she was driving, but not before he passionately kissed her one more time. He opened her door for her and went around to the passenger side to get in. Maria leaned over and opened the door for him and they drove off into the night.

CHAPTER 2

LATER THAT NIGHT

Cabin lighting in the Tesla was immaculate, Kunle observed. Not too bright that you'd have problems falling asleep, but bright enough that you wouldn't need any additional light source to perform basic functions. He observed Maria's posture as she drove, hands holding the steering wheel at 9 and 3 O'clock, she wasn't slouching but was sitting up straight. He imagined if the roles were reversed. Would Maria take advantage of the fact that there was no center console? "Am I supposed to...?" He thought to himself. I wonder what she's thinking. Was I supposed to kiss her the second time or am I supposed to wait for her to make the next move?

Kunle thought to himself as Maria breaks the silence:

Maria: This never happens.

Kunle: What never happens? You mean you don't meet random guys from Instagram and drive them around in your model S?

Maria:Ha, not even.

Kunle: What would your momma say? "I'm disappointed in you"

Maria: First of all, she doesn't sound like that (as she laughs out loud, letting out a little snort), her speech is more proper, like she speaks in cursive.

Kunle: (pulling the seat belt to the side so he can laugh unrestricted). That is funny. She really sound like that? Is it crazy that I know what you're talking about?

Maria: No, your mother probably sounds like that too (Maria laughing out loud. She thought to herself, I'm way too comfortable with this man, I don't even know him).

Kunle: My mother is African, she sounds more like she learned Yoruba in cursive and refuses to bend for the West, so speaking English is like you're inconveniencing her, even though she speaks great English.

Maria: What does she do?

Kunle: She's my mom, what do you mean? She only has one job (he said with a laugh).

Maria: You know mothers do other shit besides being mothers, right (Confused and not sure if Kunle is   the typical misogynist Nigerian man the society has warned against)?

Kunle: Ha, bad joke. She's an economist actually (he said with a what Maria perceives as a sense of pride).

Maria: Whoa! That's a complete 180. You said that almost like you're proud of her or something

Kunle: Haha. I maintained the same tone when I made the terrible joke though. But yea, I am very proud of my mother.

Maria: Guess you did have the same tone. What about your mom are you proud of?

Kunle: She's ahead of her time, just like you.

Maria: Just like me? How is that?

Kunle: I don't know you, but I know you based on what you shared with the world via Instagram over the years, but my mom is a fucking boss. She's an economist, google her, she's published a few things and ran a few organizations. She is ahead of her time. She can go toe to toe with any man and hold her own. She is a partner, not a subordinate; a MERGER, not an acquisition. She'll probably win a Nobel Prize because of her innovative way of thinking about Macro Economics.

Maria: (Puzzled. He sees all that in me?, WTF! Keeping her composure) Wow, you think very highly of your mom, huh?

Kunle: I wasn't trying to be disrespectful of mothers, it's just I'm passionate about mine and hate how societal restrictions have limited women for far too long. (Noticing that they're on the freeway and looking at the full yellow moon) Did you engage the autopilot?

Maria: Why? I just did. You're displaying a lot of what "IG people" would call "choose me energy" (she said making air quotes after engaging the autopilot) right now haha. I love it though.

Kunle: Look up, beautiful ain't it?

Maria: It is something (the bass from Kunle's amapiano mix from Tidal caught both their attention). This music, what did you call it?

Kunle: This is South African, Amapiano.

Maria: I really dig it. It's different

Kunle: Yea! Think of it as a mixture of jazz, afro beats, house, techno, EDM, soul, and then some, all in one track if done right, and it's often done right.

Maria: And it's perfect for the mood.

Kunle undoes his seatbelt and leaned over to kiss Maria. Worried, she reached for the steering wheel but Kunle did not let her get to it. He gently intercepted her hand and proceeded to give her an even more passionate kiss. He reached for her left breast and started playing with it. Her nipples were hard to the point Kunle imagined if they were numb.

Kunle: See? The car is in control (he said as he pulled away).

Maria: (Still trying to recover from the mix of adrenaline and estradiol [pheromones] and the sensation of Kunle's soft but firm hands on her nipples. In a very soft voice, almost like she was whispering because the base was just heavy enough and the vocals came in loud and clear on that evening): Wow.

Kunle: (stops bopping his head and turns the music down a smidge) Did you say something?

Maria: I mean, WOW!

Kunle: It's something, ain't it?

Maria: Why are you single? Do you have a family back home in Nigeria?

Kunle: Yea, 14 kids in one hut. I'm working on the second hut though, one that can stand an elephant attack!

Maria: (Busted out laughing) That was ignorant of me, wasn't it?

Kunle: A little, but it's okay. Some people before me gave Nigerians a bad rep, I get it.

Maria: No, but why are you single?

Kunle: I wasn't always single, but that's a story for a night you're wearing my favorite t-shirt while we look at the moon from my place.

Maria: What makes you think that would ever happen?

Kunle: What makes you think I have a shirt I love but want you to have?

Maria disengaged the autopilot because she was approaching Kunle's exit. Kunle, with his window down, was feeling the breeze and was enjoying the music. He must have felt like an eagle on a night stroll. Maria glanced at his face and she was amazed at how joyful Kunle looked. Is he going to invite me up? Do I want to go? What would happen? You don't even know this man's last name. I'm not gonna go up.

She pulled up to Kunle's hotel and stopped in front of the valet/lobby entrance. Kunle wasn't sure if he should invite her up. He broke his silence.

Kunle: I have a bottle of Macallan I don't feel like bringing back with me, wanna have a drink? I promise nothing would happen.

Maria: You promise? (as she busted out laughing)! Since you're promising, I'll come up for one drink.

Kunle: (Unsure if she was being sarcastic) Okay!

Valet: Good evening Mr. Olu!

Kunle: My man, how are you (extending a friendly hand shake, not the firm business type, and discreetly passes a $20 to the Valet)?

Valet: I'm well sir, thank you. Where do you want it?

Kunle: Somewhere where she'd beat the morning rush.

Valet: You got it, enjoy your night sir, and thank you.

Maria: (Exits the vehicle) The keys are in the cupholder in Valet mode.

Kunle: Yes Ma'am (laughing)!

Maria: Shut up (as she flashed a very joyful and innocent smile).

They walked up to the elevator and Kunle walked behind her as he admired her beauty from a different perspective. He wondered if he was being a creep.

Kunle: I see a bright future behind you.

Maria: (Busted out laughing) that's a cute line.

Kunle: It's actually not, it's a line from a song.

Maria: No it's not.

Kunle: Do you like Two Chainz?

Maria: I know his songs.

Kunle: "She got a big booty so I call her big booty." You don't think there's someone who can say "I see a bright future behind you?

Maria: You're right, it was just strange. And why did that man say thank you?

Kunle: It's brilliant is what it is. And he said thank you because I shook his hand haha.

Kunle reached for his wallet to grab the keycard and unlocked the door to his room. He had a king suite with a soak-in tub, separate glass shower, floor to ceiling windows with a king sized bed. The floor is gray, the couch is blue, and the curtains are white.

Maria: This is nice.

Kunle: (Flips on all the lights and grabbed a complimentary bottle of water). Do you want one?

Maria: Sure. I'm going to use the bathroom.

Kunle: Go for it.

Kunle grabbed the 12 years old bottle of Macallan he purchased on Monday when he thought he was going to have a stressful and boring week. He imagined he'd have one or two drinks on days of heavy stress, but he hasn't touched it. He grabbed the two glasses provided and waited for Maria to come out of the bathroom to go rinse them off. He turned on his most treasured travel companion, the Bose Sound Revolve+ portable speaker, and started playing his Tidal playlist. Maria exited the bathroom.

Kunle: I'm going to rinse these.

Maria: Okay (as she proceeds to inspect the room. She noticed Kunle's clothes hung up in the closet. One full suit, two slacks, 7 button up long sleeve shirts, running shoes and his workout clothes. She picked up the soiled t-shirt to smell it. It smelled musty but good; a mix of sweat and Kunle's perfume. She liked it).

Kunle: Don't judge me, I don't live here (as he put the glasses down and grabbed the bottle of Macallan). Bless the bottle (he double taps the top).

Maria: (following Kunle's lead double tapped the bottle) Bless the bottle?

Kunle: Yea, I'm not sure if it's a Nigerian thing, but it's a tradition my boys and I treasure.

Maria: I like it (as she watched Kunle pour generously into one glass and a small amount of scotch into the other glass)!

Kunle: (Handing the glass with the less scotch to Maria): Cheers!!!

Maria: Switch glasses with me.

Kunle: Okay (hands her his glass and poured more Scotch into the other glass).

Maria: (Seating on the couch) This is nice. How many women have you brought here?

Kunle: Honestly?

Maria: Yea, honestly.

Kunle: One

Maria: You were supposed to say zero.

Kunle: I know, but why lie when the truth is easier?

Maria: Good point. You probably just ruined your chances (she said as Kunle watched her roll her eyes).

Kunle: (Show You Off by Wurld produced by Shizzi & Walshy Fire started playing) I love this song, dance with me.

Maria: People can see into your room.

Kunle: So you know I wouldn't try anything.

Maria: What if I want you to try something?

Kunle: We're grown, you'd make a move.

Maria: (Amazed about how Kunle thinks, got up to honor Kunle's invitation) Okay playa.

Kunle: "I'll be honest, I can't keep my hands to myself. It's your world, it's your world, don't know no man that wouldn't kill for your love..." (as he pulls Maria close like he just needed to feel her breathe).

Maria: What was his saying (as she observed Kunle's firm chest {pecs}, his cologne doubled as this aroma that engaged her nose, his hands were soft and his nails were clean)

Kunle: (Singing along) "Do you mind if I show you off, show you off show you off..."

Maria: (Imagined what that meant. Does that mean he'll show me off to his friends?) I like this song.

Kunle: You're so beautiful. That's the song (as if he was blaming the song for making him say that), even though I kinda wanted to say that to you again.

Maria: (Puzzled and not sure how she should react to all this affection Kunle was showing). You love that song huh?

Kunle: Yea, what gave it away? (the song stopped and another track started Gbese by Wizkid and DJ Tunez. Kunle let go of Maria and grabbed the water and had about half of the bottle)

Maria: You're a responsible drinker, I see. Why did you buy a bottle of booze? Do you have a drinking problem?

Kunle: Haha, no. But when I have a stressful day at work, I think it's a better decision to drink, though I'd rather smoke, by myself than to go to a bar. You never know what would happen at a bar.

Maria: What's the worst that would happen?

Kunle: You drive drunk and kill someone.

Maria: Yea, but you're not driving.

Kunle: One night stand that results in a child.

Maria: Yea, good point. But you just opened this bottle tonight, it's Thursday.

Kunle: My week wasn't as stressful as anticipated.

Maria: Okay. I love this song, the saxophone is doing things to me I can't explain.

Kunle: Is your brain tingling as well?

Maria: No, but i feel it.

Kunle: Sit down let me give you a scalp massage.

Maria: A scalp massage?

Kunle: Yes, but focus on the music. (Maria sat down and Kunle proceeded to start massaging her scalp. It was like he was looking for veins that needed a straightening out to allow better blood circulation. He applied enough pressure that Maria was instantly alerted; and then added his second hand and was applying pressure with each individual finger as they each moved in varied directions and supplying enough pressure to Maria's scalp. She started to enjoy it, she took slow, measured deep breaths; her shoulders relaxed. Kunle observed everything going on and kept the same consistency for the next 45 seconds. He then stopped and said) Open your eyes. Are you still here?

Maria: I'm back now. I was on cloud 9 just now.

Kunle: (drinks from his glass as Maria mimics him. He knew he had her, he knew she wouldn't resist him if he was to make a move). Can I kiss you?

Maria: Yes please!!! I mean, sure.

Kunle got on his knees and started kissing Maria. Twenty seconds in, Kunle used his index finger to guide Maria's chin as he stood up slowly. Maria was turned on. Kunle could feel her tremble a little. When they were both fully erect, Kunle, not detaching his lips, picked Maria up like a groom trying to take a romantic picture with his bride. Maria was impressed and thought to herself, am I floating right now? Kunle placed her on the bed and Maria sat up. Kunle unhooked her bra like he wanted to win gold at the bra Olympics. Maria, simultaneously impressed, was surprised at how Kunle was able to do that. Before her mind could drift off, she felt Kunle's soft and moist lips make contact with her right nipple. It felt warm, soothing. Kunle was sucking on Maria's breast like a hungry puppy that's aware enough to know this shit can hurt, while simultaneously massaging them. Maria unzipped her pants and took them off. Kunle's hands immediately went down there and felt how moist Maria was. He imagined it was like fresh okra soup. It was slimy, wet, perfect. Kunle wanted to go close the blinds, but the lights were already dim and he didn't want to ruin the moment. Maria started to moan softly when Kunle looked up and gave her another passionate kiss. He got up to go close the blinds and Maria saw that he was fully erect; Kunle did not even make an attempt to conceal it.

Kunle returned to the bed as Maria made way for him by repositioning herself on the right side of the bed (farthest from the exit). It was obvious to Kunle that she wanted to stay but Kunle wondered if she expected him to break his promise or if she'd take the lead. Kunle kissed her.

Kunle: What time do you want to wake up

Maria: What?

Kunle: I'm going to set the alarm...

Maria: Oh right, the alarm. What time is it (as she looks around for her phone).

Kunle: It's 1:15. Do you need your phone charged?

Maria: Yes please and 8 am should be fine, I hope that's not too late for you

Kunle: No, it's perfect. (As he leans over to kiss her). Good night gorgeous!

Maria, thinking to herself. "WTF? That's it? His dick was hard and he clearly knew I wanted this. WTF? She was lost in her mind and it was obvious to Kunle because she did not respond to his goodnight greeting)."

Maria could not quiet her mind. What is happening right now? What was I expecting? I definitely was not expecting this man to be like this. He was private online and only occasionally shared. She realized Kunle had passed out in the first two minutes. She went on Instagram and looked through Kunle's pictures. She observed he was well traveled. He's been to 12 countries and 30 of the 50 states including DC and Puerto Rico. A text from Gina came in as Maria scrolled through Instagram.

Gina: Bitch!!! You good?

Maria: Haha, I'm more than good. I think he might be gay.

Gina: No, what the fuck? Why?

Maria: He turned me on and didn't do anything. Like literally had his hands down my panties, felt how wet I was, and then he stopped. He's probably one of those undercover gay guys.

Gina: Bitch what? He must be special, you never get that far with ANYONE on the first date.

Maria: I see why now, they leave you hanging like this? Never again.

Gina: Na, they usually want to just fuck you. He's different. But, isn't that a good thing? You said you're going to be celibate for a whole year.

Maria: Well yes, but I think I like him more than I realize. I'm eight months into this celibacy thing too.

Gina: Haha, true! But I want to hear all about it.

Maria: Tomorrow, I'll debrief.

Gina: Perfect. You're still down for dinner right?

Maria: Absolutely.

Gina: Great, we'll talk tomorrow. I can't wait]to hear about it all.

Maria: kk. Sleep tight.

Gina: Stop over thinking it. If you really want some, wake his ass up. Give him some dome (head/oral sex) or something. You're in charge.

Maria: Not gonna happen, I barely know the guy.

Gina: Okay then., you right. Anyway, sleep tight.

Maria: Yea, yea.

The alarm went off for a split second, but Kunle cut it off and placed his hands on Maria's shoulder.

Kunle: Wake up gorgeous

Maria: (Opening her eyes to a fully dressed Kunle) Damn, what time is it?

Kunle: Good morning to you too. It's 8 am

Maria: I'm sorry, why are you already dressed?

Kunle: Oh, I woke up at 6:30 and went for a quick 3 mile run

Maria: Oh okay, showoff.

Kunle: Coffee? I had them bring up an extra toothbrush for you.

Maria: Thank you (as she sits up. She realized her panties were on, but her bra was missing. Embarrassed as she looked around, she noticed her bra was neatly folded on the nightstand next to her, and her clothes were folded on the couch. She reached for her bra while holding the comforter to cover her breasts). Turn around please (and then she noticed Kunle was already turned around). Thanks.

Kunle: How did you sleep?

Maria: Ignoring the blue balls? I slept well. You?

Kunle: (In awe of her physique as he observed her in her bra and panties when she walked towards her clothes on the couch). I slept good actually, but I'll probably need a nap later.

Maria: Yea, me too. Busy day?

Kunle: No, not busy at all. About 3 hours of real work and then I'm free. You?

Maria: Not really, I have a 2 hour from 1–3 and then I'm done.

Kunle: Oh good. What are you doing tomorrow and for the weekend?

Maria: Why?

Kunle: I want to take you out.

Maria: So you did change your flight!

Kunle: You had the moves, haha.

Maria: Geez, thanks. I'm free tomorrow, what do you have in mind?

Kunle: You'll see.

Maria: Okay, I can't wait. Want to accompany me to dinner tonight? It's at my best friend's friend's house.

Kunle: Sure, I'm game.

Maria went into the bathroom to brush her teeth, clean her face, and freshen up. When she reemerged from the bathroom, Kunle noticed how beautiful she looked. She had no makeup on and he was smitten. Kunle grabbed his messenger bag and they both left the hotel room.

CHAPTER 3

FRIDAY

While driving home, Maria reflected on the night. She recalled how smooth she danced with Kunle. She remembered his touches and how well he moved. She was listening to an Amapiano mix Kunle sent her earlier that morning because he thought she'd enjoy it and he was right, she truly did. . Her drive wasn't long, but she wanted it to continue because she wanted to analyze the entire night to spot the red flags, something she tries to do with her friends. She made a mental list:

He's already had a girl in his room; but he doesn't deny it.
He came so close to sleeping with me, but then he stopped? Was he being a gentleman? Did he sleep with that other girl?
That comment about mothers, but then he's just avoiding talking about his own whom he's obviously proud of?

She's deep in her internal debate when a message from Kunle flashed on her screen, the same time she pulls up into her garage. She Lives on the 38th floor of a 42 story building with west facing views overlooking the Ohio River. Her condo has a white, navy blue, and dark gray wood theme; when you enter you're greeted by an abundance of natural light and sharp colors. Six of the paintings she's collected over the years on a few trips include three paintings of birds, one painting of the ocean with boats and a golden sunset, and two paintings of women in powerful poses.

She parked the car and grabbed her phone to read Kunle's text. She realized she was actually giddy and joyful, in a muted way, as she reached for her phone.

Kunle: What kind of coffee do you like? I'm in line at Starbucks and I'm trying to picture what you like. Three shots of espresso with honey or sugar and cream?

Maria: Close, but a caramel macchiato is my true vice.

Kunle: That's not even close.

Maria: I get the venti, it has 3 shots of espresso.

Kunle: You think you're smart huh (inserts a blushing face emoji).

Maria: I know I am.

Kunle: I can't stop thinking about you.

Maria: Of course you can, you need to. Don't you have meetings?

Kunle: No, no meetings today and I'm leaving the office at 12.

Maria: Good for you. Focus on your tasks and be done with it.

Kunle grabbed his Venti oat milk mocha and heads out of Starbucks with Travis.

Travis: You're really staying huh?

Kunle: Yea man, I want to explore the city a bit.

Travis: Perks of being single.

Kunle: With no kids. Why not bring your girl out here one weekend? She might enjoy it and you get to go to those museums you keep wanting to go to.

Travis: Yea, you're right.

They both got into the red Cadillac CTS that Kunle had picked up after work the prior evening when he decided to stay for the weekend. He felt like he had to be there that weekend, and Maria's initial message was the sign he needed. He booked the car before confirming if he'd get a chance to meet Maria. He wanted to check out the parks, some breweries, and the side of town people of color frequent.

While at work, Kunle could not focus. He too was reminiscing about the previous evening. He really wanted to have sex with Maria and knew if he didn't stop his advances the way he did, things would have heated up even further than they did; but one very important thing to Kunle is that he keeps his word. Under no circumstance would he have allowed things to get heated up further than they did. He opened the Notes App on his iCloud account and typed a blueprint of some of the things he wished would happen with Maria. He titled it *This Morning*. Kunle did a quick proof reading of the note for general grammar and punctuation errors. Once he glanced at it, he reached for his phone where he copied the note into a text message that he sent to Maria.

Maria was just about wrapping up her two hour meeting when Kunle's message buzzed on her gold stainless steel Apple Watch. She ignored the buzzing on her wrist, almost as if she was expecting it and expected not to read it or let it distract her until she was done with her meeting. She had the team's attention, all twelve of the participants in the meeting had their eyes fixed on her via Zoom. She summarized the meeting as she reiterated her expectations from each of the three team leads whose teams are on the call. She closed the meeting off with a remark saying, "let's crush it guys, and have a great weekend!" She spoke with the spirit of a general in a battle they're badly losing, but motivated to win and attempting to inspire their troops.

She picked up her phone after she got off the meeting and saw Kunle's message. She began to read it; but the more she read, the more shocked she was at what she was reading.

This morning:

This morning, I couldn't stop thinking about gazing into your beautiful brown eyes while I fight all the urges to kiss you!
I just want to look into your eyes until I can't bear being so far away from you, even though I'd be less than a foot away!

When my lips finally make contact with your beautifully shaped lips, it'll send shockwaves through my whole body! My knees would get weak, lips quibble a bit, heart racing faster! Man, what a privilege to taste you, I'd think.

Your soft lips and caring tongue welcoming mine! What a joy to experience! When I've caught myself, I'd massage your perfect tits a little! They're the perfect size and the right texture! Your nipples, hard like they're ready for my lips! I'd suck on them, wet and warm, I'd bite them with my lips acting as a buffer from my teeth! I'd take my time but not too much time, then I'd go back to kissing you! Lips locked, one hand on your breast, and the other firmly gripping your perfect ass!

Oh your ass! I imagined spanking it and grabbing it and kissing it and biting it and putting my face in between it! I want to bend you over and eat your pussy! I want you standing up against a dresser, looking into a mirror while you try to get a visual of the source of all this pleasure, but you can't see me!

I imagined your body would be experiencing great pleasure and you're helpless because all you can do is hold on to the dresser and enjoy the ride! When you start to moan louder and you finally turn around, I'll go back to kissing you and let you feel my pulsating dick! Then I might lift you up and carry you to the bed! Start kissing your lips all over again and then slowly kissing you all over your body, from your jaws, neck, chest, I'll pause to recharge your nipples a bit more before I continue to make my way down!

Once I'm back to your pussy, I'll let my tongue get super familiar with your clit. Giving her the right amount of firmness and motion! When you start to moan louder again, then I'd take off my pants...

...to be continued □

Yours truly in Lala Land

Kunle Olu

She had to reread the whole note now that she knew what she was in for. By the fifth read, she was turned on beyond imagination and felt a long bath was necessary. She responded to Kunle with a gif of Rihanna. It was the one where she's seated in a white chair, wearing a blue denim jacket, her right index finger pressed against her temple with a mischievous look in her eyes. No words accompanied the gif. When she replied, Kunle was heading out of the office with Travis because he offered to drive him to the airport to kill time and explore a bit. Kunle reached for his phone and looked at it, a smile engulfed his face. Maria's response was a lot better than Kunle anticipated because he was a little bit concerned about being forward and such. He drove Travis to the airport and headed back to his hotel for a much needed nap.

While Kunle was driving around, Maria was up to something else entirely. She ran herself a bath (in the middle of a Friday) while she listened to Marvin Gaye's station on Spotify. She took her time and pleasured herself. She imagined Kunle actually doing everything he said in his text message, and then some. Is this a game to him? She stayed positive and imagined Kunle's lips on hers, his soft lips on her nipples while he dominantly grabs her butt. She played with a few more scenarios in the bath, which lasted for about an hour. After her bath, she took a nice and much needed nap.

Maria woke up at approximately 5 pm to a slew of messages from Gina, Kunle, and slew of other notifications. She FaceTimed Gina, Ignoring

Kunle's text because she's been dying to catch up with her.

Maria: Okay, I see you. Looks like you're ready for the weekend.

Gina: Oh you like this look? I stopped by the mall and picked up some new Fenty items. I'll put you on, but first tell me about this mystery man.

Maria: He isn't going to be a mystery for too much longer, I invited him tonight; I hope you don't mind.

Gina: Of course I don't mind, that's why you invited him in the first place. □
Maria: Girl, this man had me masturbating twice today, over a fucking text message.
Gina: He's sexting you? I thought you don't like unsolicited dick pics.

Maria: No, not that, but some shit he wrote. (Maria sends Gina the This Morning note Kunle sent her. She waited 2 minutes while the video was paused and seemed muted).

Gina: This man ain't gay.

Maria: I definitely don't think so, but you see what I mean.

Gina: I see. Is it weird that I feel somehow, like turned on?

Maria: I don't think so, it's normal. That shit is graphic.

Gina: I can't wait to meet him.

Maria: Yea, speaking of. He's spending the weekend and said he wants to "take me out."

Gina: What are you thinking? What do you think he has in mind?

Maria: I'm not sure. It's hard to imagine. I'm guessing some fancy restaurant with valet parking, some regular old shit; but then, he's not like most of the other guys.

Gina: Wait, so what was your response to this?

Maria: I sent this gif (Maria sends the Rihanna gif)
Gina: Nice, I love it! No words?
Maria: Right? No words, but I have to go see his response.

Gina: Gotcha. What time am I expecting you?

Maria: 8 pm. Depending on him.

Gina: 7pm!!!, bitch I said 7 P.M.!!! 😏

Maria: You and I know that I'm always on time but others?

Gina: So, come at 7:30.

Maria: Deal. I'm going to get started on the salmon and I'll make Kunle bring two bottles of Riesling.

Gina: Sounds good, see you babes.

Maria hung up the phone and looked at Kunle's text messages.

Kunle: I drove by a liquor store and was wondering what kind of wine you like/feel like drinking tonight.

Maria: For the potluck? Riesling should work, get any kind.

Kunle: (responding almost instantly) Sounds good. Anything else? Also, what time should I come get you? I forgot to tell you I picked up a rental car yesterday.

Maria: When did you get the car? Nothing else unless there's something you think we should have.

Kunle: Sounds good. I picked up the car after work yesterday
Maria: So I was right, your mind was made up to

stay.

Kunle: Yea, I could feel it in my bones, but your message was the sign I needed.

Maria: Good answer. So see you at 7?

Kunle: Depends on how far away you are. It's 5:20 now and I can definitely be ready by 6.

Maria: I'm 15 minutes from your hotel and I'll send you the location at 6.

Kunle: Perfect, see you in a bit.

Maria made her way into the kitchen to start making the wild caught Atlantic salmon she was taking to the potluck. She started playing Prince radio on Spotify and started grooving. While she was doing her own thing, Kunle was still on the bed and was catching up with his emails and then social media. He laid in bed curiously wondering what the Bar on the 6th floor is like. Kunle decided to go see for himself and got up and started getting ready. He started playing Afrobeats as he got ready, dancing and in a generally happy mood.

By 5:40 pm, Kunle was ready; sporting a sharp colored red v-neck t-shirt, blue jeans, and a navy blue blazer with a light blue handkerchief in his chest pocket. He headed to the rooftop lounge to have one or two drinks before he headed out to meet up with Maria, wherever that is. Upon arriving at the lounge, it was busy. Kunle normally gets to drink for free because he's a platinum member with Marriott and one of the perks is complimentary happy hours at locations where they have an executive lounge. The Oaklander did not have a lounge, but they had an event that night.

Kunle asked for a glass of white wine because his intention was not to get drunk, but to network. He ran into a group of women and learned that they were attending a wedding at the Soldiers & Sailors Memorial Hall across the street. One of the ladies (Katie "Kate") came to have a chat with Kunle at the bar and insisted that they exchange numbers in case either party wanted company when grabbing coffee or a drink. Kunle had a slight distrust for white women because of all the horror stories he's heard/videos he's seen of Karens falsely accusing innocent black men.

As Kunle sipped his wine on the balcony, a group of three men came to the balcony and were chatting about the wedding. They seemed like brother in-laws and catching up on their businesses and such. One of them,Jason, asked if Kunle was also attending the wedding and he responded; "I'm not, at least I don't think so. I definitely did not get an invitation yet." A response to which they all laughed.

Jason: Avoid a woman named Danielle this weekend.

Brandon: No, it's truly Diane he has to look out for.

Jason: Diane is chronically single, it's like she's scared of men or something.

Mathew: That is because no one is ever good enough for her.

Jason: Yes, you look like you make really good money and are obviously smart. If given the chance, Brandon is right, look out for her.

Kunle: They both sound lovely but I'll be hanging out with a friend this weekend, hopefully she will serve as a deterrent.

They all laughed and cheered to a fun weekend, Kunle included. He finished his drink and looked at the message from Maria. Well gentlemen, I have to go meet up with my date. Enjoy the wedding but I'm sure I'll probably bump into you at some point during this weekend. Kunle departed the lounge while looking at his phone.

Maria: Come here (she sent her current location because she doesn't trust Kunle to know her address just

Kunle: Sure, see you at 7 pm or sooner.

Maria: Sounds good, please don't forget the Riesling.

Kunle: Already picked up 4 bottles, one for me, one for you, and two for others □ □ .

Maria: You have plans of getting me drunk and then leaving me with the female version of "blue balls

Kunle: No, I'm definitely not going to make that same promise tonight and I'll follow your lead.

Maria: Deal, if you try that shit again I might just not listen to you.

Kunle: Haha, that's a plan. I'm heading out now, I'll see you in a bit.

Maria: I know you're trying to be on time and all, but you'd get here at 6:15.

Kunle: Oh right, I want to drive by this park I read about online.

Maria: Which park?

Kunle: Schenley Park, I ran through it briefly, but I want to check it out.

Maria: Okay, so you'll get here at 6:30?

Kunle: See you at 6:30.

Kunle requested for his car via the valet application and by the time he got to the lobby, his car was ready for him and his favorite valet was on duty.

Valet: Good evening Mr. Olu! Where are your bags?

Kunle: Hi Daryl, I'm staying for the weekend.

Daryl: Good for you, any reason in particular?

Kunle: Yes, Maria!

Daryl: Haha, definitely a great reason to stay.

Kunle: Absolutely! See you in a bit bro.

Daryl: You too sir, see you.

Kunle got into the car and drove off, ignoring/avoiding the crowd of 10 women in evening gowns. Upon arriving at the park, Kunle walked around and took some pictures. He was scouting for the perfect location for a picnic date with Maria. On his drive to Maria's location, Kunle imagined they'd have their picnic, relax, and then walk around the park and end up at the botanical garden. He wasn't sure if Maria would like it, but he knew he would, so that was good enough for him. He sent a text to Maria when he was 5 minutes away, and another one when he was outside.

Kunle: I'm here, I'm parked in a red Cadillac.

Maria: Okay Mr. flashy red car, come outside of the car. It's the tall house with the Starbucks. Go through the lobby and press #3800 on the intercom.

Kunle: Okay ma'am.

Maria: Stop that, haha. (Watching Kunle, through the window, bend over to grab some things from the back seat) nice butt (even though she could barely see it).

Kunle: Yea? Well, if you're nice, I might let you touch it.

Kunle grabbed everything he needed to grab (the wines and a tres leches cake) and headed to the door. Before he could press the Ring doorbell, Maria opened the door. Her make up was already done (at least Kunle assumed) but she was wearing a silk robe that hugged all her curves. Kunle observed that she was not wearing a bra and that her nipples were hard. Before Kunle could continue the observation, Maria hugged and gave him a really long and passionate kiss, while Kunle was still holding the bag with the wines and carrying the cake on his other hand. He was not expecting a kiss that passionate, but he welcomed it all the same.

Maria: Let me grab that for you (taking the cake from Kunle and leading him to the kitchen).

Kunle: Oh wow, you've been busy (observing the 5 pounds of salmon, container of couscous, and pesto sauce that Maria made).

Maria: Yes I have been, but I did take a really long nap, among other things (briefly remembered her bathtub session earlier).

Kunle: Everything looks delicious (setting the bag in his hands down next to the cake on the counter).

He looks at Maria, who was just standing there observing Kunle. Before he could say anything else, Maria interrupted.

Maria: Drinks? I have some wine, some liquor by the bar, or coffee, tea, etc. You chose.

Kunle captured her soft gaze and maintained eye contact as he walked towards her closing the ten foot gap to mere inches. Maria repeated, but softer and more delicate (as Kunle observed the sun setting behind her through the floor to ceiling walls):

Maria: How about the...

Kunle: (interrupting) I just want to take in this moment and everything I want is right here.

Kunle stared into Maria's beautiful brown eyes, as if he was trying to get a glimpse of her soul; he then started to passionately kiss a joyful Maria, this time with his hands freed, as the sun sets behind them. There were twenty percent scattered clouds in the skies that formed shapes and patterns that were magical; Kunle observed one shaped like a smiley face. Maria welcomed his kisses as if she had been waiting all day for his hands and lips to get reacquainted with her body again. In one swoop and without anticipation from Maria, Kunle lifted her onto the counter by the armpits. Maria got a glimpse of the time and noticed it was 6:35; she wondered if they had time for whatever it is that Kunle is starting and she had been looking forward to...

Realizing that she might not be able to stand correctly as her legs were still trembling, Maria decided to take the risk. Kunle noticed her beautiful butt as she struggled to walk straight to the bedroom to get ready and reapply her makeup.

Maria: This will take some time; so don't get any other beautiful ideas.

Kunle: Maybe I can help if you want.

Maria: Oh I know you can, I'm just afraid Gina would kill me if we arrive any later than we already are.

Kunle: Speaking of which (as he puts on his clothes starting with his boxers); you have to tell me about the people at this dinner, so I know how to relate to them.

Pausing at the entrance to the bedroom to take a look at Kunle. "Damn," she thought to herself as she walked back towards him. Kunle realized Maria was walking towards him as he pulls up his boxers. She started to kiss him again and this time, Kunle stopped her after about two minutes to let her know that he doesn't want her friends to hate him too much.

Kunle: You want Gina to kill me?

Maria: You're right, I'll tell you about them in the car.

Maria disappeared into the room and Kunle started to play some music as he examined the apartment. It was nice and her taste in decor confirmed to Kunle that Maria is a sophisticated woman. The sun was fully set at this point, it was about 7:06. The sky displayed an array of beautiful colors ranging from a variety of oranges to red.

About 15 minutes later, Maria emerged in a form fitting dress that looked like a mix of polyester and a cotton blend. It hugged her curves and left Kunle's jaws open, literally.

Maria: Ready? Didn't your mama tell you it's rude to stare?

Kunle: Yes, but god damn it, you're gorgeous!!!

They both left the apartment and headed downstairs to Kunle's car.

CHAPTER 4

DINNER AT GINA'S

While they headed to the elevator, Kunle was carrying a big recyclable shopping bag that held the salmon, couscous, and the pesto sauce Maria made for the potluck. The bag also contained the tres leches cake Kunle picked up. Maria was holding the remaining three bottles of Riesling because Kunle and Maria finished one of the bottles, they couldn't' be bothered that it wasn't perfectly chilled. This time though, they had the wines in ice because they planned to continue drinking when they arrived at Gina's. Kunle was walking three paces behind Maria and couldn't stop admiring her every curve, like he didn't have her ass in his face just 20 minutes prior.

"God damn you're fine, "Kunle said, with almost a frustrating sigh, as Maria pushed the elevator button and Kunle closed the gap between them. Maria was blushing but Kunle couldn't tell. Without warning, he reached over her shoulder for her left breast with his right hand (the free hand) and pressed his pelvis against her butt. Maria felt a rush, she loved how Kunle did that. It was exactly what she wanted as she was still reliving what had just transpired. She got a lot of wetter and moaned slightly; this in turn caused Kunle's blood to begin rushing to the only part of his body that mattered in this moment. Maria remembered how Kunle had her screaming without care for her neighbors not so long ago; completely out of character for her. Also out of character for Maria is what was transpiring. The elevator door opened, and she turned around to look at Kunle.

Maria: Must we go to this thing?

Kunle: We should, I want to meet your friends (As he held the elevator door open for Maria to enter).

Maria: Fine. But we have unfinished business, you can't just be doing things like this and not expect consequences.

Kunle: Yea? What consequence(s) should I be looking forward to?

Maria: Well, you're going to need naps tomorrow, unless you're sleeping in. It's like that huh? We'll see, we will see! I don't want to "see," I want my back blown the fuck out. I don't know what's gotten into me.

Kunle: I have an idea what got into you haha.

Maria: Shut up big head. We're leaving the party early! They both exited the elevator and out into the car.

Maria: Can I play a song (to express how I feel)?

Kunle: Please (as he hands her his phone). How long is the drive?

Maria: 5 minutes (as she searched for Blow My Mind by Davido featuring Chris Brown).

Kunle: Seriously?

Maria: Yup, you opened the floodgates hahahahahahaha.

Kunle: Literally (they both laughed)! I wish I had more time (Kunle looks over and flashed a smile and a wink). Tell me about your friends. How many people are going to be at this thing?

Maria: About 8, maybe. Gina and her boyfriend Marcus, Wanda (she's transgendered), Jess, Shawn and Kristi, Grace and fucking Derek.

Kunle: Sounds like you don't like Derek. Why?Maria: You make up your own mind about him, but good luck. He's one of those "know it all" types that NEDS!!! you to know he's intelligent. He's smart, don't get me wrong, but not as smart as he thinks.

Kunle: Okay, and Grace? Are they together?

Maria: Yes, they met at some conference and they hit it off. He met her at a difficult time in her life and she just settled. I give them till the end of October.

Kunle: That's 3 months.

Maria: At best.

Kunle: How so, he's not good to her?.

Maria: You'll see. Take a left at this light and it's the peach house.

They exited the house and Kunle noticed the luxury cars park outside. He imagined if Maria's friends were as accomplished as she was. Maria led the way and Kunle followed. Before Maria could press the doorbell, the door was opened.

Gina: Bitch you're late!

Maria: I said 7:30, didn't I?

Gina: It's 7:40 (they both hugged each other as Gina took a good look at Kunle standing behind Maria). Oh, he's cute!!! Hi, I'm Gina (she said with the warmest of smiles)!

Kunle: I gathered, nice to meet you (Kunle instantly recognized that this was a healed person)! I'm Kunle!

Gina: I know (both Maria and Kunle started laughing).

Wanda: (Murmured) They fucked, and it looks like it was good! (Everyone stopped what they were doing and gave Wanda a sharp look) I'm just saying... shit!

Kunle: (Without hearing what Wanda just said). Hi everyone, I'm Kunle.

Maria: (Also missing Wanda's remark) Right, this is Kunle, that's Wanda, Marcus, Jess, and Derek!

Derek: Hi Maria, you're late. Shawn, Kristi, and Grace couldn't' make it.

Kunle: Yes, apologies for that, I had to go change my shirt.

Wanda: Why, Maria ripped it off when you guys were doing it (she murmurs as she sips from her cocktail)?

Kunle: Something like that (as he looked over at Maria who was headed to the kitchen)!

Derek: Nice get up! I hear you're here on business! What do you do?

Kunle: I'm a CPA.

Derek: You mean Certified Public Accountant?

Kunle: Is there another professional meaning for CPA?

Derek: I wanted to clarify in case anyone didn't know. You know, not everyone knows.Kunle: (looks around the table) I think they understood.

Maria: Can we eat?

Jess: Yes, I'm starving!

Gina: What else is new (Kunle was shocked at that remark by Gina)? Where are you from Kunle?Kunle: Nigeria, but I live in Hartford, CT.

Gina: Oh nice, I've never been to Hartford.

Kunle: You're not missing much.

Maria: I'll make you a plate babe (catching herself), I mean Kunle.

Wanda: Oh, already? Damn!

Maria: Ignore her, Kunle!

Kunle: I hope to live up to their expectations.

Gina: Oh, you're doing just fine.

Derek: I've been to Hartford, a while ago though.

Kunle: Yea? What brought you there?

Derek: I went on a college trip as part of my football team.

Kunle: Oh you used to play football in college (noticing Gina and Maria smiling)?

Derek: I was part of the cheerleading squad.

Kunle: Oh nice.

Maria: Here you go (handing Kunle a nice and well-balanced plate with couscous, salmon, grilled shrimp, and pesto sauce.

Gina: You forgot to say babe (as she looks up like that emoji).

Kunle: Haha, thanks babe (with a smile).

Everyone else emerged from the kitchen from their plates and dinner started. Kunle couldn't believe how good the salmon, couscous, and the sauce were. While he enjoyed his food, he watched Maria and her friends interact. Wanda reminds Kunle of "that friend" that's adventurous and would often engage strangers, but sometimes offend them because she has a unique sense of humor. Jess, a brunet caucasian woman from the Midwest, seemed kind and warm. She has the personality of the white girl that's been invited to "the cookout;" Kunle wonders if her cooking tastes bland (doubt it though). Derek, a black haired caucasian male from Chicago, struck Kunle as someone that seemed like he needs to be respected. Perhaps probably because he was bullied all his life until he got into college. Kunle took a bite of his food.

Kunle: Oh my god!!! This is delicious Maria, DAMN! (Everyone at the table couldn't help but laugh at Kunle).

Maria: Thanks!

Jess: So you guys are, what? Dating?

Marcus: Yes, what's the story?

Gina: Y'all need to mind y'all's business, that's what they are.

Kunle: You must give me the recipe for everything. (Kunle pours a generous amount of Riesling into his and Maria's glass).

Gina: I'll try some of that too, Kunle! Pour it up.

Marcus: You cook?

Wanda: (Interrupting Marcus) How did you guys meet? I'm tired of dating, no good guys out here.

Jess: It's not about you girl, let's enjoy Maria's story.

Maria: We somehow started following each other on IG a while ago.

Kunle: (Simultaneously shocked and impressed with how Jess responded to Wanda) Yea, I've been admiring her from a distance for a while. You can say I was "thirst trapped." But I knew that wasn't her intention though. I just admired how she carried herself. She had and still has this aura about her. And yes Marcus, I can throw down.

Wanda: Mm, interesting. I don't trust Nigerians.

Gina: Bitch I'm Nigerian.

Maria: Yea!!! When it's convenient!

Wanda: So her ass wasn't phat or nothing? Talking about, "I like her aura and shit (making a gesture of air quotes).

Kunle: (Sipping from his wine and catching himself about sounding like he is simultaneously revealing and admitting that he liked this girl too much.) Wait, you're Nigerian? (His head twisted like that guy in the meme with his head bent at a seventy-degree angle and eyes fixed on you like are you serious?)

Gina: How far?

Kunle: I dey oh, my sista! How body?

Gina: Body de!!!

Kunle: Bode DE!!! (simultaneously with Gina and both bursting out laughing!!!).

Wanda: See? I don't trust Nigerians. Who's this new bitch? Gina never sounded like this!!!

Maria: I told yall, when convenient.

Derek: Whaadathdcartt's haaaappening?

Kunle: Don't chew with your mouth open, (pausing for effect) "Bro."

Everyone was surprised at Kunle's tone and even Kunle wondered if he was being too harsh with his tone. Subconsciously, Kunle felt he had to set Derek straight because it seemed like his new girl felt some type of way about him. He looked at Maria's face and she had that look of "yes, that's my man and 'HE!' gon get all this pussy tonight," with the expression of joy on her face.

Wanda: OMG, I need a Nigerian. You got any cute cousins.

Kunle: Yea, all my cousins are attractive actually. The men around my age all seemed to be married and or they all live all over the country, except the East Coast.

Gina: Maria! Balcony (winking at Maria)?

Maria: Yes!

Kunle: (puzzled) Is that a safe word for something?

Gina: Girl time, mind ya business.

Maria: Code four twenty

Kunle: Oh, elevation time?

Maria: Yes baby (excited while twirling her hair looking playfully in Kunle's eyes)! You bout it?

Kunle: All day, every day!!!

Marcus: This is too cute, both of y'all are too cute!

Derek: Yea, their chemistry makes me wanna puke. Hashtag honeymoon phase.

Kunle, Maria, and Gina got up and went outside the balcony of the townhouse. The sun was completely gone, and darkness was about 70% in, while the moon was rising over the ocean in some remote part of the world on sandy shores. Kunle, interrupted by Maria's cough because she's an amateur smoker, realized that he was high already. Either Gina's kush (marijuana) must have been really strong or he hasn't had some in such a long time and he's now a light weight. He pats Maria on the back and slightly rubs it while admiring her amazing dress. Maria passed Kunle the spliff (joint) and he took a couple of paces back to take a puff and passes the spliff to Gina, who took a hit and passed it back to Maria.

Kunle: Aww, you don't have to try so hard to impress me.

Maria: (Choking even further mid puff busted out laugh, as did Gina): Are you not impressed?

Gina: We're keeping this one. Look at all the squares in there? They're probably talking shit about y'all. I'mma go stop it.

Gina walked back into the house and Kunle observed her. She stood about 5'1" and definitely hits the gym. Her dress is also form fitting, but longer on her because of her height. She was wearing earrings that looked like she got them on a trip overseas or at a farmer's market (pre Etsy days). Her hair was out in an afro and looks like her whole existence is in rebellion to societal constraints. She has a few visible tattoos that Kunle was curious about but didn't get to asking her about them. Kunle really admired and related to her, but loved it more that Maria is best friends with her. Her boyfriend (Marcus) seems like a genuinely good guy. He's mixed race, Italian and Somalian, and very "light skinned;" Kunle initially assumed he was white. As Gina disappeared and closed the sliding door behind her, Kunle moved towards Maria; it appeared to her as if Kunle was gliding. They were both high. At this time, the temperature had dropped about twelve degrees from when Kunle got to Maria's apartment about two hours earlier.

Maria: Oh you think you're smooth huh?

Kunle: Can I be vulnerable with you? (rubbing Maria's shoulder as if to try to keep her warm).

Maria really appreciated the gesture and the combination of Kunle's touch, and the slight breeze made her nipples erect and she subconsciously leaned towards Kunle in such a subtle way that it is very easy to miss, but Kunle did not miss it.

Kunle: You see? I feel like this is all too perfect. That's why I made that comment!

Maria: I thought as much!

Kunle: And your response was perfect...

Kunle leans in for a kiss and Maria was excited to kiss him because he had turned her on from the moment they left that elevator and every single action he's taken since then has just been making her more eager; including putting Derek in his place, understanding her in her element, and the general chemistry and how he was cool with all her friends. She tried not to let these thoughts distract her from this kiss she was about to melt into. She could taste a hint of the pesto sauce, salmon, and smoke. She loved it! It was like rainbow skittles were exploding in powdery form in her wet mouth and her saliva glands were on high alert and were high functioning. Kunle loved her taste. He could taste the Riesling in her mouth and her mouth was moisturized and so was his. Both their senses were heightened. They kissed passionately while Kunle's hands carefully caressed Maria's body, touching every essential receptor for the sensory organ (i.e. she felt everything). Kunle felt a sensation similar to the waves of an ocean gently pushing his body to shore in ninety degree weather on a shore with fine sand. He was really high!

This continued for about 5 minutes, but inside, everyone was talking about Kunle and Maria...

Derek: They've been gone a while; you think they're fucking?

Marcus: Gina's neighbor is not home. She's out of town in her four-door yellow Mini Cooper. I love that car.

Wanda: They're fucking!!!

Gina: THEY'RE NOT FUCKING!

Jess: They seem so perfect. It's like too perfect.
Derek: Absolutely, almost like an act.

Gina: Y'all just need to mind y'all's businesses.

Wanda: Everything tastes soo (emphasis on the so) good girl!

Maria: Yea, the Mac and cheese is fire (emerging front the back porch with Kunle)Kunle: I gotta try that now!

Jess: Y'all are high?

Maria: (Giggling along with Kunle) Maybe a smidge!

Kunle: Who's got the song?

Gina: Yes, let's dance!!! (She was also high).

Maria: Yes, let's dance.

Jess: (Growing even more jealous and happy for Maria) Y'all were out there for like an hour.

Derek: 38 minutes, I timed them.

Maria: (Murmurs) Creep.

Marcus: Nothing really loud, but the Samsung can handle herself a bit (pointing the remote at the 60-inch ultra-thin Samsung TV hung on the wall).

Kunle: (Kunle didn't want to dance as he was just getting the munchies but welcomed the idea. He wanted to taste more of Maria). Can I choose a song?

Marcus: Go for it, but please let me play this song real quick. (Marcus opened the YouTube app as

Kunle went to get himself some Mac and Cheese with some more of Maria's couscous and pasta; he grabbed a clean fork for Maria in case she wanted a bite. Marcus selected Ginger by Wizkid featuring Burna Boy).

Kunle: Na, you can play every song for the rest of the night (he said with food in his mouth, but with his hands covering it. He was pleased with Marcus' choice. Everything was perfect. Kunle observes Maria dancing as he takes the fork with a base of cheesecake, layered with couscous, followed by salmon, and the pesto sauce dripped over it, to his mouth. He sat his plate down and started dancing towards Maria).

Derek: Don't chew with your mouth open.

Jess: There they go again, so cute (as she got up and started to dance too).

Gina: Common Marc, let's dance.

Marcus: Cool, I love high Gina.

Kunle: (Thought to himself, "how'd I get so lucky?) You're such an amazing cook too! Where have you been all my life? (Kunle observed Maria's eyes widen up).

Maria: Waiting for you, silly (she said with a cute but sincere smile as she looked into Kunle's eyes who had his arms wrapped around her butt)!

Kunle: I'm here baby!

They both danced and got lost in each other's hands for about ten minutes, almost as if they can't remember that they had company. Gina was also similarly lost, but Marcus was the adult; Jess danced by herself and Wanda just watched on.

Kunle: Do you think they'd be mad if we dip early?

Maria: Nah, I don't care, let's go! They'd understand.

Kunle: Okay, I'll call the Uber.

Maria: Sounds good.

Kunle and Maria headed for the kitchen; Maria to make some to go boxes and Kunle to give her a hand. Gina observed what was going on but wanted to dance to the song that came on right at that moment, Essence by Wizkid ft Tems. She was hyped and was so engulfed in her dance that by the time the song was over, she waved goodbye to Kunle and Maria as they snuck out of the building.

While in the Uber, Kunle informed the driver that he'll be adding another drop-off location because he did not want to be too forward to assume that Maria was going to invite him back into her home or to spend the night with Her.

Kunle: Hey Chris (Uber driver), I'll add a second drop-off location, is that cool?

Chris: Absolutely.

Maria: Want to spend the night together?

Kunle: Thought you'd never ask! My place or yours (as Kunle continues to delicately run his fingers through Maria's dress like he was trying to diffuse a bomb).

Maria: Mine, definitely!

Kunle: Chris, sorry, only one drop off location.

Chris: You've got it!

Kunle glanced at the time displayed on the dashboard and realized it was only 9:30 pm.

CHAPTER 5

THE DATE

Maria heard a faded knock on the door as 6 Inch by Beyonce played on her Sonos while her and Kunle were covered in sweat, the result of passionate and intense love making. What Maria did not anticipate was a Kunle on drugs (Marijuana). They had a night cap after the Uber dropped them off. She had an unopened bottle of tequila, Casamigos Reposado, and six pre-rolled joints. They had smoked half of a joint and the tequila bottle is now only half full. Maria was tipsy, not drunk, and Kunle was high and only had one and a half drink really strong drinks.

Maria heard the knock again, this time a little louder; even Kunle heard it. She was in the reverse cowgirl position and she stopped rotating her waist. Kunle didn't want her to stop, but he also heard the knock. His senses were fully heightened and his imagination wild.

Kunle: Please tell me that's not your husband or a boyfriend that's being released from prison

Maria: (Giggled) Lets find out.

She gets off Kunle, but not without kissing his fully erect penis, a little longer than she should have. They both heard the knock again and hurried up. Kunle puts on his boxers and his white t-shirt. Maria puts on a robe and put her natural hair in a bun. She hurried to the door and Kunle strolled behind her, giving her a distance of about six feet. Maria opened the door and seemed surprised.

Maria: Hi Karen, how are you?

Karen: I'm well, how are you? Everything okay? I heard some noises and it isn't like you, so I wanted to check in on you.

Maria: Oh I'm okay, thank you so much (she was genuinely touched by the gesture of her neighbor caring about her safety). My friend and I got a little carried away.

Karen: It's okay, at least one of us is having a great Friday night. Can I come in?

Maria: (Moved her head to look at an handsome Kunle in his boxers and white t-shirt. Kunle was shaking his head in disapproval and she gave him a mischievous smile). I'm not sure that's a good idea as we were in the middle of an intense session, but you can come in for a quick second.

Kunle puzzled as to why Maria would invite her neighbor in while they're both almost naked. He took a few steps closer to Maria as she opens the door for Karen.

Kunle: Hello.
Maria: This is Kunle!
Karen: Hi Kole.
Kunle: It's Kuunle!!!
Karen: I'm sorry, Konle. Very nice to meet you. I don't mean to intrude, just being a good neighbor. Looks like you guys were giving it a really good go.
Kunle: Yes we were... But, now we're not. Drink?
Maria: (Puzzled at Kunle) I don't think Karen would be staying.
Karen: No, I can have a drink. What ya got? (She whispers to Maria, you lucky, lucky girl)
Kunle: There's a bottle of Casamigos somewhere, interested?
Maria: Please have a seat (pointing to the yellow velvet sofa that looks too classy, inviting, and too comfortable).
Karen: This sofa is everything!!!
Kunle: Right? That's what I said.
Maria: Ice or no ice? And also, do you want a

chaser? I have ginger beer.

Karen: Yes to all of the above!!!

Maria puts three solid balls of ice, the size of a ping pong ball, in three rocks glasses and brought them along with the bottle of tequila and ginger beer in a tray to the living room. She noticed Kunle was looking out of the glass sliding doors and Karen was engulfed in one of her paintings.

Maria: Here we go!!!

Kunle: Thanks gorgeous.

Karen: Thank you so much (as she pours a generous amount of tequila into her glass).

Maria dashed a look of shock at Kunle and observed Kunle's smirk. Kunle internalized Maria's look to say "Uh, this bitch!!!" Maria didn't quite know what to think of Kunle's smirk, she didn't like it. Meanwhile, Karen, now back on the bright yellow couch with feather cushion, was very comfortable and relaxed. As Karen was about to engage Kunle, he interrupted.

Karen: So Kon...

Kunle: I'm going to go on the balcony a look at the moon. She's calling out to me.

Maria: Yes, she's lovely isn't she?

Karen: (Looking puzzled as she tries to look out through the sliding door) Okay. (Both Maria and Karen watched Kunle disappear in his white t-shirt and boxers and Maria observed Karen stare with delight).

Maria: He's a looker isn't he?

Karen: Yes, oh my god. I shouldn't be here. I just wanted to make sure you were okay. I promise to not interrupt next time.

Maria: Were we that loud?

Karen: Not really, I heard you scream when I went to close the balcony door and wanted to check in on you.

Maria: I truly appreciate it and I definitely would have done the same if the shoes were reversed.

Karen: (Finishing her drink in one big gulp) Well, I'll leave you both to it. I hope it's a really long night for you (she said with an awkward wink).

Maria: Thank you Karen, enjoy your night.

Maria walked Karen to the door and went to join Kunle on the balcony with the bottle of tequila, and the remaining half of the joint they didn't finish. The balcony was unusually large, about ten feet long and five feet wide. It was big enough for an outdoor sofa, a coffee table, two armchairs, and a hammock. Kunle was seated on the left side of the sofa with his feet on the coffee table. He observed Maria approach in her silk robe with her nipples fully erect. The night was still chilly, but not too chilly; it was a comfortable sixty five degrees. The stars were very noticeable and the moon was shining bright. Still standing, Maria set the bottle down; she lit the joint and took a really long and impressive drag. She passed the joint to Kunle as she stood over him. Kunle moved to the side a bit so Maria can sit on his lap facing him with her back turned to the night sky. He took a really long drag too, in an attempt to make jest of Maria, but he couldn't hang because he choked. Maria leaned in and whispered in his left ear as she rubs on his nipples through his shirt.

Maria: Blow it in my mouth!!!

Kunle tilted his head backwards and obeyed Maria's instructions. Amazed at how incredible this woman is, he couldn't imagine what he did to get so lucky.

Kunle: If you're trying to butter me up before you kill me, just know I'll probably do anything you damn well please at this point.

Maria: My only interest at the moment is your dick in my mouth.

The morning sun was heaven sent, Maria imagined as Kunle observe it kiss her fresh shea butter covered and makeup free face. Her skin radiated joy and harmony, Kunle thought. He thought to himself that she truly is nature's gift to earth, at least to him in that moment. His eyes were hidden behind some overpriced designer polarized and reflective sunglasses he purchased about a year ago. Maria with her eyes closed and face directed at the sun glowed and radiated. She was listening to the gentle music from Kunle's stereo speakers as her curls bounced; Cherish The Day by Sade played. Kunle had called in a favor and somehow it came through. He mentioned to Shirley, a director at the company he's consulting with, that he would love to have a date at Phipps Conservatory and Botanical Gardens and she said she knows someone that could make it happen. Maria is truly impressed, but only with Kunle's initiative and not his reach, as Kunle thought. Anyone can reserve a conservatory but not anyone can plan a beautiful picnic, especially in a city they're just visiting.

Kunle had red wine and some sandwiches. He found a bakery that had a sandwich shop on Friday and put the order in. He said to the chef, Pierre, that he wanted to take a special lady for a picnic and wanted bite sized sandwiches that pairs well with red wine. Pierre smiled and sympathized at the love struck romantic in his bakery:

Pierre: Okay my friend, she's a lucky girl (he said in his French accent).

Kunle: Thank you my brother. I will pick it up at 9 am! Do you have a picnic basket I can borrow or buy? **Pierre**: I'll have one for you tomorrow.

Looking at Maria, Kunle remembered how she looked in her robe this morning when he poured her coffee as she read the newspaper at the coffee table. She radiated!!! Her hair was wrapped in her sateen Moyovelli Wura scarf, her face was glistening and her eye lids looked perfect. Kunle hoped to catch a glimpse of her perfect nipple at some point while they drank coffee and read the news, but he was out of luck; that damn robe was the biggest tease and Kunle loved it.

Kunle: I have to go pick something up at 9.

Maria: What?

Kunle: Our breakfast.

Maria: Okay, where are you taking me?

Kunle: You'll see, just use your allergy medication.

Maria: So we are going to be outside?

Kunle: Yes! Do you have sunblock?

Maria: Yes, I have some, all natural!

Kunle: We're going to need it as well.

Maria: What else are we going to need?

Kunle: Do you have a picnic blanket?

Maria: I have something.

Kunle: Perfect!

Maria: So that's it, a picnic?

Kunle: Maybe, just chill. You'll find out eventually.

Maria: Okay!

Back in the garden, the blanket was perfect. It was microfiber and Kunle grabbed some pillows as well. Kunle poured Maria a glass of wine and said, "it's seven pm somewhere," even though it was really 10 am. Maria was overwhelmed with the details in Kunle's plan. He had chosen the perfect spot. It was on a hill overlooking downtown Pittsburg. There was a tree to provide shade when needed, but the sun was in her glory. The joyful Maria opened her eyes and smiled with all the muscles on her face at Kunle. She said to herself, "so this is what they mean when they say 'Yoruba Demon.'" She had on oversized square Dior sunglasses that sat perfectly on her face, like it was bespoke. She had the elegance of a princess that escaped the luxurious prisons of her castle walls to discover a whole new world that had been foreign to her.

Maria: I have never experienced anything like this, I will never regret sliding in your DMs

Kunle: Do you journal?

Maria: Yes, but not consistently. You?

Kunle: No, but please document this day for our grandkids, if we're fortunate to have any.

Maria: (Choked on her wine and coughed it out) Huh?

Kunle: (Unbothered as he lights a Joint and took a long drag from it) Well, don't die yet silly.

Maria: I thought I heard you say grand kids.

Kunle: Yes, if we're fortunate. Don't you want kids? Adopted or not!

Maria: I want kids, but you're crazy.

Kunle: Perhaps. (He passed the joint to Maria who took a long drag from it). This city is really something isn't it?

Maria: It absolutely is. I wonder what Hartford is like.

Kunle: She has her charms! I'd love to explore it with you.

Maria: Is this how you trap your women?

Kunle: What do you mean?

Maria: Is this how you get women to sleep with you?

Kunle: No, I saw this place on one of my runs and thought it'll be a beautiful place for a wedding! But then I was given an opportunity to spend time with the most beautiful woman in Pittsburg. I had to do something spectacular.

Maria: Well, you're getting lucky tonight, that's for sure.

Kunle: I want to get lost in your love tonight, but before then, tell me about your favorite flower.

Maria looked around and saw an assorted field of flowers; lilac, purple, yellow, red, green, blue, violet, etc. filled the gardens around them. She leaned forward and got on her knees to get a better look as Kunle leaned on one his right butt cheek and right elbow. Maria leaned over and came face to face with Kunle; she kissed him passionately and said;

Maria: Though I may never see you again, you are the man of my dreams.

Kunle: Why would you not see me again? I've never met any woman quite like you.

Maria: Let's go walk the garden, please!

Kunle: Okay gorgeous.

They explored the botanical garden and took selfies in multiple locations. They smelled every flower and studied every rose, like a wanna be Sommelier drinking wine like they had to give a report on its composition. Kunle kept asking to take pictures of Maria without revealing them to her. She wondered what his intentions were with the pictures, but didn't think too much since these are photos that she wouldn't mind being shared publicly. She was wearing a yellow dress with navy blue polka dots. Her natural hair and curls bounced in the gentle breeze and her a-lined dress danced with the breeze as well.

Kunle: Please do a spin for me, like you're a 3 year old girl that just discovered that her dress opens up every time she spins.

Maria thought it was silly, but did it anyways, because it felt good to be seen, admired, drooled over, and adored. Kunle seemed sincere, and he was. She was comfortable. She had on zero make up and she knew she looked absolutely gorgeous. The joy she displayed reminded Kunle of that of his nieces on Sunday mornings back in Nigeria. They were always happy and their Shae butter covered skin always glistened in the Sunday morning sun. Her joy was innocent and uncorrupted by life's many forces.

Kunle: Dance with me, please. (as he sets his speaker down. I'm Hanging UP My Heart for You by Solomon Burke playing).

Maria: I'd love to.

Maria put her hands around Kunle's neck and Kunle put his hands on her waist. They had the whole garden to themselves and the only noises they heard was the music from Kunle's speakers, water fountains, and birds. They danced to the whole song and kissed through the next song, To Be Loved by Jackie Wilson.

Maria felt a rush she had never felt. A feeling she couldn't explain. She felt chills that she struggled to understand. Like she was frozen in ice but then surrounded by fire. She felt safe in Kunle's arms. Held on firm to his broad shoulders as she shed one or two unexplainable tears. Kunle was transported to an unfamiliar place. He was experiencing feelings he couldn't explain as well, but he loved them. Maria felt so comfortable in his arms. Her skin so soft and her hair smelled of lavender. Kunle buried his face in it and told her how good she smelled.

Kunle: I want to cuddle, is that something you're into?

Maria: No, but for some reason I'm sure I'll enjoy it with you, so I'm game.

Kunle looked at the time and it was midday. They packed up the tan leather picnic basket Pierre lent Kunle and made their way to Maria's condo, as Clementine by Pink Martini played in the background. Upon arrival, the two love birds fell asleep in each other's arms on the yellow velvet couch. By the time Kunle opened his eyes because his phone was vibrating, the sun was beginning to set. His sudden motion disrupted Maria's sleep, waking her up as well.

Kunle: Can I draw a bath in your tub?

Maria: Sure! What do you have in mind?

Kunle: It'll be fun to watch the sunset from your tub, wouldn't it?

Maria: I've never thought of it, but It would be!!!

Kunle got up and drew a warm bath. He poured a generous amount of Maria's organic coconut soap, sea salt, rose petals, and some roses from the ten dozen red roses he purchased for her from the garden. He placed his speaker in the bathroom and played Sade radio station on Pandora, and Cherish The Day by Sade was the first song to play.

Kunle: I think the bath is ready.

Maria showed up in her white cotton robe with a towel for Kunle and they both settled in to watch the sunset. Kunle had grabbed a bottle of Bordeaux Superieur and had two glasses ready. He handed Maria a glass and poured into the glass until it was three-fourths full. He poured himself a glass and leaned back as he puts his right arm around Maria's neck and held the glass with his left hand, as Back At One by Brian McKnight played.

Kunle: Life is truly beautiful!

CHAPTER 6

THE DATE CONT'D

Are you happy? Kunle asks Maria shortly after she kissed his right hand that rested on her shoulder, cupping her left breast. He waited two long minutes to ask that question. He didn't want to alert her to his awareness of how her feelings for him were being revealed and he didn't want her knowing about his (he was insecure and not sure if his feelings would be well received). He asked the question while he reached for his wine glass with his left hand and while observing that the candles were holding on strong and that the night was blue; he noticed the first star (he smiled and thought it was some kind of a sign [though he didn't believe in such]).

Meanwhile, Maria wanted him to. She felt like she was in some kind of movie and she was the star with the best supporting actor. She was Alicia Keys and he was Idris Elba (though Kunle looked nothing like Idris Elba). She felt like it had been a perfect weekend and she couldn't wait for it to be over so she could get back to reality. However, she felt like those moments were magic and she is enjoying each and every minute. She felt like the set had been set by the finest of designers and planners, tailored to her specifications without her contribution. She felt like someone stole her play book and had figured out a way to avoid the mountains, hills, and walls she has in place to protect her heart. She even questions herself if she was falling in love, but she quickly dismissed that evil thought, "this shit is not fucking real." She felt like Idris Elba was James Bond and she was one of his women, but the main one that ends up on vacation with Bond at the end of the movie.

Maria: What's with the philosophical question?

Kunle: Haha, I love how your mind works and understands mine.

Maria: How so? And regarding your question, are you asking if I'm happy now or if I'm happy in life?

Kunle: You knew the question was deeper than it seemed, that's why your mind gets mine. And I'm asking regarding both situations.

Maria: So why not ask the question directly.

Kunle: Because I want to know both, for clues to how to answer two different questions I can't ask yet.

Maria: Well, this moment (she paused for about 30 seconds as she stared into the blue evening that was slowly turning into night) this day has been magic, with a capital M. This whole weekend has been outstanding.

Kunle: How so?

Maria: I'll get back to that. In regard to the question if I'm happy in life, my answer is a solid yes. I'm comfortable with all my past actions and decisions, I'm at peace with what's to come, I'm in tune with myself.

Kunle: Wow!

Maria: The weekend has been magical because of our time together and I think that's because you've been consistent and full of positive energy.

Kunle: I'm stunned.

Maria: I'm not surprised (as she chuckles). This water is now feeling a bit cold, but I'd love to change that and stay like this a little longer. This is better than sex and sex with you is the best I've ever had by the way.

Kunle: Wow, I feel like that's a huge compliment. Thank you! Lean up a bit let me let some of this water out and fill it with hot water.

Maria: It is a compliment... big head and that's a genius idea.

Kunle opened the tap and turned it all the way hot. He felt a lot of the burn of the hot water, but he didn't flinch because he was doing it for love. Wait, "am I in love?" Kunle asked himself as he felt his heart skip a beat. "Holy shit!"

Maria: This is perfect.

Kunle: This is enough?

Maria: No, not yet, a little bit more. I want this moment a lot longer.Kunle: (Excited at the news) Okay!

Kunle turned the tap off and relaxed back into his comfortable position, placing the blue pillow behind him for neck support. They both sat in silence for ten minutes as they listened to Snoh

Alegra's Ugh, Those Feels Again album. Kunle subconsciously played it because he wanted to send a message to her. He wanted her to hear the line that says "I fall for you every time I resist you." And "I try not to show how I feel about you, thinking we should wait but we don't really want to." Maria loved his choice, she didn't connect the dots, but loved how he's been able to pick theperfect soundtrack for each occasion this weekend. This has been a fun weekend but she felt like it is not sustainable as she pondered on the future. "What if I don't want to? What if I don't have the energy? What if I'm upset about something?" She stopped herself and reminded herself not to fall for this "Yoruba Demon."

Maria: Good song choice (she says as she breaks the silence)

Kunle: Yea? Listen to this next part.

Maria: Okay.

Kunle: I try not to show how I feel about you, thinking we should wait, but we don't really want to.

Maria: Aww, you're catching feelings already?

Kunle: I'm just sharing the phrases that I felt were perfect for the moment.

Maria: Aww, lover boy. It's okay, you don't have to be shy. Let's get into some robes.

They exited the tub and though Kunle wanted the chance to watch her stand up so he can see her beautiful body from this angle. He imagined it'll be beautiful to watch as she'd stand up straight, as water drips down her body, grab a towel to dry off a bit. She'll then proceed to exit the shower slowly as she steps over the tub with her left leg, she'll stop and smile at Kunle as he watches her like a dog reunited with his owner. What would her ass look like from this angle? "I bet it'll look glorious," he thought to himself.

None of that happened because Kunle was a gentleman and he exited first and helped her out of the tub as he handed her a towel like a well-trained butler. Maria fancied it, she loved all of it.

Maria: Grab the joint, let's stay at this level.

Kunle: Okay! (He said in a high-pitched voice).

Maria went into the room as Kunle dried himself. He observed himself in the mirror and the voice of Michael Blackson came to his mind "I am one sexy morafucker." Maria reappeared and gave him a bag that contained a matching silk robe, but the one she handed him was men's and was brand new. Kunle was shocked and impressed at the same time.

Kunle: Men's huh?

Maria: Yup!

Kunle: Are you sure you're single?

Maria: I was saving that for Idris Elba but you'll do.

Kunle: Wow, thank you... I guess.

Maria: (Disappointed as she felt like Kunle did not understand the compliment, she turned around to kiss him as he slipped the robe on) You're welcome!

They kissed so passionately that Kunle was convinced he had met his soulmate. He observed Maria raise her leg as if she was a Disney princess and he loved it. He grabbed and squeezed her butt with both hands and she loved it.

Kunle: Come, let's light this up and get comfortable.

Maria: Yes daddy! (Looking Kunle dead in the eyes as his face lit up with satisfaction. "And he's back").

Maria led Kunle to the ottoman as Kunle redirected the sound from the bathroom to the living room. He wondered if Maria had an ex- boyfriend or husband that set up the gadgets in her condo for her. Maria placed two pillows on the ottoman as Kunle poured some hot water, from the translucent electric kettle, into two mugs that Maria had added honey and tea bags to. They both settled in and Kunle changed the tempo of music by playing Show You off by Wurld.

Kunle: I hope you'd give me a chance to show you off for the rest of my life.

Maria: Only if you don't blow it.

Unsure how to receive the answer, he felt reassured that he's not the only one catching feelings. At least it seems like she's feeling a spark. Here you go, he hands her the mug filled with tea. He laid first on the ottoman and Maria took her position, like a queen in the inner sanctum of her palace. Kunle felt like she was Missandei and he was Grey Worm (from Game of Thrones); this way of thinking keeps him loyal; he's always assumed.

Kunle: Tell me about your last relationship.

Maria: We met seven years ago and dated for 4 years. Turned out he was already married with three children that he abandoned. I ran like the devil was chasing me. I recently came to the conclusion that there's no place to run to while listening to Nina Simone's Sinnerman.

Kunle: Wow, that's crazy. I'm sorry.

Maria: Don't be, I was younger and now I'm wiser. What about you?

Kunle: Well, did he set this place up for you?

Maria: No, I hooked this up myself.

Kunle: I love your taste.

Maria: (Softly) Yea, me too!

Kunle: My past relationship was outstanding but couldn't work because we both had some growing to do.

Maria: What a way to be a man, taking responsibility and shit.

Kunle: Well,

Maria: (Cutting him off) And you're more man than any man I know, besides my father.

Kunle: That's saying a lot, thank you. You barely know me though.

Maria: I know the most important things.

Kunle: Like?

Maria: You're consistent, present, happy, creative, dynamic, and most importantly a protector.

Kunle: Wow, all from one weekend?

Maria: You know a lot about someone that shares as much as you do on social media when you spend a weekend with them.

They both shared a warm and heartfelt laugh and sipped from their tea that was soothing to the soul on that warm evening with the windows open and the moon fully shining.

Maria: So you and your ex over or still at it?

Kunle: Forget about her, I have a confession.

Maria: (A bit nervous because she is not ready for his verbal confirmation of his feelings for her.) Uh oh, anything good rarely follows those words.

Kunle: (Pausing for effect) I have a matching set of silk robes too, but the women's is medium.

Maria: That's my size, I ain't no skinny bitch, though they're beautiful.

Kunle: Calm down, you're beautiful whichever way you choose.

Maria: Wise man.

Kunle: If I were to make a life decision on a house that I'll live in forever, I'll pick the one that is fully loaded with top of the line everything.

Maria: What does that have to do with my body image issues?

Kunle: You are the fully furnished house I'll choose. (Maria was shocked but liked the analogy).

Maria: What equipment would I have?

Kunle: If you can imagine it, it's there and it'll never break and would stay shiny and spotless forever.

Maria: Wow, now I'm flattered. Your imagination is wild huh?

Kunle: Yea, I'm in my head a lot.

Maria: Tell me a story. I want to be the main character.

Kunle: Okay (as he felt a gentle breeze blow the smooth silk, reminding him of how good it felt).

Maria: Go on, Mr. Smooth Operator.

Kunle: Imagine yourself in a blue silk dress and a pair of red Louboutin stilettos. You're wearing a tanzanite tennis necklace in 18k white gold, but it's not too loud. You have a red silk scarf wrapped around your Hermes bag. How do you want your hair?

Maria: Curly, bouncy, hmm and moisturized. Wild and unrestrained.

Kunle: Okay! Your hair is shiny, like you bathed it in the finest of natural ingredients and smells heavenly (a scent only you can create). Standing next to you is Idris Elba, or his substitute, as you both wait for your car.

Maria: What was he wearing?

Kunle: He was wearing an all-black silk outfit like the one Nipsey Hustle wore in Higher music video, only his was silk top to bottom and tailored by his Nigerian tailor. He stands at the same height as you, elevated on your stilettos, and he's wearing a pair of black tuxedo shoes and a black and gold traditional Yoruba cap. He has a yellow gold tanzanite ring on and his cufflinks were also yellow gold and tanzanite.

Maria: Do you guys have traditional names for those caps, so I know how to ask for them when you go to Africa next? And what is a tanzanite?

Kunle: Good save, but it's just cap. To my knowledge, my language has one word for cap and it's fìlá which literally translate to cap, any cap. Tanzanite is a gem stone that's rarer than diamond and only found in Tanzania on the hills of Mount Kilimanjaro. It was recently discovered (in 1967) and only enough supply for our generation.

Maria: Feela?

Kunle: Perfect.

Maria: Thank you, please continue, I'm captivated by your story. Where are we going?

Kunle: You're having dinner with the president of the country you're living in because your farms and businesses are thriving, and you've been very generous in giving back to the community. Your philosophy is "The goal is to get rich with the community, not while the community remains stagnant because you're just paying slightly above the average salaries."

Maria: I said that?

Kunle: You and your partner/husband agreed on it.

Maria: I love it!

Kunle: The driver pulls up the navy-blue Rolls Royce with white interior and the roof had the stars projected.

Maria: Wait, which country?

Kunle: You pick! I pull the door open, I mean Idris, pulls the door open for you and extends his left hand as you step into the car. He bows slightly, subconsciously without realizing it, but you saw it. You didn't need his hands, but you knew how he treated you and that's why you married him and ended up in paradise.

Maria: Go on...

Kunle: The driver exits the car, dressed in some sort of uniform because Idris wanted to give a treat to his queen. He wanted to remind her that although they're living a modest life where his main source of income are his farms that has turned into cash cows. The driver opens the door for Idris as he gets in, his Bluetooth automatically connected, and plays She's Royal by Tarrus Riley. Maria smiled and realized what was happening. She loved it and loved the gesture even more. Idris slides the roof open because the air was fresh, clean, you can smell the turquoise blue salt waters that shelters the island.

Maria: See? Hair down haha.

Kunle: Right! The drive wasn't far but you wanted it to last a lot longer.

Maria: Exactly!

Kunle: Idris agreed to your request and sent a text message to the president "we're running a bit late."

Maria: Wow, that powerful huh?

Kunle: Go with it.

Maria: I am, I'm loving this.

Kunle: The truth of the matter is you were going to dinner on the water at one of your resorts with the best chef on the island and Idris knew the president also wanted to solicit donations for his reelection bid and for his political party. Even though you both decided not to participate in the local politics, Idris needed something from him.

Maria: Why is he keeping him waiting then?

Kunle: It's a power move. The car drove around that night, the sunset came a lot earlier than usual and the moon came up early and vibrant. After driving around for 10 minutes without a word and Idris playing songs such as; She's Still Loving Me by Morgan Heritage and I Feel Good by Barres Hamond, she said she was ready. Idris told the driver to head to the venue as he reached for your hands (Kunle grabbed Maria's hand and squeezed it in real life). He saw a few tears roll down her cheeks. "Are you okay?" Idris asked. You look at him and say?

Maria: Thank you for building me a dream to live in?

Kunle: He smiles back and says "you deserve this world babe. You're my rock, on which we have built this modest empire. You centered me and I greatly appreciate you.

Maria: (With tears rolling down her cheek) Wow.

Kunle: I'm getting hungry. Wanna grab a bite?

Maria: Yes, me too. Let's order in.

Kunle: Okay. I read about this Jamaican restaurant that's supposed to be really good. Let me see if they deliver.

Maria: Yes, I need flavor to seal in your beautiful story.

Kunle: Haha, did you enjoy it?

Maria: I did, please don't tell me it's over.

Kunle: The tea has gone cold, but to be continued.

Maria: Please continue.

Kunle: I have to give you something to look forward to.

Maria: You only have one story? And trust me, there's plenty I'm looking forward to.

Kunle: There is only one fantasy I want to explore consistently. There would be other stories, but that's for the future. Let's watch a comedy, you choose.

Maria: Coming to America!

Kunle: It's on Amazon Prime!

Maria: Yes.

The food arrived and they both sat on cushions placed on the ground by the fire place that Kunle had suggested they light. They laughed the evening away as they devoured the oxtail and curry goat Kunle had ordered. It was delicious. Kunle left Maria's apartment and went back to The Oaklander to prep for his week; make sure his dry-cleaning was done, catch up on emails sent by the kiss ass colleagues that want to seem like they're going above and beyond by sending emails on the weekend, and plan his week. Maria did the same after Kunle left and she also meal prepped; she didn't let Kunle leave before making love. It was slow, passionate, and extremely emotional for

Maria. She was in control and got exactly what she didn't know she needed, but love to have experienced. "Is this the end?" She asked herself. If it is, she thinks she was at peace with it and would cherish the sacred moments she had this weekend.

CHAPTER 7

TYPICAL

It was going to be a busy week for Kunle, but he was as certain as he was on Friday that it wasn't because he had a plan. He also had a feeling that he couldn't shake, as much as he tried. He had several internal battles on his morning run four hours earlier.

"Man, it was just a fun weekend, that's all. It's like one of those one night stands. Did we even discuss expectations for this? No, we didn't, so I'm probably just tripping off nothing. I wonder what she's thinking at the moment. What would she be wearing? Maybe a white shirt and a navy blue suit? Oh, and some heels. Wait, she works at a start up, so definitely not a suit. Maybe some denim, a shoulder-less strap... but wait a minute, she does have a phatty though. And her confidence is refreshing!" Kunle had more internal dialogs before coming to some sort of resolution. "Fuck it."

By midday, Kunle had ran four miles, responded to forty-two emails, found and documented his other client's disaster that Kevin needed him to turn around by Friday. He stopped typing when he felt someone's presence. He unplugged his noise cancelling Bose earphones and turned around and notice Travis in his navy blue Calvin Klein suit. He was looking sharp with his fresh fade and bright smile.

Travis: Lunch?

Kunle: I'm starved.

Travis: Yea, me too.

Kunle: Meet by the car in 5? Gotta hit the head.

Travis: Bet!

Kunle locked his computer, grabbed his grey blazer, and went to the bathroom. On his way, he ran into Shirley, the tax director at the client site, and she asked to have a drink with him after work; he agreed. It was a cloudy morning in Pittsburg and the blazer was definitely called for, Kunle thought when he saw Travis on his phone while standing by the red Cadillac 2020 CTS.

Kunle: My bad man.

Travis: It's all good, I was trying to catch Shannon, you know she stays busy.

Kunle: Facts. All good?

Travis: Yea, I got staffed on this project with her and I want to set some time for kickoff.

Kunle: Smart! Shannon knows her shit, you'll learn lots from her.

Travis: Have you worked with her?

Kunle: Yea, a few projects in a couple of years actually. She had and has my back!

Travis: Word? Any tips on working with her?

Kunle: Na, just hit the deadline and communicate when you feel like you have a question. She's not one of those intimidating managers that you have to worry about.

Travis: Bet.

Kunle and Travis had lunch at Café Du Jour on Carson Street. It's a cute European restaurant with a water fountain containing turtles in the backyard, that doubles as an outdoor dining space. Kunle and Travis opted to seat next to the water fountain even though Kunle was disappointed. He was expecting a French restaurant because that's what his best friend, Seun, had told him.

While they waited for their orders, Kunle picked up his phone to chat to some friends. However, only one person had been living rent free in his head. He imagined if Maria would love this restaurant. It has an atmosphere he would love to have dinner with her in. He imagined he'd cook her lamb and some starch; that he'd be wearing shorts and a shirt. If the weather is nice, he'd wear his sateen lounge wear and she'd wear one of her beautiful dresses. He'd love to give her a yellow rose, but only if she would let him put it in her hair. "That's it, I should send her flowers!" He picked up his phone to send a few texts.

Kunle sent a message to Maria that read "is this long enough of a period to wait before texting you?" He didn't expect her response to be swift but it was.

Maria: Ha, I'm sure "they" recommend waiting a few days. You know, to let me realize how "special" you are or some shit like that.

Kunle: Well, fuck them haha.

Maria: Yes, my sentiments exactly.

Kunle: How the hell are you?

Maria: I'm good, you know, being a boss ain't easy.

Kunle: I'll let you know when I become one. Hopefully you'll teach me a thing or two before then.

Maria: I'll teach you a few things if you'd feed me good Nigerian food.

Kunle: Oh, I got you! How's work, busy day?

Maria: It was, but I woke up energized and inspired, so I completed most of the items on my todo list.

Kunle: Damn girl, it's only 1 and you're done for the day?

Maria: More like almost done for the week, if things remains unchanged.

Kunle: I stand corrected. What does the rest of your day look like?

Maria: I have two meetings and then I should be out by 4 pm.

Kunle: Nice. I want to be like you when I grow up haha.

Maria: What does the rest of your day look like?

Kunle: Not bad, I'm having a drink with my client after work and then I should be free! Do you have dinner plans?

Maria: I wish I had clients wining and dining me. I don't have any dinner plans as of yet, but Gina might want to meet up, she wants a debrief.

Kunle: Yea, I can imagine. Let me know if you want to meet up.

Maria: Will do . I'm glad you stayed.

Kunle: Me too!

Interrupting his text was the waiter checking on their table:

Bridget: How is everything (the waitress asked)?

Travis: Fantastic, everything was perfect.

Kunle: Yes, so good. What time do you open for dinner?

Bridget: We have happy hour from 5-7 and we typically start serving dinner around 6.

Kunle: Perfect.

Bridget: Do you want to see the dinner menu?

Travis: Yes please.

Kunle: I'll take a coffee and the check if Travis is good.

Travis: Make that two.

Bridget: Two coffees coming right up.

Kunle started browsing for local flower shops that delivers. He wanted to send Maria yellow roses even though he just learnt that they signify joy, gladness, freedom and friendship. He thought that would be perfect. He found a local shop and placed a call. He ordered a sunflower bouquet and asked that they put them in a vase. He also added four dozens of yellow roses and a dozen of red roses sprinkled in between. Kunle remembered Maria smelling the roses at Phipps Conservatory and Botanical Garden and became overwhelmed with joy. He remembered when she got on all fours as she listened to the roses. He remembered their dialog:

Kunle: What's happening?

Maria: Shh, I'm trying to listen to them (she whispered).

Kunle: Okay!

Kunle whispered back to Maria. He couldn't process his emotions because he couldn't look past

Maria's beautiful pose. He couldn't believe what he was witnessing, the most beautiful flower in the universe talking to other flowers. WOW! She almost blends in with her yellow a-line dress that perfectly fell into shape, revealing the curves of her bountiful ass. Two amazing shapes that formed an amazing sight. He wanted to take a picture and show it to Maria, but he was shy. He didn't want to seem like a creep, but worked up the courage to reach for his phone as he instructs Maria not to move. She listened and didn't move a muscle. Kunle took it as an invitation to take some shots, and boy did he. He took a total of forty-three photos, some for Maria, and some for Maria's dad. He got her favorites angles, he knew how to harness the daylight for the best photos. She loved every single shot. Damn I look good, she thought to herself as she flips through the photos on his phone. After airdropping the pictures to Maria, Kunle asked if he could keep a few and Maria agreed. She selected four specific photos for Kunle to keep.

Kunle was so overwhelmed with joy as he reminisced on that moment that he felt he might start crying if he didn't stop. He added an arrangement of Vanda orchids because they stood out to him from the garden. On their drive back to the office, Kunle called the flower shop to verbally place the order and beg for urgent delivery.

Kunle: Hello! Please I'm trying to place a very urgent order, would that be possible?

Lilly: Yes, what did you do? Haha.

Kunle: Nothing, but I want to show someone she's very special!

Lilly: Oh, that! What ya got in mind (sounded to Kunle like an over joyed sixty years old white lady at the end of the line "watch ya got in mind?")?

Kunle: A sunflower bouquet in a vase, four dozens of yellow roses and a dozen of red roses sprinkled in between, and if you still have the Vanda orchids, I'll take an arrangement of those too please; all in vases.

Lilly: Wow, she's very special I see.

Kunle: She is.

Lilly: Good for her. That'll be $168 plus $20 express fee.

Kunle: Would you be able to deliver before 4 pm?

Lilly: As long as my name is Lilly!

Kunle: Haha, thank you.

Lilly: What do you want the note to say?

Kunle: Note?

Lilly: Yes, for the flowers. Do you want it to say from you?

Kunle: Let me get back to you in the next hour.

Lilly: Don't take too long now.

Kunle paid for the flowers and knew Travis was going to have questions. He played them off as he wanted to continue reminiscing on the date at the garden. He remembered their brunch. They had Chèvre Tomate Avec Herbes de Provence, a tomato goat cheese sandwich sprinkled with olive oil, dried French herbs, dried tomato, and arugula. It was heavenly. Kunle remembered the mouthwatering sensation of biting into that perfect French bread that housed the sandwich and how the wine made it even better. Maria moaning with joy as Kenny G played on that sunny morning was everything Kunle wanted.

Since he got the message that read "You're in my city," he's wanted to make an impression on Maria. Even before then. He remembered scrolling on IG and stumbling on Maria's page. She didn't share much, she only had about a hundred photos up at the time, compared to Kunle's forty. Kunle thought she was cute and liked one of her photos from Greece. He started to follow her because she was traveling at the time and she was hitting some spots Kunle found fascinating and hope to one day visit. Like any other person on social media, Kunle admired them and just kept scrolling. But that text changed everything. Oh wait, I'm supposed to be thinking of a note, Kunle snapped out of it.

When he got back to his computer, he wrote a short poem for Maria and emailed it to Lilly at the flower shop.

Of all the roses in the world
And of all the gardens in the world
You are the rose! my favorite rose
No other rose compares, not even close
Do accept these roses from the garden of my heart

They'd wither away, but you'll forever be in my heart

Kunle worked for two additional hours and spent the rest of his time catching up with his friends. He exchanged a few text with Seun:

Kunle: Yo, what's good? That "French" restaurant looked like it stopped being French a while ago dude.

Seun: Haha, I moved out of Pitts like two years ago. How was it though?

Kunle: It was dope, I think I'll bring Maria here.

Seun: Who's Maria?

Kunle: This lady I'm seeing!

Seun: Since when?

Kunle: Since Thursday!

Seun: Wait, Thursday? What are you smoking?

Kunle: That Chronic (Ice Cube's voice) haha.

Seun: Must be some good shit because how do you start seeing a bitch in five days?

Kunle: Nigga watch your mouth. LADY/WOMAN! Not the B word. Don't worry, when Jen delivers my goddaughter you'll change.

Seun: My bad dude, I knew you was gon be like that. Tell me about her? She's from Pitts?

Kunle: Yup, check your phone, I just sent you her IG profile.

Seun: Oh shit. My nigga! That's why you stayed in Pittsburg last weekend huh?

Kunle: Yea man. Had the best date of my life, no cap.

Seun: FOH. Better than when you took that chick to see Michael Buble?

Kunle: Well maybe If I was on stage playing the sax that'll be better.

Seun: Oh shit. You smashed?

Kunle: Besides the point.

Seun: Are you whipped?

Kunle: You can say that, or maybe she's worth spending time with!

Seun: Bro, you think you're ready?

Kunle: Yea, it's time. Remember when I said I was gonna risk it all this year?

Seun: Yea, but I didn't know you were talking about relationships. This is huge bro.

Kunle: Fuck yea it is, I want it! I'm ready! Bro, she's the coolest woman I ever met, and she's smart as fuck. Oh look at your phone.

Seun: I mean she's beautiful (Kunle sent Seun a picture of Maria from the garden. The picture shows a beautiful Maria, mid twirl and smelling a flower. Her yellow a-lined dress expanded but blurred out.), just be careful.

Kunle: Yea bro. How was the weekend? What did you guys get into?

Seun: You know, married men shit. We went shopping for the nursery.

Kunle: Yea? What did you buy my goddaughter?

Seun: An over priced crib and some other shit.

Kunle: Nice. That's what's up!

Seun: Did you check the chat? I think we're pregaming at your house this weekend, so get your ass home.

Kunle: What's happening?

Seun: Summer, that's what! Also, there's a concert or something!

Kunle: Sounds good, I'll check for details.

Seun: Dope. When are you flying back?

Kunle: Friday. How's Jen, hope she's good.

Seun: You know white people.

Kunle: "Make money don't spend it?"

Seun: More like putting me "through the wire."

Kunle: You good bro? What happened?

Seun: That's the problem, I don't know. She's mad at something and how the fuck am I supposed to know?

Kunle: That's not a white people problem bro, that's a you problem.

Seun: How?

Kunle: You did not communicate with your wife.

Seun: Are you deaf or is you high?

Kunle finished his conversation with Seun and checked his group chat. The chat is sacred and nothing from that chat gets out. The chat to everyone in it is the opposite of what a support group should be. These men do nothing but make fun of each other for no reason. Only family, wives, and girlfriends (current or past) were off limits. Everything else was fair game. If anyone had an issue they can bring it to the table, as long as you're comfortable with being the butt of everyone's jokes. Kunle knew he had to avoid mentioning Maria's name at all cost because they'd press for details until he folds. While he caught up with the chat and worked, he wondered what Maria was up to.

He made up multiple scenarios as to what she might be up to. Reality, however, was something else entirely. On her short drive home she reminisced about her day. Maria woke up at 4:10 am and she did not waste a single minute. She spent twenty minutes on her rowing machine, did Pilates for twenty, and meditated for ten. She then worked for three hours before heading to the shower. By nine she was seated at her desk with a freshly brewed cup of cappuccino that was delivered by the office assistant she shares with the executive team and some other directors. She spent the first three hours of work completing her task for the week. She approved some new marketing designs and marketing slogans. She had a ninety minutes lunch with Jeff, the CFO/her manager, and was back in her office listening to an audio book and planning her next getaway with fifteen tabs open on her Safari browser, all in "incognito mode." She was also catching up with Gina and Wendy while all of this was happening.

Maria: Hey girl, how are you?

Gina: So you are alive! Responding eighteen hours late.

Maria: You know I was getting my back blown out.

Gina: I knew it, you slut.

Maria: It was exactly what I needed.

Gina: So it wasn't good.

Maria: It was out of this world, like out of this fucking world and not just the sex.

Gina: Yea? You're still in the office right? Did you have a drink at lunch?

Maria: Yea, but only Merlot. Trust me girl, I'm sober as shit. I have to tell you all about it. You free for drinks later?

Gina: No, I have yoga, I'll be sweaty. Come by my spot at 8?

Maria: Lets hang tomorrow then, I'll grab dinner with Kunle.

Gina: Damn girl! How many times did you cum this weekend?

Maria: I'm not sure, I loose count each time. And yes, I know, too good to be true.

Gina: Well damn! Stella got her groove back?

Maria: She did! I'm looking up flights to Jamaica as we speak.

Gina: Why Jamaica? Lets do Nigeria! Kunle can bring us.

Maria: Shut up.

Gina: Haha, I gotta run girl. I'll FT you later.

Maria: Bye bitch.

By 3 pm, she was in her last meeting for the day. She was meeting with the executive team, Sean the cofounder and CEO, Jeff the CFO, Mike the COO (Chief Operating Officer), Mary the director of HR, and Mark the CTO (Chief Technology Officer). They were meeting to brainstorm about a proposed acquisition of their company by a giant tech company. Mark and Maria could never agree on anything. He's always undercutting her, trying to demonstrate that he could do her job better than she could (he always ends up looking like a "fucking idiot"), sometimes he'd make remarks that Jeff would have to tell him he was out of line. None of his antics works on Maria. Never once did she loose her cool, at least not in front of them. But often times she wishes she could call him a "pig face, shit eating, ugly ass bitch." But no, "mama raised" her to be better than that. The meeting ended the way they always end, everyone looking to Maria to save them like she was some kind of angel with all the answers. The thing about Maria is that she does not settle, and you can see it in every aspect of her life.

"I do all of this? And I'm this fine? Kunle's ass is lucky. But he's fine too though. And smart, quick witted. And is only slightly annoying. Was it the weed or was that the best sex I have fucking had? Must be the weed." She thought to herself. When she got off the elevator on her floor, 38th, she saw a trail of flowers, all neatly arranged and placed in front of her apartment door. A total of six arrangements were placed there and at the center was the yellow and red rose arrangement. Lilly had placed them to form a star shape, which Kunle found simultaneously beautiful and creepy when he got the picture from Maria. Lilly gave Kunle an extra two flower arrangements of red roses because of his generous 50% tip. When Maria got the note and read Kunle's corny poem, she couldn't help but get overwhelmed with emotions. She called Kunle on FaceTime, but he did not pick up, so he texted.

Kunle: Hey, need a few, but can text if urgent.

Maria: Okay, don't reply, but I got the flowers and the note. They're too beautiful. Did you write it?

Kunle: Yea, I had to come up with it on the spot. I'm not used to buying flowers haha.

Maria: You are so sweet. Why are you single again?

Kunle did not respond for three long and painful hours, even though Maria was able to take a nap. When she woke up she saw two missed calls from Kunle and a text message that said "I was searching for you, silly! Are you hungry?" She was in-fact hungry but did not respond to Kunle right away. She wanted to be certain that she still wanted to see this man again. Long distance relationships are never easy, she felt and what is she going to do about Anthony? She looked into the sunset as she sat on the couch on her balcony, thinking about her current situation. Before sliding into Kunle's DMs, she had been seeing Anthony, the young attorney from Detroit. He was quite a looker, book smart but somehow incredibly stupid, stood six foot two inches, caramel skin tone, and a total asshole. He was exactly the kind of men that Maria was tired of dating, but somehow she ends up agreeing to grabbing drinks or dinner or brunch or coffee. Anthony had managed to retain her attention longer than two months and she was wondering if she has lowered her standards or if she was evolving. "Anthony hasn't texted me all day, but Kunle is over here begging to have dinner with me."

She picked up her phone and responded to Kunle's text.

Maria: Haha good save. Yes, what do you have in mind? And how was your meeting?

Kunle: Have you been to Café du Jour? Or that Jamaican restaurant I told you about! The meeting was good, she tried to poach me.

Maria: Café du Jour sounds fancy, is it? Oh and she's trying to get you to move to Pittsburgh?

Kunle: Cool. I can be there in 30. Yea, I'll tell you all about it at dinner.

Maria: Okay, see you shortly. What's the dress code?

Kunle: None you have to worry about gorgeous.

Maria: Cool, see ya.

CHAPTER 8

CHEERS TO LOOSER GHOSTS

It was a cool seventy degrees that Monday evening, but the wind chill made it feel like sixty five. Kunle wasn't his usual chatty self, he had something on his mind. On their drive to Cafe Du Jour, he listened to Maria recap her day. He asked detailed questions such as "so you have an assistant? That's cool!" Maria was careful enough not to divulge too much information about herself to Kunle; she saw him as the random hot stranger that hopped her fence when she's been deprived of sex for too long and while ovulating and heavily stressed. "You fuck him, but you don't trust him," she had told Gina earlier.

Kunle asked her details about her coworkers. He wanted to know what they were like, what kind of office politics Maria has to play, and wanted to know the overall complexity of her corporate life. She answered his questions honestly and accurately, after all, it's public on LinkedIn and she saw that Kunle viewed her profile after she browsed through his. Upon arriving, Cafe Du Jour was an instant favorite of Maria's.

She was wearing a royal blue cropped sweater (that Kunle couldn't tell which brand it was but knew it was quality) with blue denim and cream colored Adidas sneakers; she was comfortable. When they walked out in the garden at the cafe, she slightly pulled her sweater with both hands at the neck. Kunle took it as a sign that she felt cozy there, that she liked it. He requested to be seated outside. There was a couple dining inside (but only the lady was currently at the table), a group of three older ladies. A waiter approached Kunle and Maria and walked them out to show them their dining options. Another couple were dining outside and both Kunle and Maria nodded at them, you know that nod that only cool black people understand.

Maria: This is lovely.

Kunle: I imagined cooking you dinner here earlier!

Maria: Yea? Always trying to score brownie points I see.

Kunle: Nah, for real. I'd make you lamb. You do like lamb, right?

Maria: I do. What else did you imagine?

Kunle: My outfit, silk. You'd be laying on a hammock or a swinging chair of sorts with a glass of wine and a book.

Maria: I love that. What am I wearing?

Kunle: Depends on the weather, but a dress or my sweats.

Kunle pulled a chair out, intended for Maria, but she took the another chair.

Kunle: Oh, I was pulling the chair for you.

Maria: Very chivalrous of you. I'll take it next time, thank you (as she is seated facing the entry into the courtyard with her back against the concrete fence).

Kunle: Sure.

Maria: Do you know what you want?

Kunle: Yea, it depends on what you get though.

Maria: We'll take some sparkling water with lime, he'll have a Macallan neat, make it a double; and I'll have a glass of Merlot.

Kunle: Hold on, we'll take a bottle of your finest Merlot; no to the Macallan.

Ant: I'll give you some time to checkout the menu and I'll go grab that wine for you.

Maria: Thank you (echoed with Kunle). Tell me more of this beautiful fantasy you had this afternoon.

Kunle: Well, it'll be on a Sunday or a day the streets are quiet. Maybe not here. Somewhere quiet. The only sound you'd hear is the sound of the water fountain and some Afrobeats music of sorts.

Maria: (Looking up from the menu) Would it be sunny?

Kunle: Yes, because you'd be wearing your oversized sunglasses.

Maria: I'll be wearing your soccer shorts and one of your muscle tees, no bra.

Kunle: Hashtag freethenip.

Maria: Haha, exactly. Is that really an hashtag?

Kunle: Yes, why are you acting like you don't spend hours on social media.

Maria: Fun fact, the name for hashtags is octothorpe, according to the OECD.

Kunle: Interesting. I guess you know that because you don't spend hours on social media daily!

Maria: Smart man. I know what I want. I'll take the North African Porkchop.

Kunle: I definitely did not see you going for that?

Maria: You thought I'd order the mushrooms or salmon?

Kunle: Yea. I'll take the New York strip steak.

Maria: How do you like your steak?

Kunle: Medium well.

Maria: Nice! Good thing we're still getting to know each other.

Kunle: (With a smile) A picture is starting to form!

Maria: Yea?

Kunle: Absolutely. You're like a complex Russian Doll. Oh, I hope they play Pink Martini again after dinner, I'd ask for a dance (as Clementine by Pink Martini started playing on the speakers that weren't too loud on the partly cloudy night with visible stars). We'll stay out till it is later.

Maria: You know this song? You have a really eclectic taste in music.

Kunle: Thank you, it's the African in me, with a K so you know its real.

Maria: (Laughing louder than Kunle anticipated) Is that right?

Kunle: Absolutely.

Ant: Are you ready to order?

Kunle: Yes! The lady will have the pork chops and I'll have the steak medium rare.

Ant: (Pours a little bit of the wine in a glass and handed it to Kunle for a taste) Give this a try sir.

Kunle: Thank you, just pour it.

Maria: You don't want to impress me?

Kunle: I mean I have drank wine at most of the wineries in Napa and some in Italy and South Africa, but I don't want to appear pretentious.

Maria: I like that but I wouldn't think you're being pretentious. I'll just think you're trying to impress me.

Kunle: If I were watching myself I'd think I was being pretentious.

Maria: Haha.

Ant: I'll get your order in.

"Maria?" Both Kunle and Maria looked up at Ant, a dark figure that blocked some of the evening light that shinned towards the garden.

Maria: Tony?

Anthony: Oh shit, I knew I heard your voice. How've you been?

Anthony walked over to Kunle and Maria. Maria became uneasy, Kunle observed because he decided not to pay any attention to Anthony. Maria's mind began to race because she knew this would not be a good encounter. She decided to "ghost" Anthony because they simply were not compatible. He was too intense, too cocky, too bossy, too square. He didn't pay enough attention to her and she did not feel heard. She tried to communicate her needs, but he always made everything about himself. "So you think I should break the law to appease you?" Maria briefly remembered Anthony's response when she asked him to stop telling her not to smoke in her own apartment. "A lady does not entertain such things." Maria felt like Anthony was looking for his country club, golf playing, lemonade serving in plaid skirt on a hot summer day, wife. Truth is she'd play the role excellently, but she felt like she would hate every moment of it.

Maria: What are you doing here? Grabbing dinner obviously, duh.

Anthony: Yea, I came here with some clients for dinner. I just won a case, that major case...

Maria: (Cutting him off) The Curtis case you wouldn't shut up about? Good for you?

Kunle: Oh yea, I read about that. I'm Kunle, congratulations.

Anthony: Sup little man? So this is the dude you've been seeing behind my back?

Maria: Well, yes.

Anthony: I knew it you fucking slut.

Kunle: Watch your tone (he said as he stood up).

Anthony: How about you mind your fucking business while I talk to my woman.

Maria: WHOA! Your woman? Just leave, don't embarrass yourself.

Kunle: I'd listen to the lady if I were you.

Anthony: Or what?

Kunle: Or be ready for the consequences, esquire!

Anthony: Cute, real cute. You can have her, she wasn't good enough for me anyways.

Anthony stormed off back into the restaurant. Truth is he was there on a date. He was with Yao, an intern from his firm that he had been messing around with for about a month while he was trying to court Maria. Maria suspected that he was seeing other people and never questioned it because she wasn't really interested in him. Truth was that she was bored and wanted company any time she wanted it. Although they never had sex, Maria once allowed Anthony to attempt cunnilingus with her. She hated it! She remembered their interactions on Bumble and how she only agreed to grab a beer with him at the Pirates' game. All he did was talk about himself and how important he felt he was to everyone and everything he encounters. They had been silent for about five minutes and she began to wonder what Kunle was thinking about. She noticed Kunle went silent after he said Wow in response to Anthony as he stormed away.

Maria: That was embarrassing! Sorry about that.

Kunle: Who was that?

Maria: That was Anthony.

Kunle: I gather.

Maria: He's the reason I'm here. We started seeing each other in mid March but it wasn't going anywhere so I tried to end it. He was persistent. He said "no one would ever love you with that attitude! And I love that attitude."

Kunle: What in the name of gaslighting is that?

Maria: So I ghosted him.

Kunle: So we just saw a ghost?

Maria: Yup, in living color.

Kunle: Well, here's to loser ghosts.

Maria: Cheers (they both toasted, clicking their wine glasses). Have you ever been ghosted?

Kunle: Yes, I think. She told me we are not gonna sleep together anymore the last time I saw her. Texted her one weekend I was home and she had deleted my number.

Maria: That's not ghosting, she warned you haha.

Kunle: I see. So you didn't warn him and that's why he's calling you his "woman?"

Maria: No, not even sure where that came from. We never slept together. He gave me head once, and it was terrible.

Kunle: You didn't let him find his footing?

Maria: He thought he was perfect, so I didn't want to bruise his ego.

Kunle: He didn't try to have sex with you after?

Maria: No he did, he couldn't get it up.

Kunle: (Bursted out laughing, almost spitting his wine) No way!

Maria: Yup. Oh, the food is here.

Kunle: Mmmm, I can use some food. Good call on the wine by the way.

Maria: Yea, why are you not drinking something heavier?

Kunle: It's a work night and I want to be sharp tomorrow.

Maria: Responsible, I like it.

Kunle: I would smoke if you have some though.

Ant set the plates as Kunle and Maria sat up and positioned themselves to eat.

Kunle: Is it okay to smoke in the garden?

Ant: I don't mind, but it's against the policy.

Kunle: It's all good, thank you.

Kunle and Maria enjoyed their dinner in silence as what sounded to Kunle like Nora Jones' Pandora playlist set the tone for their dinner. They tried each other's food and Maria ended up eating a third of Kunle's meal. He didn't mind and she allowed him to feed her. Maria was coming off her high from the joint she smoked while waiting for Kunle to pick her up. Barring the incident with Anthony, it was a pleasant dinner. Twenty minutes after their dinner was served, the pair were done eating and were already on their second bottle of wine.

Ant: How is everything?

Maria: Great, put everything on this card.

Ant: Perfect! Are you ready for the bill?

Maria: Yes, we have dessert at home.

Ant: Sounds good, I'll get the bill.

Kunle: (After Ant left and looking puzzled). What are you doing?

Maria: What do you mean? Oh, don't worry. My treat.

Kunle: Well, thank you! Can I have a dance though?

Maria: Absolutely!!!

The pair got up to dance as Come Away With Me started to play on the speakers. Maria paid attention to the music and her surroundings. She saw the silhouette of the turtles in the pond as the water fountain perfectly complemented the music. Kunle's perfume had faded, but not completely. It was as if it was only there for Maria to smell. She hugged him a little tighter and pressed her breasts on his firm chest. She perfectly fitted into his broad shoulders and she rested her head on his chest. She felt safe.

Kunle, however, was enjoying the moment, but couldn't stop thinking about Shirley's proposal. She had offered Kunle a director position, for him to start as soon as she officially takes the reigns from the retiring Chief Tax Officer. Kunle's total package was going to be more than double his current earnings but he'd have to relocate to Pittsburgh. Kunle was ready for the next phase of his life and this offer was coming two years earlier than he had anticipated. It was a great offer! Kunle started to think about what he'd have to do to get his affairs back in Connecticut in order. His long term friends with benefits would certainly miss him, he thought. But he'll be closer to Maria! The lady that smells like roses and the finest oils; that flows like the ocean and her presence feels better than the cool ocean breeze on a hot Caribbean afternoon.

Maria: Are you okay? Something feels off!

Kunle: I'm perfect Angel, just a few things on my mind.

Maria: I'm here if you need a listening ear.

Kunle stopped dancing and lifted Maria's face with his fingers and brushed back her curly hair with his left hand. "I know angel," he said as he passionately kissed her. "Let's get out of here," Kunle also whispered in Maria's left ear, after kissing her for about a minute.

Maria leaned over and signed the bill. She gave a generous tip of thirty percent and the pair left.

Kunle: Fancy a walk by the moon light?

Maria: Why, yes! I love walks.

Hand in hand, they walked and roamed the streets of Southside Flats for about an hour. They talked a bit about philosophical topics, sports, politics, but Maria noticed a theme in Kunle's questions; they were about the future, and life in Pittsburg. "Don't fall for it," she thought to herself, "it's all a ploy. Is it?" After their walk, Kunle drove Maria back to her apartment and she asked him to come up for a smoke and cake. Unsure if she meant the literal cake or the other kind of cake.

Maria: Wanna come smoke with me and have some cake?

Kunle: Only if Anthony wouldn't show up.

Maria: Funny, and he better not.

Kunle: I'll kick his ass.

Maria: Hope it doesn't get to that.

Kunle: Sure, I'd love some cake (he blushed a bit).

Maria: Cool. Come on.

When they got back to Maria's apartment, she dimmed the light as Kunle got comfortable, untucking his shirt, loosening the three top buttons, and folding his cuffs. The pair lit up a joint and smoked, while they listened to Erykah Badu. After smoking half a joint, Maria disappeared into her room for a couple of minutes. She reappeared wearing her silk robe and she started dancing towards Kunle. She loosened the robe when she got close to Kunle, revealing her royal blue lace Victoria's Secret underwear. Kunle was delighted and became fully alert. Maria started to tease Kunle by dancing slowly and passionately on Kunle, on the bright yellow couch. She knelt on the couch, over Kunle, as he looked up to her. She began to gently rotate her waist in rhythm with the music. Kunle took a deep breath and tried to kiss her. She resisted and delicately grabbed his locs. She continued to tease him until he was fully aroused, which only took about five minutes. Kunle stood up and the pair slow danced for about fifteen minutes. While they danced, Kunle gave her a thorough butt massage and by minute thirteen, her nipple was in his mouth. They did not make it to the bedroom!

By the time they were both satisfied, Kunle observed that it was eleven. Maria noticed Kunle looking at his watch and asked him to stay. Kunle accepted without objection.

Maria: I want you to stay.

Kunle: I'd love that (Kunle said as he kissed her on the forehead).

Maria: Come on, let's go to bed.

Kunle: Sure, let me use some of your mouthwash.

Maria: I'll join you.

Kunle observed how cute they looked together in the big and well lit bathroom mirror. He observed Maria's smile, even though she was brushing her teeth and her mouth was stuffed. They made their way to Maria's bedroom and they both had a wonderful night's rest.

Maria's six am alarm went off and they both woke up.

Kunle: Good morning angel!

Maria: Good morning zaddy!

The pair kissed without regard or concern for any potential morning breath. As they kissed, Maria searched for Kunle's morning wood under the covers. He was fully erect and Maria disappeared under the covers shortly after. Kunle thought to himself, "It's going to be a wonderful day, I can feel it!"

CHAPTER 9

SUNSETS AND THE BOOGIE MAN

It was a cloudy Pittsburgh afternoon. Kunle and Maria were headed to the airport. Kunle had asked Travis to take an Uber to the airport, sacrificing their "work bro" time. Travis could use Kunle's counsel, but Kunle was only focused on one thing: impressing Maria! Kunle had planned everything he could. He booked Maria a first class seat and paid for an upgrade for his own seat from economy. He knew he'd probably get upgraded, but he wasn't willing to take the risk to test his assumption. He also took the liberty of booking Maria a room at the Marriott downtown Hartford for one night in her name and told her she can stay there until she wants to and just come over to his place during the day; she was welcome to stay the night at his apartment, only if she felt comfortable enough. He didn't book the room to impress her, but he booked it because it was the rational thing to do; if you're going to spend a weekend in a random guy's city, have your "fuck you money." He wanted to spare her of any expense.

Also, he was hoping this would be the first of many flights together, so he wanted to make a great first impression. Maria didn't see anything special or notice how nervous Kunle was. She herself had expended a lot of energy calming her nerves. "What would papa say? He'd be disappointed. And Bobby (her brother) wouldn't get it either, even though she told him she was spending the weekend in Connecticut. Good thing I'm grown, and I'm set for life; I can do whatever the fuck I want." She had this "boss" essence to her. She was able to tap into a side of her that she rarely ever taps into. She was in charge, like she was the star and director of her story. This is the side that Kunle experienced on the car ride to the airport. He didn't hear her conversation with Gina when she Facetimed Maria earlier that day.

Maria: Hey girl, how are you?

Gina: I'm good, my mind is still rational, unlike some of us.

Maria: You've got that right. This shit don't make sense, but I'mma do it.

Gina: Do what? Travel with a random stranger to his hometown in the middle of nowhere, a place where the closest person you know lives four hour drive away? Do that?

Maria: Damn girl, but you're right. I'm just gonna see where this goes, no pressure. Imma just live. He seems like he does that well and I think he's doing a good job thus far.

Gina: My point exactly. Girl, you don't think you're doing too much too soon.

Maria: I'm having a good time, that's it.

Gina: Let's fuck him together then.

Maria: Excuse me? (As she stopped folding her blue jeans to be packed in her carryon luggage because Kunle doesn't check a bag).

Gina: I mean we used to talk about having a threesome when we were younger and if you're just having fun, let's fuck him together.

Maria: No. What if I end up really liking him?

Gina: You mean what if you end up in a relationship with him?

Maria: Well, yea.

Gina: That's what I mean girl, what if?

Maria: At least this time if he turns out to be married with children, I would have enjoyed my time a bit more! Plus, girl, once they sell that company, I get a $40 million dollar windfall! Fuck, let me live before all this shit, life, gets complicated.

Gina: Well, I see you've thought this through.

Maria: Duh. If we end up in some kind of relationship, I'll set up a trust fund and stash my money away from anyone's grab. Trust me, I've got this.

Gina: Okay, okay! But for real, how's the sex?

Maria: Girrrrl!!! It feels better than ice cream on a super-hot Houston afternoon.

Gina: Okrrrrrrr! Have fun girl and please be safe.

Maria: Yea. Kunle booked me a room at the Marriott downtown Hartford. Said I can stay there until I feel safe enough to crash at his spot. And I didn't even need to ask.

Gina: Shit, if he's being this thoughtful, maybe he's serious. What do you think?

Maria: He's doing and saying all the right things to communicate his seriousness. I think he stopped trying to hide it.

Gina: Shit. That's good. How do you feel?

Maria: I'll know after this weekend. So far all signs are green.

Gina: Well, I trust you to trust your judgement.

Maria: Fuck is that supposed to mean?

Gina: I mean, you're a smart ass bitch and you've got this, and you know you've got this.

Maria: Better! Haha.

Both Maria and Gina laughed, and Maria giggled in real life on the Clear ("TSA Precheck") line. Kunle observed the giggle and recognized it. It felt familiar to him. Truth is he'd do the same from time to time and is often embarrassed by it.

Kunle: Good memory?

Maria: Yea?

Kunle: I'm asking because it seemed like you just recalled a good memory. That giggle, I do it too sometimes.

Maria: Oh yea? You're a weirdo?

Kunle: Well if that's how you see it, that's a "you" problem. But yes, I am "that."

Maria: I love that you're so confident in who you are.

Kunle tried to stroll through TSA, but he forgot that the big buckle belt that he's wearing to appear cool for Maria (since it seemed to him that she doesn't mind being impressed) often sets off the body scanner, so he had to come back and take it off. Meanwhile he had just watched Maria glide through the scanner like an angel that trained in the ballet, effortless. She was watching

157

him from the other side, and observed his neatly ironed white shirt cleanly tucked into his grey pants. The buckle on his belt matched his shoes, and she liked it. His sense of style matches hers, she felt like she might not have to "upgrade him." She felt justified for not spending her twenties trying to chase men that were not up to par with her.

Instead, she had focused on herself. After a four years spell on Wall Street with Goldman Sachs, she went to Wharton to get her MBA because she saw herself as more of a leader than a salesperson. She needed some other skills/tools to lead, but she's already got the smarts. She needed to spend time then to set herself up for her thirties. She had three sexual partners while in grad school. None of them knew of each other because she made sure she did not get entangled with anyone in her cohort. In her class, she was in the top ten percent and in the present day, she's in the top ten percent (if title, income, job responsibility are metrics used to measure and compare).

As the gate agent started to announce the boarding process, Kunle got up and grabbed his suit bag and looked down at Maria, who was comfortably dressed in black jeans, plain cream colored t-shirt, and her cream Adidas, Yeezy Boost:

Kunle: Are you sure about this? There is no going back! Think of this as a spaceship and we are traveling through this wormhole. We're not sure what is on the other side. It could be an amusement park with sunny weather and a waterpark, or it could be an amusement park decorated for Halloween to scare you. I'm just saying I'm ready, and would love for you to join me.

Maria: (Trying to dampen the mood) Cool speech bro!

Kunle: You are not serious (in his Nigerian accent and Maria couldn't help but laugh loud enough for the three people behind Kunle on the line to hear her).

Maria: Sorry!

Kunle: Looks like it'll be the amusement park after all!

Maria: Yea, but which one? (She winked at Kunle and moved her aviator sunglasses from her forehead to cover her eyes, as she turned around. Kunle Smiled as he followed her down the jet bridge).

On the flight, they both drank whiskey and with a splash of coke. She liked the taste. "A lime would be perfect with this," she said to Kunle. Neither Kunle nor Maria looked at their work computer. It was as if they were on a mini vacation. They watched the first Iron Man Movie on that Delta flight that had a flight attendant that paid Kunle a bit more attention than Maria was comfortable with. And for the first time, she was convinced that she's developed feelings for Kunle a little too fast. "Why am I already being protective of him? I just met him and he's not mine, yet." She said to herself after she interlocked her arm with Kunle's when Paris, the beautiful flight attendant, asked Kunle if he'd like a double "just how you like it?" She saw Gina's point and began playing with the idea of the threesome. Was Gina serious or was she really saying it to gauge her level of interest in

Kunle? She played with a lot more scenarios in her head. She thought about the worst and the best things that could happen with Kunle. She played with multiple scenarios. She concluded that she had no evidence to expect anything terribly bad, so she gave herself permission to enjoy his presence. She had told Kunle to cancel the room early enough for him not to get penalized. "But you better have your credit card ready if you mess up."

The flight landed at Bradley International Airport at 6 pm and by 6:50 they were in an Uber ride to Kunle's apartment. On the ride home, Kunle wondered if he left anything perishable in the fridge because he had been gone for a little over three weeks. He spent his first weekend away in San Francisco, his second weekend in Houston Texas, and his third weekend in Pittsburg. He realized that his apartment must be a hot box, so he turned the AC on from the Nest app on his phone, discreetly.

They got to Kunle's apartment just in time for the sun to finally set; you know that moment when she literally sinks? Right before our eyes following with an array of color display that's often so captivating; This is one of the activities Kunle enjoys the most from his apartment, his sanctuary. No matter how long a day, week, or month he's had, all his stress melts away anytime he walks into his apartment, especially on evenings like this.

Kunle and Maria got off the nineteenth floor of Kunle's apartment building, Downtown Hartford. When Kunle opened the door, he knew exactly what to expect, but wasn't quite sure how spectacular it would be. They were greeted by the most amazing sunset you can see from any apartment in Connecticut, at least that's what Kunle believed. The skies were on fire and displayed a bright orange color that was glorious to stare at. The floor to ceiling windows instantly drew Maria in, when Kunle went in and held the door open for her. His apartment had an open floor concept with no walls separating the Kitchen from the dining and living room. The huge center island took center stage in the kitchen, making it great for entertaining.

Kunle: Bienvenido.

Maria: Wow, this is lovely. Very modern!

Kunle: Well, thank you! The sunset is giving it what I needs right now! Let me get us a some water. The room is right there and that's the bathroom, make yourself at home. You can push my clothes to the side if you need closet space, behind that door (Kunle had a couple of shirts on the bed, but nothing else. He cleaned his apartment before he travelled).

Kunle moved the bags into the room and changed into something more comfortable. Maria peeped into the room and saw that the sunset was still visible from the floor to ceiling windows in the bedroom, including the closet.

Maria: I mean, wow. This is seriously nice.

Kunle: Yeah, that's what I thought when I first saw it too. Thank you!

Kunle grabbed one of the six bottles of wine in his fridge. He grabbed the HXM Inspiration bottle of Riesling by Rheinhessen, a German Riesling. On the sweeter side, because Kunle liked such wines, and so did Maria.

Maria: I need shorts and a t-shirt.

Kunle walked into the room and handed Maria a frosted wine glass with the Riesling in it. She was grateful. He also gave her a brand new pair of gray polo sweatpants that were so comfortable, it felt like she was wearing cotton wool. Kunle had purchased it because Macys no longer had his size, medium, but wanted to see if the small would fit, which it did, but extremely snug. But he felt so comfortable that he decided to save it for his next girlfriend. He also gave her a pure white cotton t-shirt. Maria loved both, even though she had wanted Kunle's oversized sweatpants.

Maria: These are perfect.

Kunle: I'm glad you're comfortable in them. Come, let's watch the sunset.

Kunle led Maria to the couch and handed her a pair of sunglasses, just as These Arms of Mine by Otis Redding started to play from the record player through the Bose speakers. Maria paused in her tracks and looked back at

Kunle with a look that simultaneously expressed shock and approval. She sat down on the navy blue couch that was low to the ground, and sat her wine glass down on the white coffee table that was even lower to the ground. Kunle grabbed one of the two round glass stools that almost hooked to the couch as if it was designed for it, and placed it next to Maria so she could be even closer to her wine. Maria examined the place thoroughly. She liked his taste in everything. The design was modern and she appreciated the vision. She asked Kunle about all the art and what inspired his decoration/theme.

Maria: Where did you get that painting from (She said pointing to a painting of Zadar, Croatia at sunset)?

Kunle: Zadar, Croatia. I call it the Bifrost!

Maria: You've been? And Bifrost like from Thor?

Kunle: Yes, exactly like from Thor.

Maria: Why?

Kunle: Well in Zadar, there is this pedestrian bridge that connects the old city to the new city and the first time I saw it at night it was lit up. So I joked around and called it the Bifrost. A couple of days later, I was walking around and found a woman selling paintings of the sunsets, which are magical by the way, and I bought that.

Maria: What about that one (pointing to a painting of the silhouette of a woman with an afro)?

Kunle: Lagos Nigeria. The first time I went to Nike Art Gallery in Lagos, you have to go, I saw so many beautiful works that were way too expensive for me. My uncle told me to go to the art market instead and look for something there because that's where the unknown artists sell their work. That's where I bought that one! They have some specular works there too.

Maria: So all of these paintings have a background story?

Kunle: Yes, pretty much.

Maria went on to ask Kunle about his other seven paintings, as she observed each like she was at a gallery; wine in hand, sunset lighting the evening with magical hues of red, orange, yellow, pink, blue, etc., Long Hard Road by Sade playing in the background! She was a "joy to watch," Kunle thought to himself, as he sat relaxed with one foot on the coffee table, and followed Maria around the huge living room with his eyes. After about ten minutes, Maria came back and sat on the couch.

Maria: Is that a blanket? Let's cuddle.

Truth of the matter was that Kunle was expecting Maria to want to cuddle because he realized he didn't increase the temperature until it was about sixty-seven degrees. He turned the temperature up to seventy degrees because he knew they were sitting directly in line of the vent that was blowing cold air directly at them. Maria grabbed the gray blanket as Kunle sat up on the couch and opened his legs for her to relax her back on his stomach and head on his chest. She sunk in and instantly felt comfortable. The cashmere blanket felt soft, Kunle's arms around her felt reassuring, and the sunset was magical. The wine sent a chill wave down her spine, but Kunle's body heat kept her warm. The pair spent the next thirty minutes watching the sunset, Maria dosing off, until Kunle's phone rang, interrupting the silence, it was Andre, "Dre."

Dre: Yo, what's good G, where you at?

Kunle: At the crib bro, how've you been?

Dre: You know how I be, chilling! Listen, what's popping this weekend? I'm trying to get into something.

Kunle: I know there's a Nigerian concert tonight and I got my shorty with me (remembering that Maria could hear him), I mean I have a lady with me.

Dre: That's cool! Are you trying to roll?

Kunle: Yea, pull up around 9/9:30. Seun, Chris, and Olu are coming through too.

Dre: Oh word? It's a boy's night?

Kunle: Yup, plus Maria, the lady that's with me.

Dre: Dope. She from Hartford?

Kunle: Nah man, Pittsburgh.

Dre: Bet, I'll bring a bottle of Macallan.

Kunle: Dope!

Kunle hung up the phone and told Maria the plan.

Kunle: So we're going to this Nigerian concert, it's Kizz Daniel, at about 11. The guys would start getting here around 9, or in about one hundred and ten minutes. I have to make something for us to eat.

Maria: Do you have anything to cook?

Kunle: Probably not. There should be some lamb and salmon in the freezer. Maybe some ribs too, but I'm not sure. I'll probably just order something. What do you want for dinner?

Maria: Your city, what would you recommend?

Kunle: Oh, I got just the thing. Rasta pasta with shrimp and salmon from Island Fishhead. It is to die for.

Maria: Okay, I'll have one of that.

Kunle: I'll order three, and some fried chicken. Maybe a jerk chicken too, just in case we're hungry after the club.

Maria: Okay. I love your space (as Kunle searched for the restaurant's number); it's very homey.

Kunle: Thank you, I'm glad you like it. (Kunle received a text message from Bella, his longtime friends with benefits). I have to tell you about Bella.

Maria: First of all, did you order the food? And secondly, who's Bella and why do I have to know about her?

Kunle: She's my long time sex partner. We're both on the same page about what we have going on, but I can't read people's minds, so I think I should warn you about her, to avoid a situation like we had at Cafe Du Jour.

Maria waited in anticipation as Kunle placed the order for the food to the restaurant. This Jamaican restaurant has good service and Kunle knows the owner because he couldn't resist going daily after they opened. He would always orders in abundance and the owner would give him freebies. Maria didn't know what to expect. "I knew this was too good to be true. He probably has a baby mother and shit." Her mind wandered until Kunle hung up the phone.

Kunle: So Bella is this lady I met while protesting. We have different views on some issues, but we were on the same side of the BLM protest. I found her holding a sign I made and forgot at a rallying point; I thanked her for carrying my cross for me. She replied "it's our cross to carry."

Maria: Get to the point!

Kunle: Haha. We exchanged numbers and both agreed that we didn't want anything serious. I'm telling you because things rarely work out how we intend in cases such as this. Someone almost always ends up getting hurt.

Maria: So you think she's caught feelings?

Kunle: We've been messing around for about eight months.

Maria: WOW!

Kunle: Yea, I like having a consistent partner. The streets are deadly.

Maria: If you're anything like you are with me to her, you're in trouble.

Kunle: I mean, I'm nice to her.

Maria: I see. Like you're nice to me?

Kunle: No, not like that. I'm interested in having a really long future with you. I don't see anything else in my cards. I understand if you don't feel the same way.

Maria: We'll see. So what happens now?

Kunle: If we, you and me, decide to be exclusive, I'll dead it. I kind of want to end it now, but I don't want to be the only one jumping into this ocean.

Maria: I'm with you! I'll give you my answer by the end of the weekend.

Kunle: Take longer if you want, we have till the rest of our lives, so no rush. How long do you need to get ready?

Maria: If you're ironing my dress, thirty minutes. You?

Kunle: Since I'm ironing your dress, add the ironing time to one hour.

Maria: Okay girlfriend (teasing Kunle for taking longer to get ready)

Kunle: No, I have to dust and rinse the glasses and plates.

Maria: Oh right, you've been gone a while.

Kunle: Right.

Maria: Wanna get started? I can help!

Kunle: Sure: Maybe you can unpack your bag, pick out your dress, and shoes, and let me see how long it'll take to iron. While I start the cleaning.

They both got up and Kunle changed the playlist to soca. He wanted a groovy atmosphere filled with joy. He sent a response to Bella and told her that he's in town, but he met a girl that has taken him by storm. Bella was stunned because of late, she has developed a lot more affection for Kunle than she anticipated. She missed him terribly and realized that she wanted more. The news of Maria wasn't welcome, but there wasn't much she could do. She decided to keep her feelings hidden from Kunle.

By 8:30 pm, Kunle the food had been delivered and Maria was showered. Kunle had ironed her dress, which took less than five minutes, and he was getting in the shower. By 8:45, he was showered and half dressed. His white button up shirt with grandfather collar was on the hanger, but he was wearing a slim fit premium black jean. He picked out gold colored cufflinks and black tuxedo shoes with a bow. Maria was still wearing Kunle's sweats and t-shirt, but Kunle had ironed her sexy black dress, strapless and form fitting! Kunle couldn't wait for her to put it on. They sat down and ate while they watched music videos from various countries in Africa. Maria wanted an insight into the pop culture and Kunle suggested the music videos. By 9:30, Seun and Chris were parked outside and Kunle buzzed them in. They came with a bottle of Jameson Caskmate and the party got started. "It is going to be a fun night, it looks like;" Maria said to Kunle as he handed her a glass of whiskey with a big ball of ice and a splash of cranberry juice and lime. Kunle responded, "I hope you're ready for the boogie man."

CHAPTER 10

IS THAT IT

"Holy mollie, was that it? Holy shit, that was it!!! That was the relationship talk! What the fuck?" Maria thought to herself as she listened to Dre, Seun, Chris, and Olu debate modern dating, but their only exposure to it, really, is via social media. Seun and Chris are both married, Dre is in a long term relationship, he just wouldn't fucking marry Kelly because he's a dick, and Bola is contemplating a divorce. Kunle found the conversation funny; as he flames it from the sideline with sipping from the Jameson in a frosted glass with a big ball of ice in his right hand, and his left hand in his pocket. He leaned against the sink behind the huge marble highland in the kitchen that makes it a chef's kitchen. Bola , Chris, Dre, and Maria were seated around the highland on bar stools and Seun was standing at the edge of the island with his hand in his pockets.

Kunle noticed that Maria was frozen, she looked cold. She looked at Kunle and she met his eyes, staring lovingly back at her with a warm smile. What Maria did not understand was that in order for her to be there, Kunle had to break too many "bro codes." She's not very liked at the moment, because this was supposed to be a "boy's night." But to Kunle, they weren't boys anymore, they were men. He figured they'd understand that it was time for him to date with purpose and would only sacrifice boy's time for a woman truly worthy. He figured they'd be only slightly upset, but would respond accordingly, which they did. So there should be no reason for Maria's mood change. Kunle swayed over with the bottle of chilled riesling and had a conversation with her, speaking at a volume only Maria would hear.

Kunle: Babe, are you okay?

Maria: I'm good, how are you?

Kunle: I'm chilling. Ready to dance with you.

Maria: Yea? I can use a dance! I also want a massage.

Kunle: I can do both at any time, but can only do them one at a time.

Maria: What that fuck? I'm not sure both would feel good simultaneously anyways.

Kunle: So choose which one comes first! I'd suggest the dance first and the massage, before bed.

Maria: Yea, that's what I was thinking. I was starting to lean towards getting the massage first though.

Kunle: Haha. (Kunle announced to the group that it was time to leave). Guys! Let's bounce.

That meant it was time to go. Now, for some reason, Kunle's friends are always dressed like there's a fashion show and somehow they're going to be on stage; in other words, they were always stylish. And they always complement each other; "Yo, that's fresh bro." "Them joints are fire." Maria observed as everyone readjusted to leave. She disappeared into Kunle's room and re-emerged with lipstick on, a pair of hoop earrings, puffier hair, and stilettos; it took her five minutes. Meanwhile, Kunle was struggling to put his cufflinks on and buckle his belt; she helped him with the cufflinks. The guys were mesmerized and Kunle made sure to embarrass them as a way to compliment Maria. "I know guys, she Fine! Fine!!!" Kunle said as he kissed Maria's forehead after she successfully fixed his cufflinks.

Kunle put on a green fedora hat, as Maria looked on, puzzled, until Kunle re-appeared from the room wearing a matching green dinner jacket with black lapel to match his black pants. Everything looked bespoke and Kunle had on the sleekest pair of loafers. Maria was instantly captivated by Kunle and his outfit, so much so that she wanted to ask one of the guys to take a photo of them, but she didn't act. She had to act cool because she didn't want Kunle to think she was going to accept his relationship proposal. "What the fuck does he mean if we work out? When did we start the 'work?' I definitely handled that shit appropriately." Maria thought to herself as she watched Kunle with so much joy. She didn't understand how she was capable of wanting to hate someone and simultaneously be so ecstatic to experience life with them. "Probably like wanting to see dad after failing to show up to soccer." It was a conflicting feeling.

The crew headed out to the elevator and Kunle admired Maria's dress and how it comfortably hugged her curves and not one stitch was stressed; the dress is true to size! Maria noticed that Kunle was behind her so she waited for him and extended a hand, so Kunle grabbed it. Seun seeing this felt he had to engage Maria.

Seun: So where are you from Maria?

Bola: Y'all look picture perfect, let me take a photo.

Maria: Georgia. I'm from Atlanta. (Resisting the urge of being sarcastic and asking if Seun knew anything about people from Georgia). Have you been?

Kunle: What do you know about people from ATL?

Seun: Shit, that they're peachy.

Bola : I said stop, Y'all look picture perfect, let me take a photo.

Everyone laughed as they got into the elevator and headed towards the lobby. When they arrived at Toad's place in New Haven, Kunle had shared a blunt with Dre and the drinks everyone had at Kunle's apartment had started making the crew a bit wavy. But not Maria! She didn't drink much, only had one drink that she babied for approximately two hours, and then half a glass of wine. She also did not join Kunle and Dre when they smoked even though she really wanted to. She doesn't feel completely safe yet, so she needs her guards.

The group had a section (pretty much a vip section but don't say the "VIP" part out loud because you have to be noble and no one really gives a shit) at the venue, so they were able to bypass the line that wrapped around the block. It probably had eighty people in it, Kunle estimated. Maria appreciated the access, but still looked a bit cold to Kunle. As they walked into the venue, Kunle offered Maria his arm and the pair locked their arms as they walked in, side by side. Maria thought it was weird but didn't really care because she doesn't think she'll be back in Connecticut anytime soon, so she went with it.

At the venue, Kunle ran into about six people he recognized, four women, and two men; Kunle made sure to introduce Maria as his "date." They were warm and Maria wasn't appreciative of how long Kunle spent talking to Tania. She stood about 5'4" and fit; probably weighed about one hundred and thirty pounds. Tania had natural hair and was wearing a tasteful rumpa that fit loosely with short pants and six inch heels. She reminded Maria of Gina. Kunle was sure to get Maria a bottle of Rose Imperial by Moet because he realized she stopped drinking the Jameson at his apartment when she opted for the riesling after he offered her a second drink. The concert was packed and looked like it consisted of about 80% Africans, 65% women, 33% men, and 2% other. Maria was well hosted as Kunle generally stayed by her side and his friends occasionally checked on her to make sure she was comfortable all night.

Kunle and Maria spent about 50% of the night dancing because the music was so good. The concert only lasted for about one hour and they all thoroughly enjoyed it, especially Maria. Kunle was openly expressive of his affection towards Maria; he didn't care who could be watching or what anyone thought. Maria enjoyed every second of it. At some point, she relaxed a bit; probably after Kunle almost punched a drunk raver when he tried to grope Maria. Maria had to restrain Kunle because Maria was standing between him and the man that tried to grope her from behind. It all happened so quickly. Kunle had stepped away from the section to hangout with his pals when he looked back and observed Maria pushing a random guy away. He sprung into action, but Maria was able to defuse the situation on her own and restrained Kunle from escalating it. "I got this babe," she said as she realized that Kunle's heart rate was elevated.

Kunle: What the fuck happened?

Maria: He grabbed my ass, so I slapped him. He came back like he was going to do something, so I pushed him out of my face. That's when I felt the chair move and saw that it was you who pushed it.

Kunle: Oh my god, I'm so sorry. Are you okay?

Maria: Yes, I am okay. I know Karate.

Kunle: Excellent. I'm sorry I wasn't there.

Maria: I guess you have to follow me everywhere and fight my battles for me.

Kunle: Ha, really funny. Wanna leave?

Maria: No, absolutely not. Unless you're ready to go.

Kunle: No, but I'll need to calm down a bit.

Maria kissed Kunle passionately and then topped off his drink. Kunle had been drinking the same drink for the past two hours because he did not want to get drunk. He wanted to be alert so Maria could be safe. She sat him down and started to give him a subtle, but brief, lap dance as Kunle's crew acted as a wall of privacy around the section.

The pair spent the rest of the night dancing, practically sober. Maria, seeing Kunle ready to fight for her, turned her on more than she'd initially liked to admit. After acting calm and cool for ten minutes, she pushed Kunle to the chair shortly after the DJ started playing No Underwear by Dexta Daps. Kunle was incredibly surprised, but enjoyed the 45 seconds the lap dance lasted for. When the

DJ announced that he was about to play the last song, the group left the venue. Dre, Seun, Chris, and Bola said their goodbyes to the pair and Maria asked Kunle to get more weed if possible; which was, Kunle was able to secure some more kush.

As they drove home, Kunle could tell that Maria was tired, and so was he. It had been a long day for both because they traveled to Connecticut. When they got back to Kunle's apartment, the pair changed their outfits and got ready for bed. Maria put on Kunle's sweat shorts and a white t-shirt with no bra. While Kunle was brushing his teeth after flossing, Maria walked into the bathroom to wash her face and get ready for bed.

Kunle: I have massage oil if you still want that massage, and yes, you can pass out while I massage you. It'll be soothing; I added a few drops of peppermint oil into the massage oil for the desired effect.

Maria: I would absolutely love some. Is it okay if I fall asleep with all that oil on my body?

Kunle: Don't worry, I have multiple sheets.

Maria: What about the mattress? Duh?

Kunle: I believe I bought a mattress protector. Plus I can wipe you down with a warm towel.

Maria: Is that how they wipe you down at your massage parlors?

Kunle: No. They actually use a dry towel or a slightly wet towel.

Maria: That's oddly specific.

Kunle: Yea, I only get massages on vacations and that's mostly been on Caribbean or African beaches and hot towels were hard to come by.

Maria: Mm, okay playa. Where do you want me?

Kunle: On the bed, obviously. It's ready for you.

Maria: No it's not.

Kunle: What'd you do to it, It was ready.

Maria: I was joking.

Kunle: Oh (as he spanked Maria's butt). Being bad, I see. I'm going to smoke a little, you're welcome to join me.

Maria: Sure, only if you promise to take care of me.

Kunle: With my dying breath.

Maria: Good, let's get high.

Kunle and Maria headed to the kitchen and finished one of the three joints Dre left for Kunle. They continued listening to Dexta Daps and similar sounds, and about fifteen minutes after they had smoked, Kunle turned off all the lights and Maria was impressed with the way the lights in the surrounding buildings and streets lit the room, just enough that they could see each other, but no one could see inside through all the windows.

Maria: Oh, that's cool.

Kunle: I know, that's not the best part though. Want some of that pasta? We still have a fresh one, I'll put it in the oven.

Maria: Why not the microwave?

Kunle: I prefer the oven taste.

Maria: Sure! Where's the ice cream?

Kunle: I'll bring it. Sit on the couch as close to the window as possible, I'll come join you.

Maria: Why?

Kunle: I want to show you something.

Maria: Okay.

Kunle joined Maria on the couch as she leaned forward for him to sit and stretch out behind her. He took off his shirt and boxers and was naked.

Maria: What are you doing?

Kunle: I've always fantasized about a moment like this. High while I enjoy the night with a woman that was heaven sent. Look up at the moon.

Maria: Oh shit, she's gorgeous.

Kunle: I know, right?

Maria: And this ice cream is the truth. I love butter pecan.

Kunle: Me too, it's the best. I love nuts, so I always get this when I get ice cream.

Maria: Big nuts or small nuts?

Kunle: Shut up.

Maria: I'm so high and this is so perfect!

Kunle: I'm so high, I can feel an insect on my skin. Don't panic, there are no insects here (he said as he giggled).

Maria: I'm so high, and this is very different.

Kunle: I'm so high, I can't rhyme right now.

Maria: You can't keep up huh? How many women have you done this with?

Kunle: Just you, no one else.

Maria: Sure (with a hint of sarcasm in her tone).

Kunle: No, I'm dead serious. Believe me I've wanted to, but I avoided the urge because I did not want anything serious. You are different.

Maria: Did we have the relationship talk earlier?

Kunle: Relationship talk? Not that I'm aware of. Isn't it too early?

Maria: That's what I said, then you said some shit like if we workout?

Kunle: Oh, when you asked me what's next with Bella and I? Oh no, I was being dramatic, maybe.

Maria: Well, I like consistency in my partners too.

Kunle: Good. Are you entertaining anyone else besides Anthony at the moment?

Maria: Besides Anthony? You're funny. No, no one.

Kunle: I'm a lucky man.

Maria: How so?

Kunle: I was able to win your attention.

Maria: By doing very little to get it too.

Kunle: Don't worry, I'll make up for it by doing the most to retain it.

Maria: Good. How about that massage?

Kunle: Let's do it.

Kunle and Maria migrated to Kunle's queen sized bed that faced the wall of windows. Maria wondered if she could still see the moon from the room. "Let's use the futon," Kunle said pointing to the convertible futon by the window. "We can still see the moon from here." Maria loved that Kunle was enthusiastic about giving her a massage, but in reality, Kunle just wanted her to have the best experience.

The massage lasted for about twenty minutes and Maria thoroughly enjoyed every minute. She moaned for a good fifty percent of the massage.

Maria: I want to take a hot shower! Come join me.

Kunle: Only if I can regulate the water temperature.

Maria: HOT SHOWER!!! (she said sarcastically, raising her voice).Kunle: As long as it's not a burning hot shower, we're good.

The pair got in the shower and Kunle suggested the pure castile peppermint soap because of the sensation Maria is already feeling, it'll compliment it. Maria and Kunle both couldn't help but to get aroused as they lather soap all over each other's bodies, both carefully avoiding the hair. Kunle liked how the soap allowed his hands to glide, slide, and skate all over Maria's shea butter smooth body. Maria loved how his every touch felt; she climaxed twice during the shower. After the shower, Kunle turned the AC off and the pair made wild and passionate love.

Maria felt like she encountered an entirely different Kunle. She could tell that he was more himself at home. Much more confident, relaxed, wild, and he even felt stronger. She liked it. She had enjoyed how Kunle tossed her around for two solid hours. She liked how Kunle accidentally knocked down the contraption he calls a night stand down and didn't even stress to pick it up, he just kept drilling like he was drilling for oil. She, as she continues to try to catch her breath, wants more, more of it, all night long. But when it was all done, she couldn't move, even though Kunle was up and about. Kunle reemerged with two glasses of water, and turned the Nest thermostat on.

Maria: What temp do you sleep in?

Kunle: In the winter, sixty seven if it's above twenty outside and seventy when it's below ten. In the spring, summer and fall, sixty eight. Tonight? Sixty eight.

Maria: That's cold, but perfect.

Kunle: Don't worry, "I've got the right temperature to keep you warm."

Maria: Okay Sean Paul, come to bed.

Maria and Kunle got comfortable under the cashmere blanket that felt heavenly when combined with Kunle's rock hard shoulders and chests holding her. Within two minutes, they were both passed out. Good thing Kunle closed the blinds shortly after he brought Maria some water.

CHAPTER 11

BACON

Maria woke up to the sweet smell of beacon. It was a pleasant and welcomed smell, as the aroma instantly put her at ease. She could faintly ear the soccer game Kunle was watching, Chelsea vs Manchester City, big game and he's a Chelsea fan. The time was 11:30 and Kunle had already gone grocery shopping and just got coffee ready. The frying of the beacon on low heat, so the smoke detector doesn't go off, and minimized but not muted game on the TV was Kunle's way of waking Maria up, and it worked, perfectly.

Maria woke up in such a positive mood that when she came out of the room, Kunle thought she looked like a model. She was wearing olive green lace panties, one of Kunle's white t-shirts without a bra. The backdrop for Maria was the beautiful morning seen through the wall to huge windows that made up 50% of the walls in Kunle's apartment. Maria paused to take a look to her left when she saw how it looked like Kunle was transposed.

Maria: Your space is really nice. You have okay taste.

Kunle: If it's just okay, I'm glad it's "okay" (gesturing air quotes, in his muscle t-shirt, locs in a bun, and Diesel jogger jeans) and enough to get you here.

Maria: Good morning zaddy (in a sarcastic tone as she walked up to Kunle who was about to pick up his coffee but she interrupted him with a gentle kiss).

Kunle: Morning, fine ass woman (he said pulling her closer, by her left butt cheek, with a little force and she loved it.

He kissed her shortly after gazing directly into her eyes, he then closed his as he went for a passionate kiss filled with delicious coffee breath; she left her eyes opened in awe (widened pupil)).

Maria:I love this big dick energy!!!!

Kunle: So I had little dick energy before?

Maria: More like medium dick.

Kunle: Well, welcome to the dick party!

Maria: Thanks for showing up!!! (Both laughed a bit, but Kunle kept his eyes fixated on Maria).

Kunle: Here's the plan. Wanna do a quick hike before I have you laid out with me like two fat slobs?

Maria: (Shocked at Kunle's analogy) Who, why?

Kunle: We'll get high, I'll feed you, that's if you would allow me to engage all your taste buds, eat you out after, and then we'll watch James Bond movies. At least that's what I have in my head.

Maria: So the hike is to not feel guilty?

Kunle: Exactly! Plus I ain't young no more, all those theatrics last night requires maintenance.

Maria: About last night, GOD DAMN!!! Knew you had it in ya, but damn.

Kunle: Too much?

Maria: Just the right amount of much.

Kunle: So yes to the plan? I can also start cooking and we skip the hike all together. But you'll have to hop in the shower and give me time to cook you something delicious.

Maria: That sounds so tempting, but let's hike. I love this plan.

Kunle: Cool, go get dressed, I'll put the coffee in coffee travelers.

Maria: To go cups, got it. But why not just go to the gym? I don't want to get my Creezys dirty.

Kunle: (Bursts into laughter). Creezys? I love it! Do you have names for your other shoes?

Maria: Yea, don't you? I've seen your closet. That shit is EXPENSIVE.

Kunle: When did you see my closet?

Maria: Last night, you left the light on, so I went in. There's a fucking floor to ceiling window in your closet.

Kunle: Hashtag big flex. Like what you saw?

Maria: Hell yea! Well, if you didn't make good money, I'd say wasteful, but you're good for it.

Kunle: How do you know I make good money? You know these firms don't pay that well.

Maria: I looked you up on Glassdoor.com and the pay is not bad, plus the trajectory is amazing.

Kunle: When I say pay well, I mean in terms of what you put in. That's why I work according to what they think I'm worth, I'm paid a lot higher than my peers.

Maria: So you work harder?

Kunle: Smarter! (As he pours coffee into a Lexus branded travel mug, followed with Baileys.) Has to be the perfect amount.

Maria: Smarter, how? And are you making Irish coffee in the morning?

Kunle: Yes, it's the weekend. Plus my life feels like a vacation right now.

Maria: (Haha, laughing) I love it. Smarter, how?

Kunle: Get dressed, I'll tell you in the car. I'll clean your Creezys for you if it gets too dirty, I have a kit.

Maria: Deal!

Maria went to brush her teeth. And realized she didn't pack a toothbrush.

Maria: Damn, do you have a spare toothbrush?

Kunle: I have a new soft one in the drawer, top shelf.

Maria: Thank you.

Maria pulled the drawer open and discovered its content. She shut the bathroom door shortly after and gave it a thorough inspection. She noticed multiple containers of oils, some branded hotel toiletries (Salvatore Ferragamo, Gucci, etc.), half used Sheamoisture bottles of shampoos and conditioners. She went through the drawers trying to see if Kunle was on prescription medications, she didn't find any, only Ibuprofen. She finished brushing her teeth, washed her face with Kunle's tea tree and hemp face wash, applied his witch hazel, and moisturized with his Grape-seed oil (light sunblock). She exited the bathroom and disappeared into the room and showed up in a sky blue Lululemon tracksuit and her Creezys. Kunle had changed into his knee length soccer black Adidas shorts, Adidas sneakers, and a muscle shirt. She stopped to admire his pecs (pectoral muscles).

Maria: Are you on any prescription medication?

Kunle: No. I've only ever been prescribed vitamin D and a muscle relaxer once when I pulled a muscle while working out!

Maria: Okay! Thanks for the medial history. You look good. Was I gone that long?

Kunle: Yes ma'am, about fifteen minutes.

Maria: Okay, not bad. Which of the coffee cups is mine?

Kunle: Whichever! Listos?
Maria: Si.
Kunle: Vamunos!

The pair left for the garage attached to Kunle's apartment, where Kunle unlocked a brand new, but completely covered in dust and pollen, blue Lexus LC 500.

Maria: That's your car?

Kunle: Yup! I don't name my shoes, but I do my cars.

Maria: I assumed. What's its name?

Kunle: Correction, his! And yes, but only if you tell me some names of your shoes.

Maria: Deal (she said as she opens the door and saw the dashboard light up). Wow, this is clean.

Kunle: Thank you, meet M'baku.

Maria: Like from Black Panther?

Kunle: Exactly, I know I fucks with you. When was the last time you hiked?

Maria: It's probably been over four years.

Kunle: So an easy hike?

Maria: Medium. This coffee is amazing, perfect mix.

Kunle: You're welcome, cheers (he said with a smile as he exited the garage and both toasting with their coffee mugs)!

Maria told Kunle about her shoes. One is named Bella

Kunle: Bella?

Maria: Yes, they're by Valentino Veragani. Think top one percent; the I'm getting dropped in a car with a silk dress on type personality.

Kunle: I love the imagery. What else?

Maria: What else? There's the Wanda. Wanda picked it up for me one day after brunch on Fifth Avenue. She said I needed a comfortable pair of heels that makes my booty pop. I already had six at the time, but she insisted. We were also drunk. And then there's the Maria; three inch heels, extremely comfortable. They're by Christian Louboutin with the red bottoms.

Kunle: Nice; what else?

Maria: Those are the ones of note. Others are casual shoes, unsung heroes.

Kunle: Unsung heroes indeed!!!

Kunle pulled up in a parking lot and while pointing at the map he said;

Kunle: We'll do this reservoir. It's two miles each way and should be approximately four hundred calories burned. Cool?Also you still have any coffee left?

Maria: Cool! and about half.

Kunle: Perfect.

Kunle lit up a joint in the car and the pair smoked, three puffs each and they started their hike. The pair hiked and exchanged tales about random subjects. "Tell me a time where you had to shut a bitch down," Maria said to Kunle at some point. After the hike, both were slightly sweaty because it was humid and they hiked pretty fast.

Maria: Oh my god, that was nice.

Kunle: Yea, and an easy workout right?

Maria: Yea! Still, why not the gym? I don't think you answered when I asked earlier.

Kunle: Because I treat my workouts like work. Monday to Friday in the gym, increased heart rate. But when I hike, I don't get my heart rate up to the hundred and seventy beats per minute like I do when I run or bike before lifting weights. My weekends are mine to spend relaxing, chilling, and enjoying the little things in life; no stress.

Maria: I love that.

Kunle: Yea, me too. See!, so I'm efficient during the weekdays and chill on weekends.

Maria: How did you say you work smarter again?

Kunle: You're driving.

Maria: You're trusting me with M'baku?

Kunle: It's just a car (he said as he got into the passenger seat and tossed Maria the car keys, a mere gesture because it is push to start). But long story short, I work smarter by delivering the best work product with minimal reviews required that goes directly to our national office and the partner in question.

Maria: Minimizing billable hours! I see, smart.

Kunle: Told ya.

Maria: (After adjusting the seat and mirrors and started driving) This is so smooth.

Kunle: Yup, that's my boy.

Maria: My dad has one, but his is convertible and does not let anyone drive it. He gets upset when my mom drives it.

When they got home, Kunle immediately started making breakfast. He put the turkey bacon in the oven, along with the salmon he had been marinating. He had already chopped the vegetables, because he woke up at seven am, and poured olive oil on the stove. Maria went to take a shower and came out of the shower in Kunle's white cotton robe. By the time she was out of the shower, Kunle was almost done with breakfast.

Maria: Can I help?

Kunle: Yes, find something for us to watch. Light up a joint first though, food is almost ready. The one we were smoking is right there. I'll go take a rapid shower after a few puffs.

Maria: I love how you're a weed head but not a real one, you don't smoke much like me.

Kunle: Yea, most people over do it.

Maria: This game is almost done (looking over at the TV). Is there another one?

Kunle: No, this is the last one. Well, there's one at 3 pm, but it's two bottom league teams playing. I don't care much for them; I'll get the notifications.

Maria: Let's finish this one then, I'll set the table.

Kunle: Okay gorgeous, I love a woman that helps in the kitchen, because I do.

Maria: Where are the plates?

Kunle: That shelf (pointing to one of the eight top cabinets in the kitchen area).

Maria: These are cool.

Kunle: Yea! A gift from my mom. I owe her a call back.

Maria: Call her, I'll call mine in the room after I set these plates.

Kunle: Cool.

The pair spoke to their beloved mothers and when Maria reemerged from the room, Kunle was done with his quick shower and had a spread. Scrambled eggs with, diced, assorted bell peppers and corned beef in it; Hawaiian rolls; turkey beacon; strawberries; pineapple juice; and Brut for mimosas.

Maria: Wow, what a spread (she said to a Kunle that was seated up and about to make himself a plate).

Kunle: Yeah, I'm starving.

Maria. Yes, me too.

Kunle: We just spoke to our mothers high.

Maria: Yea, I do it all the time. I tell her everything.

Kunle: Told her about me? Seat, let's eat.

Maria: Only that I'm seeing someone that's too good to be true.

Kunle: I picked us something to watch, Silvie's Love.

Maria: Great choice, I've heard good things.

The pair ate silently for a good fifteen minutes while the movie played. Maria paused the movie and turned sharply to Kunle.

Maria: This is so delicious. I'm high, but this shit is good. The spices are perfect.

Kunle: Chef Kunle at your service.

Maria: You'd have to show me, please!

Kunle: Only if you'd show me that ass for dessert.

Maria: Deal. Do you have actual dessert though?

Kunle: Yes, apple pie and some fruits. Also, more ice cream.

Maria: Perfect. Now, I have a question though, it's been burning on my mind.

Kunle: Go for it.

Maria: I already asked this, but it doesn't make sense why you're single.

Kunle: That's not a question.

Maria: If you quit interrupting, I'll get to the question.

Kunle: Good point.

Kunle topped up Maria's mimosa and put a strawberry in it. She sat up at the intersection of the sectional sofa and assumed a yoga position with both legs folded and tucked. Kunle thought she looked comfortable and beautiful in the robe with her curly hair with blonde highlights damp. Kunle Gazed into her eyes and handed her the mimosa as he turned to face her on the couch, putting both feet up and stretched on the coffee table.

Maria: Why are you single? I mean you seem great and I haven't seen too many red flags.

Kunle: Well, I was single by choice. I've been searching for you, well someone like you. I genuinely believe that most people will not know what to do when they meet the partner that they've been searching, "praying," and asking for. I've seen friends and family fuck up a good thing. I'm not about to do that. You are the kind of person I have always wanted to end up with, and when I met you, I recognized you and I think I did because I've been doing all that is necessary to not fuck it all up. In order words, I've been doing all the "work" everyone should do on themselves.

Maria: Whoa! That's a detailed response.

Kunle: It's the truth. Been searching for you for some time.

Maria: What about me is it that you want to spend a lifetime with?

Kunle: Well, I can name body parts and shit if you want.

Maria: I'm serious.

Kunle: Well, for starters you are so kind. I mean, so graceful, peaceful, elegant, respectful, tasteful, successful, adventurous, though I'm still discovering this about you. Adventure is huge for me. And the best part, you're allowing me to explore my imagination openly with you. That shit is rare. You are also beautiful, naturally. Oh and that ass? I want to colonize it and make your boobs my military bases.

Maria: What about colonizing my ass (she said as she blushed)?

Kunle: That was a joke and I saw you smile.

Maria: Fair enough.

Kunle: Does that answer your question?

Maria: Somewhat. So you've spent time since your last relationship preparing yourself for the next relationship?

Kunle: Yes, but not necessary preparing for a relationship. More like preparing for the life I want to live.

Maria: What kind of life is that?

Kunle: Well, at thirty five, I decided I want to switch careers at forty five and be living on an island with mostly black people. I want a few small businesses, a ranch, etc. I would love to be married to someone who would buy into my vision, but I'm okay if they don't. As long as their vision has me on a beach and only working four hours a day in my mid to late forties.

Maria: Mm. Okay, I like that.

Kunle: Any more questions?

Maria: A ton, but can't think of how to ask them at the moment.

Kunle: My turn! When are you going to be ready to settle down again?

Maria: Who said I wasn't?

Kunle: I assumed you weren't after the whole Anthony situation. Made me question your taste in men and look at myself in the mirror, so to speak.

Maria: What do you mean? Anthony was a waste of time, but I had time and wasn't entertaining anyone. I took a year off from the dating scene and was going to continue when I met him. He had a good head, but it seemed the head didn't have too much sense. I too am ready to settle down and know exactly what I want. Why do you think I'm here or slid in your DMs?

Kunle: Mm, go on...

Maria: Go on about? I already told you about Anthony, so quit bringing him up.

Kunle: I mean, what kind of man do you want to end up with? Or do you want me to automatically assume I'm the man of your dreams?

Maria: Well, you're already acting like it. I love, love, love, the way you carry yourself and handle me. You're very transparent, considerate, cognizant of what I want and need. I don't have to change you, at least not too much. You know exactly who you are and I love that. When Tony called you little man, it didn't faze you and that tells me that you're comfortable in your skin and have nothing to prove to anyone. Also, you were raised right, with sense. You're quite charming, handsome, good genes, amazing in the sack, and take your health very serious. I saw the oils and shit in your bathroom, healthy shit in your fridge, etc. Also, you're very patient.

Kunle: I'm not that patient, kids get on my nerves.

Maria: They get on most people's nerves. It's okay. And finally and my favorite quality in you so far, you are happy. Like you're a happy person and you seem content.

Kunle: I am, thank you for all the compliments.

Maria: Just the truth. What red flags am I giving off?

Kunle: Besides being perfect?

Maria: Yes, besides that. Is my sarcasm a turnoff?

Kunle: No, not to me. I know it comes from a good place, so you're good. I'll let you know if that changes.

Maria: I've dated men that had issues with it. I have a tendency to speak my mind.

Kunle: Boys, you dated boys that had issues with it. And can we make a promise to each other?

Maria: Too early for promises.

Kunle: It's an easy one. Let's promise to be always truthful with each other.

Maria: Oh, I can do that. Pinky swear?

Kunle: Yes, let's do it.

Both extended their right pinky finger and performed the ceremony of the promise. Kunle imagined they were both ten years old and had the naivety that that age affords.

Kunle: I also promise to never go back on a promise, without discussing it with you first.

Maria: Deal, does that mean you will not be making promises?

Kunle: Yes and no. I'll only make those I know I can keep.

Maria: That's fair. Now what?

Kunle: Well, I want to bury my face in your breasts, and maybe you'll sit on my face with that beautiful ass, at some point, if you want. Take a nap, I definitely need one, and then go out for dinner. I made reservation at Max Downtown for 6 pm. I want to watch the sunset by the lake with a cigar after.

Maria: Damn, you really have a whole itinerary.

Kunle: I just want you to see some of the things I enjoy, to aid you in your decision making.

Maria: What decision is that?

Kunle: The decision to give me a chance to prove that I'm worthy of your attention, unwavering love, affection, dedication, loyalty, and partnership.

Maria: See, words like partnership is what gets me.

Kunle: Yea, you're definitely not an acquisition, more like a merger.

Maria: What makes you say that?

Kunle: Please don't take this the wrong way, but you're a complete woman. You definitely make more money than I do. When it's all said and done, I make $210k.

Maria: That's actually more than I anticipated and more than my take home.

Kunle: Still a merger to me. But that's not my take home and that's my salary, not factoring in non W-2 items.

Maria: Well, I'm a millionaire, so maybe I'll be the one acquiring, if I decide to do so.

Kunle: I'm not for sale. You'd be getting a huge bargain if I was.

Maria: We'll see about that. How does ten nights in the Maldives sound?

Kunle: Depends on when. I already have vacation plans for this year.

Maria: I'm paying, I'm sure you can cancel your plans.

Kunle: Oh, it's like that huh? I probably could, but this is where my ego comes in. Can't be too "available" (Kunle said as he busted out laughing).

Maria: I don't understand what's funny.

Kunle: I'm assuming we're not being for real.

Maria: I am dead serious. I've been wanting to go, but thought I'd go with a "bae," but I'm not waiting to be in love anymore.

Kunle: Wait, you're serious?

Maria: Yes.

Kunle: Oh shit. Maybe while I transition to my next role.

Maria: What do you mean next role? You're leaving your current role?

Kunle: Undecided yet. My Pittsburg client offered me a role over drinks on Monday.

Maria: Oh yes. Is it a good offer?

Kunle: It's a great offer, but I haven't decided yet.

Maria: What's stopping you?

Kunle: My plan did not have Pittsburg in it!

Maria: Tell me about your plan.

Kunle: I can't, not yet. You're not invested enough yet. But what do you think about it? When do you plan to retire or no longer work for money?

Maria: I can retire now if I want, but I'll be bored. I decided to get rich after college, since that's what most people care about.

Kunle: What does it mean to be rich?

Maria: Be a millionaire. What does it mean for you?

Kunle: Same, but also be able to dedicate time to what I want to dedicate it to.

Maria: What do you want to dedicate time to now?

Kunle: Setting myself up for a perfect forties. Laying the foundation required in all aspect of my life.

Maria: I dig that.

Kunle: Is it okay if I rest my head on your beautiful thighs?

Maria: Sure!

The pair finished the movie, but Kunle passed out about twenty minutes after putting his head on Maria's thighs. Maria finished the movie and wondered if she was embarking on a journey similar to Sylvie's; "If I let distance and status dictate or keep me from exploring this relationship, will I regret it?"

CHAPTER 12

THE ONE THAT GOT AWAY

Max was busy and there was a wait time of about twenty minutes, even though Kunle had made reservations. Upon arriving, both Kunle and Maria were both shocked at how busy it was. Turns out there was a rock concert downtown Hartford that night and Kunle immediately knew the solution to an alternative fancy dinner location would be to literally get out of town. He knew that meant he'd not get to watch the sunset as he had wanted to, but was okay with it.

Kunle: How hungry are you?

Maria: Listen, brunch was quite large, so I can wait.

Kunle: Perfect. I know another place, but we'd have to drive. Based on that concert it'll be hard to get a table anywhere decent around here tonight.

Maria: Yea, I was going to ask if you wanted to order in.

Kunle: That's an option, but we're already dressed up and that red dress deserves a professionally made cocktail.

Maria: Ha! I like that and damn right it does!. So what are you thinking?

Kunle: Do you like French food?

Maria: Yes, very much so!

Kunle: Good, let's go to my favorite restaurant around here then. They have this lamb chops that melts in your mouth. They claim it's marinated overnight in red wine or something. It's really good.

Maria: Sounds heavenly. Do we need a reservation?

Kunle: I don't think so, but I'll call just in case.

Maria: Why didn't we go there first?

Kunle: Because I wanted an easy evening where we walk everywhere. I didn't anticipate this rock event.

They left the restaurant and walked back to Kunle's apartment to go get his car. "I wish I knew I was driving; I'd have thought to dress more youthful, but this would do." Kunle said as he unbuttons the third button on his long sleeves orange Lacoste linen shirt, matched with white linen pants, looking like someone's uncle that's in the summer mood. Maria thought it was cute.

Maria: You look quite sophisticated actually (she said as she opened the passenger side door and gave Kunle a smile). Giving me dad vibes.

Kunle: What do you mean dad vibes?

Maria: Like my dad (she paused, looked Kunle dead in the eyes as she tilted back in such a "come at me bitch" stance. Immediately after which both Kunle and Maria burst into tear jerking laughter for both of them).

Kunle: Get your fine ass in the car then, before I change my mind and order in.

Maria: Maybe I want that, daddy.

Kunle: Okay then. (He said as he shut the door while looking Maria in the eyes) Fine food doesn't travel well, so how about Thai food? They seem to have mastered the art of transporting food.

Maria: Your mind continues to amaze me. How's a woman supposed to say no to that?

Kunle: What do you mean?

Maria: That was your pitch for Thai food wasn't it?

Kunle: (Feeling like he was about to be on the eve of discovering his first red flag in Maria) How do you mean?

Maria: I mean it's a good pitch, well-reasoned. Now I want Thai food because Thai food seems to travel well, they know how to pack them containers.

Kunle: Oh (he said, gently sighing and relaxing his shoulders, hoping Maria wouldn't notice).

Maria: Yes daddy, put the guns away (she said as she gently closed the door). You're not supposed to slam these.

Kunle: Come here, you beautiful fine ass woman.

Maria remembers that night being magical and recalls the exact moment she decided to spend the rest of her life with Kunle. There was Thai food, candlelight, four bottles of red wine, and the silkiest of music was playing and the sound was just perfect because Kunle turned the bass all the way up on his Bose speakers, but the volume was low, so they could converse while they pig out on Thai food. They both felt the base that was hitting them in waves, like they were both in sync. He lit a candle and left the blinds open so the streetlights and buildings around his downtown apartment could set the mood. The best part was the late sunset that was their backdrop. They both had clear sight to the setting sun because Kunle placed his small moveable dinning set at the perfect spot. She decided to give herself to Kunle the moment he lit a cigar while Essence by Wizkid ft Tems started to play, shortly after he said, "a moment like this deserves a Cohiba and Havana Club Seleccion de Maestros."

That was nine months ago, and now she hasn't spoken to Kunle in about four months, despite all his calls, texts, flowers accompanied with poems, wedding date invitations, and love letters. They broke up after Kunle invited Maria's family to his villa in Tanzania. He agreed with Maria that there might be a good way to sow the seed of their partnership in Maria's parents. It worked horribly, at least they thought, because Maria's mom, Mercy, refused to give Maria her blessing to start working and planning towards that future with Kunle. Maria replays the conversation over and over again. It was on a glorious Sunday morning, sometime between eight and eleven am. They were sunbathing by the pool in Kunle's ocean front villa, and the boys, Kunle, Maria's dad, Martin, and her older brother, Malcom, were out fishing with two fishermen on a fishing boat.

Maria: What has been your favorite thing about this country?

Mercy: Oh my god, it's hard to pick. I really love the safari, that was AAAAmazing!!!!

Maria: Yea? That's your favorite?

Mercy: I loved how Kunle was entertaining us with his back stories of the animal's lives. He's quite a storyteller.

Maria: Yea, I love that about him.

Mercy: But no, I also loved that Martin got to climb Kilimanjaro.

Maria: To the first summit.

Mercy: Shh, he's going to tell everyone he climbed Kilimanjaro (they both laughed).

Maria: Well he'll get plenty of opportunities to climb the whole thing, but Kunle suggested they both climb Mt. Meru together if he can get his trusted pal, Peter, to come out of retirement and accompany them. He really likes that man.

Mercy: Yea, he has a way with people, that Kunle. You can tell by his interactions with the locals that he really sees them like his brothers and sisters. It's quite neat.

Maria: He plans to spend his next chapter here. I'm very excited for us.

Mercy: What do you mean, us? I know you love him, but you both plan to come live here?

Maria: Yes, and we have a very solid plan too.

Mercy: I didn't send you to an Ivy League university to come and lay useless on a beach with spotty internet.

Maria: I understand mom, but Kunle is having a cell tower installed next year.

Mercy: I don't care, I don't want to talk about this anymore.

Maria took a moment to reach for the tissue next to her bed and noticed about twelve used tissues scattered on the floor that surrounded Kunle's most recent letter that's accompanied with a CVS printed photo of him and a German shepherd he's named Tony (a joke about Anthony). He was standing in front of his 75% complete villa in Dar Es Salaam. She noticed how the "PS: I miss you terribly" stuck out at the bottom of the page. It's been four months since she told Kunle that she couldn't get her mother's blessings, even though her dad was excited for her. She remembered Kunle fighting back tears that Friday evening as they had dinner on a beach in Barbados, right after she told him she has to let him go. She had planned the trip to her and Kunle's taste. They were due to fly back the next afternoon, but the vacation was nothing short of magical. It was the closure Maria felt they both deserved. After dinner, Kunle went for a walk alone and didn't come back to the ocean front hotel she had booked until 10 pm, completely sober. He came back and gave her the best, and most memorable for Maria, kiss he's ever given her. "I know there's no convincing you because you've thought of all the possible compromises, outcomes, and you couldn't find a way to make it work. I respect your decision." She remembers Kunle saying on the balcony where she was looking at the night sky before being interrupted by Kunle.

She wiped her tears and continued to reminisce about the conversation with her mom as Snoh Alegra played on her Sonos.

Maria: Okay, sorry. (Maria responded to Mercy)

Mercy: I also love that camp by the hot spring.

Maria: I thought you didn't like it because you were scared.

Mercy: Oh no, I loved it. I now realize I had nothing to be afraid of.

Maria: Yea, you didn't. This part is my personal favorite, girl time with my main chick.

Mercy: You've got that right. Cheers!!

They were drinking mimosas with real Champagne from France that Kunle instructed everyone to get two bottles from the US before coming. Dada, the assistant Kunle hired (Mercy called her maid) topped them off with a smile. Dada has a preference for Maria over Mercy. As soon as she stepped away, Maria noticed a faint chatter amongst the boys.

Maria: They're back!

Mercy: Perfect timing! (she was excited because she did not want to revisit the conversation with Maria).

Martin: Oh my god honey, you guys should have came along with us.

Malcom: Yes, we saw whales, dolphins, it was phenomenal.

Kunle: We also accomplished our mission! We'll be having freshly caught salmon and lobster for dinner at six by the sunset. Martin, Top G is grilling!!!

Mercy: Well, where is it?

Martin: They're inside. Kunle, please bring the cooler and let me show off to my wife.

Maria: Yes please, and Kunle would you do me a favor and narrate this great tale of this catch for my father as colorful as you always do for me?

Kunle: With pleasure (as he disappeared in the Tribe swim shorts he got from one of his carnivals in Trinidad).

Mercy: How close were you to the whales?

Malcom: A very safe distance mom, it was still exhilarating because our little fishing boat felt some of the waves they created.

Maria: (Laughing) Kunle did that to you guys too? I told him not to.

Martin: It was the best way to experience it. I enjoyed that little boat, even though I was terrified.

Malcom: Yea, you were pretty scared in the beginning dad, and when we saw the first Whale.

Martin: Well yea, I was enjoying the gentle dolphins.

Kunle reemerged dragging a large blue cooler.

Kunle: Are you guys ready for the story? Dada is bringing some cold Savannas (light South African beer).

Martin: My man! Please start the story (he said as he opened the cooler).

At this point, Malcom and Maria were seated on the outdoor sectional sofas. Mercy sat (leaning on the arm and supported by a pillow) on the sofa with her legs stretched out on the sofa, spotting a basket beach hat Kunle welcomed them to the island of Zanzibar with.

Kunle: So it was a calm Sunday morning, a solid eighty percent of the fishermen were off, so the water was calm and didn't have too much traffic. Malcom and I watched the sunrise before setting off on the fishing expedition.

Malcom: Yea, I saw Kunle on the beach through my window so I went to join him with a cup of coffee dada was bringing to him.

Kunle: Yes, Malcom was heaven sent, and came right in time for the amazing sunrise.

Malcom: Yea, you love both sunrises and sunsets equally, quite interesting.

Maria: And moon rises too.

Kunle: Right! Malcom joining me helped relax him for the expedition. After about fifteen minutes of sailing, we saw the first dolphin in the dark blue waters of the great and majestic Indian ocean. And then there was another one, and another, and another all coming out of the water in a synchronized manner. Malcom said "y'all seeing this?" "Amazing!" Martin responded while I just smiled. Magid cut the engine to the boat and we just sat there for fifteen minutes, watching what looked like thirty to seventy dolphins playing, taking it all in. And then the first whale came out of the water like it was showing off. Martin almost fell backwards I thought, even though the whale was a good thousand yards away.

Martin: I shook, it came out of nowhere.

Kunle: Yes, it totally did. But I was expecting it, I've seen it now four times. It took a little longer today, I guess they felt the presence of a great man, Malcom! (Everyone laughed).

Malcom: That's right.

Kunle: While all this was happening, Magid and James, he didn't want me to call his traditional name, had set up the fishing gear. They handed them out and the fishing began. Malcom got the first bite, it was this fish right here, can you please hold it up, Malcom?

Malcom: Sure (as he reached into the cooler and dragged out decent sized fish).

Kunle: Great man indeed, thanks bud! And then Martin felt a sharp pull from his line. "Oh, it's big." (Kunle didn't repeat the joke he made because his response was "mmmm." With a loud laughter, which everyone on the boat echoed. Kunle didn't want to make the "that's what she said" joke because of the optics, but everyone knew that what he meant). Magid rushed to help, but Martin said (Kunle paused and looked at Martin).

Martin: I got this!

Kunle: Please, continue with the story (as he sipped his cold and refreshing Savanna).

Martin: So I took a solid stance and put the rod on my thigh.

Kunle: (interrupting) Left thigh.

Martin: (Confused as to why it matters) Right. And I started this tug-of-war battle with this beast). So I'm reeling it in, it was heavy. Quite a workout actually. (Kunle disappeared into the house and reappeared with a four foot salmon he was lifting by the head). And then I saw it's head, I knew I struck gold.

Kunle: Like the lion of this family that you are, you reeled in this beast that would feed us tonight.

Mercy: Wow, that's huge.

Maria: Wow dad, that's amazing.

Kunle: The ocean really felt Martin's presence, the end!

Mercy: (Clapping) That really was a colorful story!

Maria: You're welcome.

Martin: Yes Kunle, you're going to have to help me tell the story to the boys back home. This trip has been nothing short of awesome.

Mercy: Let's see how it tastes first before making plans of how to tell the tales, pun intended.

Kunle: You've got it boss (he said as everyone smiled).

Everyone sat around the table in the shade, with a refreshing beverage.

Maria: Kunle, wanna take a walk with me?

Kunle: Sure love.

Malcom: Bye love birds.

As they departed, Malcom made a comment.

Malcom: I've never seen Maria so happy.

Martin: Yea, they've been on a honeymoon for some time now.

Mercy: She needs to wake up.

On the walk, Maria did not mention to Kunle her conversation with her mother because after all, it was just a seed. Kunle knew better than to ask because he was sure that if there was anything good to report, Maria would share as soon as she was ready. Kunle and Maria were both connected deeply at a soul level. It was a romantic two miles walk. At times they held hands, chased each other and kissed as a reward for a successful take down. It was cute!

Maria: Thank you for this! I wish the other two knuckleheads made it down here for this.

Kunle: Yea, me too. They'd regret not coming.

Maria: They will because daddy's already sending pictures to the Whatsapp group chat.

Kunle: Haha, I don't doubt it.

Maria: I recorded your little story. I'll play it at my dad's 65th birthday in December.

Kunle: You'll keep it from them for four months?

Maria: Yup. I hope you make it, I'm gonna start planning when we get back home. I'm making a video for him.

Kunle: Your dad is turning 65? Wow, that's neat. He's such a young 65.

Maria: Yea, he still got that charming dad thing.

Kunle: He does. He said he'll consider retiring here. That it's way more lovely than Florida or Belize.

Maria: Oh, he said that?

Kunle: Yea, Malcom liked the idea, but knew your mom would be a really hard sell.

Maria: Yea, she will be.

Kunle: Oh well. Let's head back?

The walk back was somber for both. Kunle held Maria's hands because he imagined she was feeling defeated, which she was. They both knew she has the hardest job, convincing Mercy to let her go. It was a hard sell. Mercy is her lifelong friend, council, confidant, mother. Somehow putting about eight thousand miles between them seems like it was too much to ask and Kunle understood.

Maria snapped back to reality and decided to respond to Kunle's letter. Despite never responding to Kunle, Maria was happy he kept at it. She had given up trying to convince her mom about the move. She realized there was no convincing her and she decided not to even bother anymore. She opened Microsoft Word on the MacBook Air Kunle bought her for her birthday and started to draft her response.

"First of all, fuck you for that Tony joke..."

CHAPTER 13

AM I STILL YOUR FAVE

Maria was wearing Kunle's favorite "bougie" dress of hers; it's the hips loving, body fitting, curve hugging, royal blue silk dress. In length, it is about five inches from her knees and has spaghetti strings. He especially loves how he feels like Maria looks so comfortable, sophisticated, sexy, and grown in it. It has become her favorite dress too because she wanted those qualities highlighted to the right man/people. It was a reunion that she had simultaneously dreaded and couldn't wait for. What if he has secretly been seeing someone? She had blocked Kunle on every platform possible, so there was no way for her to satisfy her curiosity without her letting Kunle know she was snooping. She thought, "what if his letters were just bullshit to keep me hooked on his magic and he really does have mal-intentions? I trust him, so I'm just going to be straight up and ask him."

Meanwhile in Kunle's camp, he is looking forward to this. He however understood the need to be calm and relaxed, so he decided not to attempt to impress her by wearing her favorite shirt, the silk one he had made in Tanzania, but she'd certainly love his perfume, Turkish, it was her favorite. He didn't want to impress her in any way possible because; what if she has changed and no longer favors those things? After all she didn't talk to him for a good four months. "Nothing! Not an email, not a text, phone call, FaceTime, nothing." Kunle lamented as he got ready for the date. He had kept himself busy the days leading up to the encounter; soccer at the park at six. By the time he gets home, he's wiped. Although he still moves like a young man, he'll be laid up every night and sleeps like a baby. With some music, a good book, vodka with freshly squeezed lemon juice, or just a good movie and dinner, he's content. He looked in the mirror and realized he had this spark in his eyes as he applied some shea butter to his face. The one that got away is coming back? He thought. He understood Maria's decision all too well. "Who am I to expect something as precious as "The Ark of Covenant" to just casually walk out of the front door with me?

You've gotta steal that shit, not ask permission."
He sighed because he understands the bond
between a mother and her only daughter, so theft
was never an option. "I miss this woman too
much."

Maria had insisted that they meet in Miami, she
wouldn't tell him the name of her hotel, only where
they were going to have dinner. She had chosen the
Cuban restaurant that was recommended to them
by a Cuban living in Cuba that they met at Hotel
Nacional. He has properties in Miami and various
parts of the Caribbean. Kunle never asked him
what he did and when Maria asked, Kunle said "it
wasn't important, only that we are all here and
enjoying this view and this live band I'm about to
ask to play La Bamba." Even though Kunle had
visited Miami since the breakup, he never tried to
go to that restaurant. For one, the restaurant has no
name, and Maria has the number to call to book a
table. Secondly, he didn't want to experience it
without her. He felt as if it'll trigger memories he is
actively running from.

Maria was at the restaurant fifteen minutes before
Kunle, who was ten minutes early for their
reservation. She watched him walk in and
immediately dashed at him and jumped on him like
a twenty years old soldier returning from war to his
high school sweetheart, and kissed him with a

passion that is unexplainable. That wasn't her plan however, she didn't have one. She just knew she wasn't right and had to get right and felt like Kunle was the only one that could make her right.

Kunle: Why hello! (He said as he looked up at a bright teary eyed Maria)!

Maria: Hi! (She responded as she fought back tears) I have missed you so, so much.

Kunle: Is that so? Tell me all about it at our table, which is where, by the way?

Maria: Oh my god, right.

She got down from his arms and Kunle watched her walk away. He observed her curves, elegance, ease, and how she commanded everyone (two other couples) in the room's attention. Every woman wanted to be her and every man wondered how Kunle got so lucky, he thought to himself. He watched her without taking one step, until she turned back to look at him.

Maria: Well, you coming or what?

Kunle: Only if I will not lose you a second time.

Maria: Come here and find out Mr. Olu. (Maria stretched her right hand and opened her palms to

Kunle as everyone switched their gaze from Maria to Kunle, including the waiter, Cubita).

Kunle took a few paces and reached for Maria's hand. Like a scene from a movie, he gently pulled Maria closer grabbed the back of her head (when he was close enough) and kissed her so passionately that it felt like he was trying to melt into her. He then stopped, hugged her so tight, slowly released her, and kissed her on the forehead.

Kunle: Before we start, I'm sorry I put you through that.

Maria: I'm not following.

Cubita: Welcome Mr. Olu, what would you like to drink?

Maria: Macallan 22 years old, neat.

Kunle: Yes, exactly that. Can we sit?

Cubita: Sure and right away sir.

Kunle: It's that kind of place?

Maria: (with a smile) It totally is, I was shook when I saw the menu.

Kunle: Where is it?

Maria: It's okay, I already ordered for you and already paid.

Kunle: Oh you're trying to buy back my affection huh?

Maria: I'll check in a couple of hours if it's working.

Kunle: Couple of hours? You're that confident huh? Nice necklace (he said looking at her eight carat solitaire tanzanite in 18 carat white gold necklace).

Maria: This? The love of my life got it for me... It's okay to be excited about that statement.

Kunle: (A blushing Kunle) I would be if you shout it out on the hills?

Maria: I promise I will, someday.

Kunle: I'm looking forward to it.

Maria: So what did you mean about putting me through that?

Kunle: I meant to say I didn't mean to put you in a position to choose between me and your mother.

Maria: You didn't, at least not yet.

Kunle: Good. How the hell have you been?

Maria: Honestly?

Kunle: Only way to live!

Maria: Miserable. Really fucking miserable.

Kunle: Why?

Maria: I was missing you. I'm still missing you and I hope you can forgive me.

Kunle: The only thing to forgive is you ripping my heart out and feeding it to sea lions.

Maria: Where the fuck did you get sea lions from?

Kunle: Exactly, I don't even know if they eat meat, but imagine me watching that shit; you ripping out my heart and tossing it to them as they enjoy it and I die slowly.

Maria: Well, you seem completely fine to me.

Kunle: I had hope, hope kept me together.

Maria: How much did you miss me?

Kunle: Too much. The first month was really difficult. I kept trying to find something to fill the hole.

Maria: How big is this hole?

Kunle: Big enough for me to move to Pittsburgh hoping to bump into you.

Maria: You moved to Pitt?

Kunle: Yea, two months ago.

Maria: You finally accepted that offer?

Kunle: They came back the 3rd time and caught me at a low point.

Maria: I hope you got what you wanted, salary wise.

Kunle: Yea, they did right by me.

Maria: Good, congratulations babe.

Kunle: Babe?

Maria: Shut your fine face.

Kunle: What about you? What have you been up to?

Maria: Well, I bought a place in Miami, I've been spending some time here.

Kunle: Nice! Congratulations! Where?

Maria: Hollywood, you'd love it.

Kunle: I don't doubt it. Is that why you chose to meet in Miami?

Maria: No, I chose Miami because I want to try this restaurant with you. Have you been here before? I'm assuming you haven't.

Kunle: No, I was here six weeks ago and thought about this place when I ordered a Cuban sandwich in South Beach.

Maria: Who were you with?

Kunle: Collin. He invited me out because he wanted to cheer me up

Maria: Did he?

Kunle: He tried; I was distracted. Went to KOD and then to Liv.

Maria: Oh I'd be cheered up too.

Kunle: I wasn't cheered up. Anyway, how are your folks? Work? Life? Seeing anyone? Getting married anytime soon?

Maria: Getting married? What? To whom?

Kunle: I don't know, you shut me out for four months.

Maria: I'm sorry, I truly am. I was trying to convince my mom.

Kunle: You're forgiven, but just know it'll take me some time to let it go.

Maria: I understand. How's the deviled crab croquettes?

Kunle: Scrumptious... It's magical.

Maria: I think so too.

Kunle: Go on! Did your mom come around?

Maria: No, but I don't give a shit anymore. I cut her a cheque for two million dollars because when I told her, she said "I did not send you to Ivy League colleges to sit your ass on a beach wasting your life away." Or something like that.

Kunle: Note to self, never bring money up with Maria, she'd cut you a cheque and tell you to fuck off.

Maria: I will. I have been dodging her calls for the past two months.

Kunle: Before or after you gave her the cheque?

Maria: Before.

Kunle: You really have to stop blocking people that love you.

Maria: Mind your business.

Kunle: Good point, but your happiness is somewhat my business, as long as you're in my life.

Maria: I thought you said, "you can't rely on me to make you happy." What's changed?

Kunle: Nothing, but I cannot be a reason why you're not happy. You cutting your mother off to have dinner with me doesn't sit right with me.

Maria: I did not cut her off, we go to therapy together. Also, I'm hoping you'd want to see me after this dinner. I have a whole weekend planned for us.

Kunle: I need another drink, what are you drinking?

Maria: Damn dude, really?

Kunle: Maybe some cocaine too, it'll be my first time, but maybe it'll numb the pain I've been running from.

Maria: Well, I need another drink as well and I'm drinking the same thing you are.

The two sat down and caught up. Maria told Kunle about her retirement from "corporate America " and how she is setting up a nonprofit that sponsors black and brown people on trips to Africa if they have a skill that people of the country they're going to could benefit from; teachers, nurses (subsidize their trips), ex-convicts with nonviolent drug offenses. She's almost ready to incorporate but felt it wasn't right to do it without Kunle, whose idea it was. What made Maria and Kunle work so well is that they're both the same people, at least Kunle thought. Their core values aligned, even though they grew up with different backgrounds. After spending months and reflecting on the whole situation with Maria's mom, Kunle knew if the shoes were reversed, he'd try to convince his mom too, but taking time away from Maria wouldn't be necessary. He especially loved that they both communicated so well because they're intellectual equals, maybe Maria is smarter. When she told him about the nonprofit, Kunle shed a tear.

Kunle: You really do love me.

Maria: More than you can imagine.

Kunle: Trust me, I believe you because my love for you cannot be quantified by anything on this planet. The story of my love for you would be told for generations and on various planets.

Maria: I'm not fucking you tonight.

Kunle: Is that why you're not wearing any panties? (Kunle Grabbed his phone and sent Maria a text message) I just had that done this morning at a clinic downtown. The doctor's lab's number is right there and I signed a HIPAA waiver, just for you.

Maria: (Gasp in surprise) Why was this necessary, have you been sleeping around? Have you been with anyone since we broke up?

Kunle: I'm just letting you know I'm clean, if that's one of the reasons you're contemplating sleeping with me.

Maria: Olakunle, answer the damn question. Did you fuck someone else?

Kunle: Do you want the truth or a version of it?

Maria: The whole fucking truth.

Kunle: Tell me more about this nonprofit before I do.

Maria: No, tell me now, I promise to be understanding.

Kunle: No.

Maria: No? What do you mean no? You wouldn't tell me? Or no you haven't slept with anyone?

Kunle: Yes, I haven't slept with anyone, but I've been with someone.

Maria: Who? What does that even mean?

Kunle: We spent time together. She gave me head a few times, but you know how that goes.

Maria: You didn't climax?

Kunle: Nope.

Maria: Why not just have sex with her?

Kunle: Hope!

Maria: Mm, hope? Who is it?

Kunle: Regina.

Maria: GINA????

Kunle: No, not your Gina. Calm down, damn.

Maria: Oh, okay. Where'd you meet her and are you still seeing her?

Kunle: Well, she's a flight attendant for Delta. She's gorgeous, you'd like her too.

Maria: Don't tell me she was a flight attendant on one of your little first class flights.

Kunle: No, I met her at a bar in Hartford.

Maria: Oh, okay.

Kunle: Damn, my little first class flights?

Maria: You know how I am about sharing you.

Kunle: Actually, I don't know. We didn't get to any of that.

Maria: Well, let me remind you. I have to approve of it.

Kunle: Okay, but you were not responding to my letters.

Maria: Well, maybe if you had mentioned some bitch named Gina, I would have responded.

Kunle: Regina! And yes, but I wouldn't do that to you babe.

Maria: Don't even try to "babe" me right now, I'm not happy with you.

Kunle: I couldn't get it up.

Maria: What do you...

Kunle: (Cutting her off) I couldn't get it up.

Maria: You were sprung huh?

Kunle: Very. But she was understanding and still being patient. I think she's hanging on to hope.

Maria: Hope that?

Kunle: That you wouldn't come back into my life.

Maria: Oh, okay.

Kunle: What about you? Who have you been with?

Maria: No one.

Kunle: Not a single soul?

Maria: Well, I went on a blind date when I thought I was meeting Gina for drinks but turned out to be some guy, Obi. He is Nigerian actually.

Kunle: Oo... okay...

Maria: Gina thought it'll cheer me up.

Kunle: Did it?

Maria: Not even a little. I left after 10 minutes, but not without apologizing to him.

Kunle: I see. Anyone else?

Maria: Bumped into Anthony, god. At a happy hour.

Kunle: How did it go?

Maria: He came to apologize and tried to ask me out. I told him to lose my number and my face. He didn't like that very much.

Kunle: I bet. What's funny?

Maria smiled at Kunle's struggles, internally. She wasn't too upset about it, but she felt more ashamed for him.

Maria: Just trying to picture you not being able to get it up.

Kunle: Keep that energy, you'll see.

Maria: That is not funny.

Kunle: You're not "fucking" me tonight, so...

Maria: Whatever. I've missed you so much.

Kunle: I missed you as well. What's changed though? Why are we here and why now?

Maria: Remember that night you advised Gina about her parents not liking Marcus? You said, "it's your life and your happiness, do what would result in peak happiness."

Kunle: I sound wise.

Maria: A fucking genius, my genius. I hope you're still mine.

Kunle: As long as the oceans have water babe, I'm yours.

Maria: Don't say shit like that, I'd kill you if I believe that statement and you start acting funny.

Kunle: I meant it.

Maria: Okay. Well, I decided to prioritize myself and my happiness. I cannot see a way to "peak happiness," without you.

Kunle: Well, have you...

Maria: Stop (interrupting him and almost pleading with him), let me finish.

Kunle: Go on.

Maria: The joy we both felt and lived through those first six months are unmatched. Like I don't think it was real. I live it over and over and over and over and over in my mind. I need you in my life and I'm willing to do whatever it takes to have you back.

Kunle: Don't say shit like that, you know I carry a heavy price tag.

Maria: Oh, I know. I'm ready. What's it going to cost me? I'll shave my head, will that do it?

Kunle: No, you'd still look beautiful.

Maria: I'll clean your condo for two months straight.

Kunle: Mm, no. I have to think about it.

Maria: Let me know, I'm willing.

Kunle: I got it.

Maria: What?

Kunle: I want you to have lunch or dinner with your mom.

Maria: I'll see her at my dad's birthday party in two weeks.

Kunle: Yea, spend some time with her before then. That's my price.

Maria: Done. I didn't want to do it, but no matter what she says, I choose you.

Kunle: Don't do that! Always choose family.

Maria: I'm trying to make you my family, babe.

Kunle: I understand, but the way I see it, your mom should be skeptical of someone trying to steal her daughter away. All I'm asking is that you come to a compromise with her. She's your best friend and I wish I had other desires in life. I wish I wanted to stay out west, but as a black man in America? That's a risk on its own.

Maria: Thank you, for being you.

Kunle: (Flashing a smile) This restaurant was everything I expected.

Maria: At $500 a plate, it better be.

Kunle: Damn, that's a hefty tag.

Maria: You're worth it though, babe.

Kunle: Trying to get used to it or trying to wear it out?

Maria: Trying to get it into your head that REGINA's GOT. TO. GO...

Kunle: Haha, good try!

Maria: Where are you staying?

Kunle: Our hotel, Winter Haven.

Maria: Ha, same room?

Kunle: No, that one was occupied and I got a double upgrade.

Maria: The platinum life?

Kunle: You already know it, platinum life!

Shortly after the desert was served, Maria became very anxious to leave.

Maria: Let's get out of here.

Kunle: Okay.

Maria: Cubita, we'll pack this to go.

Cubita: I'll get you both fresh ones.

Kunle: You're awesome, thank you.

Maria: I know I am, thank you too.

Kunle: You are not just awesome, you're the best. You are also forgiven.

Maria: Can we pick up where we left off?

Kunle: You're my heaven on earth.

Maria: Don't worry, you'll still read all those poems you wrote me to me, naked. But, can we pick up where we left off?

Kunle: It depends, what's next?

The couple left the unnamed Cuban restaurant and Kunle realized that Maria got a car that looks just like his, but hers was silver.

Kunle: Nice car.

Maria: Thank you, reminds me of you. A LOT.

Kunle: I bet haha.

Maria: Wanna drive?

Kunle: No, I want you to drive me, passenger princess; but where are you taking me?

Maria: To ecstasy!

Kunle: Wait, I forgot my condoms because I was in a rush to come here, full disclosure.

Maria: If you've truly forgiven me, we don't need it.

Maria tipped the valet and drove off into the beautiful Miami night.

CHAPTER 14

REMEMBER?

On the drive home, Kunle's thoughts were occupied with questions he's derived from various scenarios he's played in his head. "Can I trust her? Why is she so eager? Maybe she's ovulating or some shit. But wait, we scheduled this two weeks ago." Meanwhile, Maria's mind is occupied with thoughts from the past, all the way back to the weekend she decided that Kunle was it. He was the last private jet to leave an island infested with wolves (men that don't quite meet her standard). Only that he wasn't just a private jet, he was T'challa on the Royal Talon Fighter and was here to take her to Wakanda.

It was the first Saturday night she spent with Kunle in Hartford, Connecticut. They had ordered dinner, Thai food, because there was a concert downtown Hartford that night and the restaurant Kunle had made reservations at was super busy and had a long wait. Kunle had made a perfect pitch for Thai food and she had agreed. Kunle then lit a scented candle with a single wick and left all the lights in his 19th floor apartment off, it was simply magical. The candle's scent was lavender and the sunset was their background. "It was a magical night!" They made love like two lost souls that are destined to be together, but had been lost in different universes and realities. The only thing they both knew was that they had to find the other person, but they are not aware they're supposed to be searching for something and so they don't know exactly what they're supposed to be looking for. Somehow, they've found each other now, and there is no way she was going to let anything come between them, at least she thought. She made love to him that night like she wanted to make love to Kunle's soul and form a "soul tie." At some point during their multiple rounds, Kunle noticed the moon through the window while she was on top of him. She tilted her head backwards and her big curly hair blocked the moon a little that Kunle could see the silhouette of her long neck and her four inch hoop earrings.

That night, sex was intentional. Both her and Kunle took their time. Slow, steady, passionate, reckless, nasty, respectful, and thoroughly satisfying. Maria squirted that night, the first two times of many. She shivered in ecstasy after she squirted the second time, Kunle recognized that she was overwhelmed, so he went to fetch her some water. When he returned, he found her shivering and curled up like she wanted to be cuddled, so he set the water aside and laid next to her, spooning her to sleep, but not before he pulled the cashmere comforter over them. She had never been as lifeless, yet so safe, until that day; which was the only time she ever felt that way. The next morning, she woke up to a peaceful Kunle, who held her so firmly with a body temperature that was heaven sent, very warm, which made being wrapped in his arms feel so heavenly.

Maria felt like there was some innocence to how Kunle was. She had to disturb him to get up, but he went back to bed. That morning, Maria made breakfast. Some pancakes, eggs, turkey sausage, turkey bacon, and off course, a joint and mimosas. When Kunle woke up, she told him to stay in his boxers, and go brush his teeth. She turned the temperature up to seventy four degrees.

Kunle: Hey gorgeous!

Maria: Hey sexy. I've got breakfast covered (she said as Kunle hugged her from behind while she was beating the egg. His body was still warm and she could feel the warmth through his Chelsea football club jersey, matched with his gray boxer briefs that she was wearing. A bra was not needed and it wasn't missed. Her nipples reminded Kunle of torpedoes in a 90's movies).

Kunle: I'd love to kiss you, every morning if you'll have me!

Maria: How about we start with this morning, and the next fifty?

Kunle: Deal. How can I help?

Maria: Just go wash up and sit your sexy ass on that couch while you do what you'd usually do on a Sunday morning.

Kunle: I'd be cooking and making coffee.

Maria: Yes, make coffee, I love how you made it yesterday before the hike.

Kunle: Okay. If I didn't know better, I'd ask what got into you last night.

Maria: Haha, funny. Last night, was that real?

Kunle: (Spanks her on the ass) Was that real?

Maria: Very, please don't start again, I don't think I have the willpower to resist you. But I also want to take care of you how you've been taking care of me.

Kunle: Okay babe, just one kiss, please!

They both kissed and Maria dropped the spatula on the floor after about ninety seconds of Kunle's soft lips gently caressing hers, like two chocolates bars melting together, into each other, on a hot summer day. Meanwhile, Kunle's hands were busy squeezing her ass and tits. All of a sudden, Kunle felt a sharp shiver from Maria and then the spatula dropped.

Kunle: I'll make the coffee.

Maria: I ---u – mm- - just – li-te-ra-lly felt weak in the knees.

Kunle: What you mean?

Maria: Like, I just felt weak in my knees. You know? Like my legs became jelly for a quick second.

Kunle: I have that effect on women.

Maria: Ha, not funny.

Kunle: You sure you don't want me here?

Maria: Listen to instructions young man, carry on like you're done with breakfast or you ordered breakfast.

Kunle: Okay!

Kunle made his perfect Sunday coffee; French pressed coffee with Baileys, at a six to one ratio of coffee to Baileys. Maria observed as she made the eggs. He served Maria first, in a white graphic mug that read "Coffee Me, Please!" with the cartoon of a lady in panties and t-shirt in front of it, just like Maria, only that she's wearing a blue Chelsea soccer jersey and Kunle's boxer briefs. He then carried what was left in the French press over to the coffee table where he sat down, planted his ass on the blue L shaped sectional couch, with a soccer game on, he wasn't really interested in it. It was Brighton vs Watford, some bottom league teams.

Kunle: Wanna watch a movie?

Maria: Remember, I'm not here, it's just you in your space.

Kunle: I don't think you're ready for that yet.

Maria: Trust me when I say the next fifty mornings, I want to spend with you.

Kunle: Well, that wouldn't be possible.

Maria: I meant the next fifty mornings I can spend with you, I choose you.

Kunle: Please don't tell me you're quitting your job to come hang out with me.

Maria: Calm down homie, you ain't all that (even though she currently feels like he's worth doing that for). Why you just gotta ruin everything? Thinking everything is about you, it ain't.

Kunle: (Genuinely feeling like a fucking dumb ass) Babe, I am so sorry. I didn't mean to be a dick.

Maria: I'm just fucking with you babe, calm down princess.

Kunle: Haha, (holding his nose down trying to sound like a little five years old girl) calm down princess. Real funny.

Maria: Aww, did I hurt your little feelings?

Kunle: You're not here, remember? I'll get comfortable.

Maria: Right, give me a show.

Kunle readjusted the pillow and laid down on the couch, facing Maria with his back turned against the floor to ceiling windows. He got up to close a few of the blinds as his TV is from 2014, and even though it's 4K, it's not Quantum LED or (QLED), so he felt he needed a little shade, but in reality he doesn't and Maria knew this.

Maria: What are you doing? That's a nice view, that's the state capital building.

Kunle: Yea, you can still kinda see it, I just need a little shade.

Maria: Here's a little shade. If you adjust the settings on your TV appropriately, you wouldn't need shade (she says with a wink in the her right eye, she looked really cool, with her hair in a bun).

Kunle: She's not here, she's not here. You're not here. You don't exist to me.

Maria: I'll fix it for you after breakfast.

Kunle: Please. See, I need you in my life.

Maria: Is that so Mr. Ola-ju-mukeee?

Kunle: Ola-ju-mo-ke! And yes, I desperately need you haha. Come fix my plumbing please.

Maria: Fixed, you're good for at least two more decades.

Kunle: Fuck you too then.

Maria remembered serving Kunle eggs, pancakes, turkey bacon, turkey sausage, mimosa made with pineapple juice, Simply Pineapple, that she was surprised was Kunle's only brand of Juice he'd buy. She remembered the conversation when she opened his fridge.

Maria: I see you're loyal to the Simply brand.

Kunle: Yea, their ingredients are straight forward. Look at the ingredients in any of those juices, I bought four yesterday.

Maria: It says 100% pineapple. I don't trust it.

Kunle: See, drink enough water and only that juice and your pussy would probably taste like pineapples.

Maria: Does that add to the desire for you?

Kunle: Yes, hell yes. I'll eat your pussy for breakfast, with or without it tasting like pineapple.

Maria: Good save, I was about to be like you're not about to be my dietician.

Kunle: The way your skin is glowing and your eyes are white, I need to take dietary tips from your fine and healthy ass.

Maria: That's what I thought. You're on the right track though, my job would be easy.

Kunle: What job is that?

Maria: The job to coach you into taking your health, and me, very serious.

Kunle: And I.

Maria: Huh?

Kunle: I think "and I" is the appropriate phrase.

Maria: Whatever, you know what I meant, don't be a dick.

Kunle: Sorry, it's the Big4 in me.

Maria: Well, leave that shit in the office.

Kunle: Yes ma'am.

Maria remembered how Kunle spanked her ass when she bent over to pour him a glass of chilled mimosa. "I deserve this," she remembers Kunle proclaiming out loud, shortly after he spanked her ass. She loved it. It was like no one's ever really taken care of him like that before. She loved that he appreciated her effort because she thought she overcooked the eggs, but they were perfect for Kunle, he preferred his eggs burned a little. They sat back and watched "Casino Royale."

She remembered how they spent that Sunday on the couch and how she didn't want to leave the Friday after they both spent their days working from

Kunle's apartment's community library; an old bank's conference room that was left intact. The conference room table sits about twenty people comfortably, but they had it to themselves.

Maria: I don't want to go (she said as Kunle grabbed her duffle bag, because she only planned to spend the weekend).

Kunle: So don't go.

Maria: That's what you said on Sunday and I'm still here. I have shit to do in Pitt.

Kunle: I know, I'll be there in two weeks.

Maria: Are you going to take the job?

Kunle: I don't know yet, it feels too easy.

Maria: Remember how you said "it's easy because you've done all the work" about my work thing? Maybe think about it that way, unless you don't feel like it's challenging enough.

Kunle: I'll sleep on it some more.

Maria left reluctantly, on the five pm flight and was in Pittsburgh in no time. Unknown to Maria was that when Kunle got back to his apartment, he was momentarily relieved, but when he went into the bathroom and realized everything was back to how it was, like she was never there, he suddenly felt gutted. He started to miss her so dearly.

He texted Seun, who came over to hang out with Kunle and Maria on Wednesday, and asked if he wanted to chat. He called him back instantly on FaceTime.

Seun: Guy, how far ("what's up")?

Kunle: I dey man, madam just left (I'm good, wifey just left).

Seun: Madam? She don become madam (She's been elevated to "wifey" status)?

Kunle: Guy, what else can a man need in a woman?

Seun: Na lie (it's a lie). You can't be serious.

Kunle: Deadass, I'mma wife her up, if she'll have me!

Seun: Why, you don't think she likes you that much?

Kunle: I think she loves me, but she can easily change her mind. You know these women, some of them might just stop talking to you over something trivial.

Seun: Yea, but she didn't strike me as such. Y'all were too cute together. She has to meet Jen. Jen specifically asked to meet her. She said and I quote "I want to meet the woman that has managed to get Kunle's attention.

Kunle: (Bursted out laughing) Bro, she's still mad I didn't like Veronica?

Seun: Off course, how the fuck are you gonna get my wife's best friend to fall in love with you only to say the same I'm not ready to get married story.

Kunle: Because it wasn't a story. I simply wasn't and I told her; talking about "but you said you never know what can happen." Something I mentioned while we were talking about if I wanted children, a question to which I responded, "they'll be nice to have if my wife and I can have them, you never know what can happen."

Seun: Bro, it was in the context of marriage.

Kunle: Yes, but I was talking about my own future, it was implied.

Seun: And she inserted herself in your future and now you're there talking about "if my wife and I can." Duh.

Kunle: Why do you sound like Jen?

Seun: Because Jen has a point.

Kunle: Y'all don litigate the shit out of this huh?

Seun: Yes, hell yes bro.

Kunle: Well, only thing I owed her was the truth and I told her. And I didn't even smash. What do y'all expect from me?

Seun: Well, whatever you did, she's in love, still.

Kunle: She's not invited to our wedding then.

Seun: You are not serious. When are you seeing her again?

Kunle: Two weeks, but work is going to be calm the next month, so I'm thinking about pulling up on her or having her meet me somewhere.

Seun: You gon fly her out?

Kunle: Yea, but she can fly herself out if she wanted to too.

Seun: Who asked you?

Kunle: Shut up. I'm thinking Cuba.

Seun: Haven't you been there already?

Kunle: I have, but I haven't been with Maria. I want to see how it'll make the trip better. Trying to see if the whole marriage thing would work with me.

Seun: By flying her to Cuba? I'm confused.

Kunle: By inserting her into my life, every aspect of it.

Seun: I see. That's smart actually.

Kunle: Yea, I'll notice red flags I'm not comfortable with in those aspects of life easily and quickly.

Seun: But so far she's madam already!

Kunle: Yup!

Seun: Na, I'm glad. I'm happy for you man.

Kunle: Appreciate it my guy! How Jen and the baby?

Seun: They're good, I'm about to go grocery shopping, trying to get her to come with me.

Kunle: Aww, y'all cute.

Seun: What's the move tonight?

Kunle: I don't know man (as he pours himself a generous amount of Jameson Black Barrell on the big ice ball with a splash of coke), I think I'll just chill tonight.

Seun: No happy hour?

Kunle: Na man, just gonna enjoy my space.

Seun: Lit. I might pull up if Jen goes to bed early, if you're sober enough to hang.

Kunle: Big if, but hit me up.

Seun: Aight.

Kunle sat on the couch as he played Snoh Aalegra and other R&B music from 1990s and 2000s on his "impressive" (as Maria puts it, which brought a smile to his face) speakers. Multiple thoughts running through his mind. "How do you know when you've found the one? She's too perfect. Is this what happens when you know exactly what you want?" He asked himself, these and other questions, as he sips his ice-cold drink. He had a conversation with himself, a version of himself that's required for "THAT" conversation. Let's call this version of Kunle Bobo (a Yoruba translation of "Guy"):

Bobo: Look at this fool, he don' fall too fast (for some reason, this version of Kunle sounds like Eddy Griffin).

Kunle: And? Your point is?

Bobo: Looking like a fucking simp.

Kunle: What the fuck is that supposed to mean?

Bobo: I don't fucking know, I'm you. Little bitch ass, pussy whipped, lover boy.

Kunle: You're supposed to be helping make a rational decision.

Bobo: Why are you so fucking dense? Don't you get my drift yet?

Kunle: You're trying to sound extra negative so I can see the extreme side the consequences my decision could bring me?

Bobo: Ding, ding, ding! That was, actually, well put!

Kunle: I created you, you little shit.

Bobo: Sorry, had to wake you up.

Kunle: I was never asleep, unless Maria is some kind of kryptonite.

Bobo: Boss, you think?

Kunle: Boss?

Bobo: Yea, you're up man. Welcome back to your sweet life.

Kunle: Um, I neve---

Bobo: (Interrupting Kunle's thoughts) What am I wearing?

Kunle: Can you be serious?

Bobo: I'm dead serious man, what's my uniform? Obviously I look like you!

Kunle: There are 20 others that look like you. You all are wearing tailored muscle t-shirts, very clean. It's all black, black tailored cashmere pants, and black tennis shoes with white soles.

Bobo: I like that, we're sleek. I'm guessing Jeff made the pants (Kunle's Nigerian tailor connection).

Kunle: Ose (thanks)!

Bobo: My name is Bobo, why are we speaking in English?

Kunle: Because them feds be everywhere. We gotta let them know we mean no harm.

Bobo: You mean feds like your self imposed reality check with your own mind?

Kunle: O get e! (You got it, translated from Yoruba).

Bobo: Fair. So Maria! We fucking love her man!!!

Kunle: Yea man, she's everything. I'm afraid I'm dreaming and shit. I don't want to wake up. I should probably put a "do not resuscitate clause on my life insurance."

Bobo: Yea, you probably should change your beneficiaries too. Dara isn't your only niece anymore. You have six of them little bundles of life now.

Kunle: Yea, Jen's baby gets 50% and the other six gets the rest equally with Dara getting 20%.

Bobo: Favoritism?

Kunle: I'm only a man. Plus, when I agreed to be a godfather, that shit is serious man. If y'all motherfuckers in my head don't get it yet, FUCKING GET IT.

Bobo: (Kunle imagined Bobo ducking in the courtyard overlooking the ocean with the afternoon sun and blue skies as the back drop) I'm sorry boss, I'm just your conscience.

Kunle: Well, that's the rule. That's law.

Bobo: Why are we talking about your will when we should be talking about Maria?

Kunle: You're right. We love her. She's the one. Tell your homies.

Bobo: Yes sir.

Kunle: Any questions?

Bobo: How are you so sure? It's not like you have a crystal ball or something, yet you're certain.

Kunle: Well, let's see. She's pleasant, playful, super intelligent, humble, kind, soft, well mannered, great boss, great partner, has a great sense of humor, gets my jokes, has just as much energy as I do, loves to do the same things, does not question my decisions, and loyal. I'm sure I'm missing a lot more things to love about her because she's like the sunshine that would illuminate the rest of my life.

Bobo: WAWU!

Kunle: Any more questions?

Bobo: No sir.

Kunle realized the sun was starting to set. He had dozed off and when he opened his eyes, he smiled at the amazing sunset. "Maria should be landing about now," He thought to himself. So he decided to text her:

Kunle: Hey beautiful!!! How was your flight?

Maria: It was great babe, thanks for checking!

Kunle: You bet. Hope it was smooth.

Maria: Like Kenny G on the sax.

Kunle: Aye!

Maria: I knew you'd appreciate that analogy! I'm definitely starting to understand you.

Kunle: I appreciate that. I promise I'll catch up.

Maria: You're doing okay.

Kunle: There should be some flowers (sunflowers) waiting for you.

Maria: I love it! Thank you. Can you please read me the poem on FaceTime?

Kunle: Sure thing babe (as he calls her on FaceTime)

Like the sun shining on the river

Your presence gives me fever
Your smile I didn't know I needed
Yet your tenderness is the creator intended
A love like yours is rarer than tanzanite
Don't leave me babe, you're not my kryptonite
Like the sun shines and heals everything
My heart is full, my brain tells everything
Like the sun shines and makes the world whole
Please stay in my life babe, I'll give you, my soul.

Maria: (Wiping her face) I love you.

Kunle: I love you too, silly.

Maria: (After a long and dramatic pause) Did that just happen?

Kunle: It totally did, we're both in love.

Maria: Good answer.

Maria snapped out of her head and she is now back in her silver Lexus LC500, where Kunle sat neatly dressed as the breeze blows his silk shirt while he gazed into the night. She turned to ask him:

Do you remember everything...?

CHAPTER 15

DEPENDS ON THE MEMORY

"...I probably do, it depends on the memory."
Kunle said to Maria as she drove down Oceans
Drive that Miami night. They're now approaching
South Beach and the night is lit by street and car
lights. The roads were infested with tourists, half of
which looked like they were of college age.
Somehow, Kunle was enjoying it all because he'd
forgotten how good Maria drove his Lexus. He
used to always let her drive and she didn't mind. "I
love how she feels," she once said. It became
apparent to Kunle that he was still madly in love
with her because he realized that he never really
stopped loving her. The fact that his face lit up and
he's having a hard time getting rid of a stupid smile
on his face; an expression also shared by Maria.

You can see her blushing, and the way her hair bounced with the Miami breeze brought Kunle an enormous amount of joy that is impossible to quantify.

Kunle: Man, fuck you.

Maria: Wow, I wouldn't tolerate any disrespect without dishing it back, so fuck you too (she said as she gave Kunle a sharp and confused side glance).

Kunle: (Still looking out of the passenger's side window:) Yea, I said it. I understand you choosing your mother, but I just want you to know I was so hurt by that.

Maria: (slowing down at a light while Kunle turned to look at her) Babe, I know and I am mad at myself as well. I hope you can forgive me, please.

Kunle: I will. I almost questioned your love for me, I feel like that was the next phase in the grieving process.

Maria: Well, no further need to grief babe. My last step was having a conversation with my mom. We started therapy together, you know?

Kunle: Yea, tell me more about that! Why? You have mommy issues?

Maria: It appears so. She's okay with us moving to Tanzania now!

Kunle: I guess therapy does work.

Maria: She said it before therapy. That's why I suggested we should go to therapy.

Kunle: What the did she say and what did you say to her for her to say it to you?

Maria: I said I'm going to be with you with or without her approval and she said we needed to talk. So, she took me out for a spa day and told me a story of some Nigerian dude she used to be in love with and how he ditched her for some girl from his village.

Kunle: Oh, I see.

Maria: Basically, she was projecting her fears (traumas onto me).

Kunle: I could have told you that.

Maria: Well, she had never mentioned dating anyone besides my dad and some boy named Joey while she was in high school. So how am I supposed to know?

Kunle: Because you have to assume that your parents are never telling you the full story, as they should. But her dating the Nigerian dude is a curveball I wasn't expecting.

Maria: Yea, I have a great relationship with my parents, not my fault you and yours are not open.

Kunle: We're open babe, it's just there has to be boundaries. You've finally grown enough for her to tell you about this Nigerian man. See, I feel like the stories our parents told us about their lives corresponds to a behavior they're trying to correct in us, so they draw from a real story in their past with real characters and they're able to change the outcome to get their desired objectives. There was never a reason for her to bring home ol up, and she didn't.

Maria: Interesting how you see things.

Kunle: I mean, they're parents. They can't be open and honest about everything.

Maria: You're something, you truly are.

Kunle: I understand babe. So now you're in therapy with your mom?

Maria: Yea. She was so in love with the homeboy that she thought about trapping him with a pregnancy.

Kunle: Oh shit, now I'm gonna be worried about you trapping me.

Maria: And I'll gladly pay you child support and do all the work.

Kunle: There'll be no need for child support, I'll be a stay-at-home dad.

Kunle remembered the first time he took a trip with Maria and the villa they stayed in. It was in Christ Church in Barbados. They stayed in an oceanfront three-bedroom villa; they had the place to themselves. Maria wondered why Kunle booked a three-bedroom villa and Kunle simply responded, "it's perfect." She never asked the question, "perfect for what?" But somehow, she knew exactly what Kunle meant. Breakfast and lunch were freshly made in the villa and dinners were had while they watched sunsets. "Never waste an opportunity to watch a sunset," Kunle once said. They had a staff of 3; a chef, security guard, and a maid. Maria couldn't believe that she's dating a man that enjoyed wearing linen on vacation and whenever he could. It seemed like Kunle didn't wear anything else anytime they left the villa on that vacation. It was linen in bright colors, yellow, red, blue, green, white, black. Maria's favorite night was when Kunle wore the black linen Polo shirt and white linen pants, topped with a hand painted black and white Fedora hat. The hat had inspired the outfit and Kunle simply said, "I have a shirt for that" when he bought the hat. The hat features the map of Africa on the roof and on the sides, hand painted in black and white, and the drawing of the map included Seychelles, so Kunle especially loved and must have it. Kunle's outfit was completed with a pair of simple loafers.

Maria wore a yellow bodycon dress and a royal blue Kimono. She matched her outfit with a paisley blue, yellow, white, and pink brim hat. She was wearing a very simple Tory Burch leather slippers that seemed to bring it all together. Kunle appreciated her elegance and how the night's gentle breeze seemed to call his attention to her curves and her big curly hair.

Maria: I'm having a bad hair day.

Kunle: Yes, you are. Where's the volume?

Maria: What are you talking about? You can clearly see the volume, it's even bigger than normal.

Kunle: That's what she said.

Maria: Oh, grow up.

Kunle: Are you mad I didn't complement your hair?

Maria: No... Maybe a little.

Kunle: I knew you were fishing for a compliment haha.

Maria: Asshole.

Kunle: I did complement it though.

Maria: When? How?

Kunle: When I came back from my run, I said all that...

Maria: ...Beautiful hair (interrupting Kunle). You did compliment me.

Kunle: Yes, but to be honest, I just haven't found the words to express how incredibly stunning you are. How your elegance brings a smile to my face and your aroma brings a chill down my spine, every fucking time. How your smile warms my heart and your hair makes me proud.

Maria: Aww. You're proud of my hair?

Kunle: I'm proud of me for not fucking up the opportunity to be with you.

Maria: I don't think you realize how rare you are.

Kunle: Nah, it's you that's clueless how rare you are. What do you mean though?

Maria: I mean I'm the real lucky one here. A lot of women would probably go a distance to date you or a man like you.

Kunle: Good thing you're not a lot of women then.

Maria: Good thing I want this and I want it with no one but you!

Kunle: You want what? You want this dick?

They were interrupted by their server who was accompanied by another server as they wheeled out a tray of food. Two roasted jumbo lobster tails paired with some couscous and mixed vegetables. They opened another bottle of Riesling from Germany they had at the restaurant.

Tristian: Salud!

Kunle: Salud!

Maria: Like I said, I'm the lucky one and it's mine.

They sat out on the terrace of the restaurant and enjoyed the jerked lobster tails. It was simply delicious. "Best lobster I've ever had in my entire life," Maria said about halfway into her food. Kunle smiled and replied "I've had better, but definitely the most memorable lobster I've ever eaten."

It was a cloudy evening on the island. Kunle and Maria spent the morning mostly on the beach. They did a two-mile jog, stretched, not on the front porch made of mahogany wood overlooking an infinity pool and the ocean, but on their private beach. Kunle remembered asking Maria if she wanted to have sex on the beach and she declined his invitation because the neighbors could see them. After their little stretch/beach yoga session, they made out for about 10 minutes, and they stayed on the beach and soaked up the eight am sun. They then walked down the beach to a small café where they had their coffee and read a bit. Maria was reading Love in The Time of Cholera, a book Kunle gave her to read because he had read it and loved it; Kunle was reading financial and political news as well as tax law updates. They stayed at the café for about two hours and then went to Kirby Gallery, where Kunle bought the painting of a Caribbean woman with big curly hair. It was titled Pricilla by the artist, but Kunle renamed it to Maria, but he did not tell her.

After dinner, the two went to a bar on the same beach, about ten New York City blocks from their villa. The evening's breeze was gentle and the clouds were almost all cleared. The two walked on the beach holding hands and using their spare hands to hold their "fancy" leather slippers/loafer. To their left was the blue Caribbean Sea and a magnificent sunset in front of them. Both had their shades on, Kunle in aviator shades as slight sweat started to drip down his shea buttered face. Maria, wearing John Lennon sunglasses that fit her face like a glove, told Kunle about one of her favorite college memories, but Kunle barely remembered the story because he wasn't paying attention. He had stopped listening because it was about her college boyfriend. He wondered what she meant when she said "I want this," but he did not want to interrupt her story. By the time Maria realized he wasn't engaged with the story, they had reached their destination. The pair put their shoes on and climbed up the stairs from the beach. They looked like a thriving, healthy, wealthy, sophisticated, and humble couple. Their smiles gave away their humility.

There was a band playing sweet old school reggae music and their lead singer is a voluptuous woman with an angelic voice. Kunle quickly realized that he could make requests, so he requested Feel good by Beres Hammond. He got up to request the song as soon as Maria went to the bathroom, and he tipped the band fifty dollars. He told them to please play it in thirty minutes and they agreed. At this point of the night, Kunle switched to whiskey from wine and so did Maria. They both drank fifteen-year-old Macallan neat. It was as if they were both babysitting their drinks, taking about twenty to thirty minutes to finish each drink. To be fair, the drinks were generously poured; probably due to the fact that it was twenty five dollars each and it seemed as if the waiter sympathized with them and was generous with the pour.

By the time they were about finishing their second drinks, the band made an announcement. "The next song is a special dedication from Kunle to the love of his life, Maria. Ain't love something?"

Kunle smiled and looked Maria straight in the face.

Kunle: Don't worry, I'm not proposing.

Maria: Worry? I would say yes.

Kunle: I'll keep that in mind for next time. But for right now, would you please do me the honor and indulge me with this dance?

Speechless, looking straight into Kunle's eyes and telling herself, "yup, he's perfect," Maria slowly grabbed Kunle's open palm that he had stretched across the table where they sat in the corner of the room. They both stood up and Maria passionately kissed Kunle; he was not expecting it.

Maria: How can a girl resist you?

Kunle led her to the dance floor and when Dennis (the bass player) saw the couple get up, he nodded to Kunle, and the band started to play following three taps of the drumsticks by the drummer. Kunle and Maria slow danced as the voice of the singer, Victoria, sent chills down both their spines and left Kunle with a tingling sensation in his skull. Other couples joined them on the dance floor.

"Oh what a night, what a night, what a night, oh gosh what a night." Kunle busted out singing as he exited the car in Maria's Miami villa. He noticed a Jay-Z blue Mercedes Benz G-Wagon that he admired, but before he could say anything, music started to play from Maria's outdoor Bose speakers.

Kunle: Remember Barbados?

Maria: I remember. How can a girl forget one of the most magical nights of her life?

Kunle: The same way a girl abandons a boy for four months.

Maria: Doesn't mean she forgets the day the man of her dreams pledged his eternal love to her.

Kunle: And yet, she ghosts his ass.

Maria: I'm serious. What's that song again?

Kunle paused in silence as he recalls the moment she was talking about. They had spent the night out slow dancing after they had had a few drinks and a delicious meal. Kunle remembers the exact moment he told Maria "I don't think I can enjoy this world with anyone else but you." After they left the bar with the band, they walked on a beach in Oistins. Kunle hates himself and Maria for refusing to tell him the specific name of the beach because they fucked on that beach and the least he could do is remember the name of said beach and she refuses to tell him and made him promise he wouldn't go back there without her. At the time, that was their most special place on the planet. Maria floated the idea of buying property there, but Kunle cautioned her that they've only been together a few months. He did promise to invest in an ocean front villa when they've established a more solid relationship.

As far as Kunle was concern, the sex on the beach was subpar and one of his worst performances with her. However, Maria loved it regardless because she climaxed as soon as thirty seconds into the act, but wasn't known to Kunle, who only lasted about two minutes because he felt like they were in front of people's houses, so they have every right to "videotape them and sell that shit on Porn Hub or some shit like that."

After they had their fun on the beach, they stopped by a Chicken Barn and bought a bucket of chicken and some biscuits. When they got back to the villa, Kunle set the mood as he dimmed most lights because the villa had mostly glass walls facing the Ocean; "a view that should never be Obstructed," Kunle once said. But by the time he got back to the bedroom to change into his night clothes, usually a t-shirt and sweats unless he's feeling fancy then he'd wear silk, Maria pounced on him like a very hungry lioness. As he opened the door to the bedroom, he didn't have a chance because on the other side of the door stood a Maria in lingerie, holding a bottle of fine Barbados rum. He couldn't believe his eyes. "I really did hit the jackpot with you, didn't I." Kunle said before he started passionately kissing Maria after taking a shot of rum, without a glass. She tasted of rum, as did he, a hint of the cigars they had smoked at sunset, she smelled like roses coated in roses, to further mess with your senses. They were both incredibly turned on and had sex for about three hours, which included multiple rounds of sex where either were thoroughly exhausted, but somehow managed to summon up the energy to keep going.

By the time they have had their fill of sex the couple migrated outside to smoke a joint. While smoking, they were cuddled up on a blanket on the beach, their private beach. The moon was showing off to them how bright it can be and Maria was loving every single minute of it; she said to Kunle; "I think this is a dream, like you are a dream." Kunle, who cuddled up under a light cotton blanket with her, passed her a joint. She was laid up on his chest as they faced the moon, with nothing obstructing their view. She felt Kunle's breath and enjoyed the rhythm of his heart. It was calm, measured, at peace. She loved laying on his "my big chest" and was especially appreciative of it because they were both bare skinned and their body heat combined was heavenly. The night's breeze was calm and perfect for the occasion.

They laid on the beach for twenty minutes after finishing the joint before Kunle suggested that they go inside. Maria really wanted to stay, but they both had the munchies, so they went inside. "Go to bed," Kunle said to Maria, I'll grab the food. He reemerged with a tray containing the bucket of fried chicken Kunle had put in the oven, which he had started to preheat before they went out for a smoke, for a good 10 minutes. He made sure it was hot because they both loved their food hot for some reason. When he got back, he observed a naked Maria who was on her phone, laying on her belly and resting on her elbow and her feet crossed as her calves were raised at a ninety-degree angle. She was ready for some food and she was not disappointed. They both sat on the bed and ate the food naked as the night's breeze cooled their evening through the balcony and windows in the master bedroom. Kunle remembered feeling abundantly blessed and told Maria, as she licks her fingers, with chicken crumbs on her lips and her hair messy, "I honestly don't believe I'll enjoy this world as much with anyone else, or that I want to for that matter. You are just the right amount."

Kunle snapped out of his head and realized that Maria is playing How Deep is Your Love by Mut4y, featuring Wurld, a song he sang to her, as he chewed chicken, and somehow did it so elegantly, in Barbados, that faithful Night.

Kunle: I remember, it just depends on the memory.

Maria: Dance with me.

Kunle: Not to this song, let's ease our way back into it.

Maria: I respect that, I'll play one of my favorites then.

Kunle: Then I shall dance with you.

Maria changed the song to These Arms of Mine by Otis Redding. They both danced and Maria found herself moved to tears by the beautiful music and the moment, shortly after they started dancing. She didn't know Kunle realized it, but he did. He responded by saying "I miss you too."

Maria: Do you remember...?

CHAPTER 16

YES HONEY, REAL HARD FEELINGS

Maria and Kunle quietly danced for a solid 15 minutes before Kunle decided to "ruin" the moment.

Maria: Here we go again, you couldn't just let me throughly enjoy that could you?

Kunle: Well, I could have, but I'm just not ready for what's to come next. And believe you me (as he glanced down at his bulging pants), I want you. But I need to process this further before I open myself up again. I need to re-examine things...

Maria: Do your cost benefit analysis (cutting Kunle off).

Kunle: Well, sort of.

Maria: You know what I love the most about you?

Kunle: My charming personality?

Maria: No, the fact that you refuse to tell a lie.

Kunle: So my charming personality!!!

Maria: I'm being serious.

Kunle: I'm sorry babe, but as you observed, I'm just being honest.

Maria: Tell me more, why are you hesitant? You think my intentions have changed?

Kunle: No baby, you came back into my life like Deanerys Targaryen riding on a fully grown teenage Drogo's back. Right now, you haven't gone rogue yet, but I've seen what life is like without you and the journey back is not something I'd survive the second time. The easy thing to do would be to run back to that familiar feeling, but that might cause the most damage.

Maria: Wow, damn. You know I love it when you make references to GoT.

Kunle: Well, yes! I also do it because I really want you to hear me.

Maria: Say more.

Kunle: About?

Maria: Play out the story for me.

Kunle: Then that would be me exerting undue influence on you.

Maria: Not really, I just want to understand you more.

Kunle: Ah, I see what you might think this is. Well, me telling you the story would be me cheating; here's why. You'd think I'm revealing my cards, but in reality I would be revealing only what I want you to see, but I'd be planting a seed.

Maria: So what is this then? Not that I'm playing a game.

Kunle: It's human nature to play games. To be a winner, you either play the game better than most or be above it. What this is, is me being incredibly guarded and attempting to be as thorough as ever with my intentions and heart. No games, just being objective and realistic with my emotions and what I intend to subject my soul to. I have to be absolutely sure before allowing myself to re-ignite that love flame and fall for you all over again.

Maria: Babe, talk to me. What are you afraid of? You think I'd leave you again?

Kunle: Yes. My hard feelings, down to my soul, were involved and that has only ever happened in my life two other times and only involved women twice.

Maria: Your hard feelings? Let me guess, your love for me and your mom?

Kunle: Yes love, my real hard feelings. And an ex-girlfriend.

Maria: This is new, didn't know you loved her that much.

Kunle: Well, now you know and not the ex you have in mind.

Maria: Are you over that? Please don't tell me you guys reconnected after we separated.

Kunle: I am over her to the extent humanly possible and we did reconnect. We actually reconnected, and it made a lot of things clear.

Maria: Like what and what does that mean?

Kunle: This is not about my past, but my present and my forever.

Maria: I'm a part of your past, and I'm your forever. If you're afraid I'd do you like your ex, I can promise you I would never, whatever it is she did.

Kunle: So how do you know you "would never" if you don't know what she did?

Maria: You know what I mean!

Kunle: It's not that. It's me trying to understand if I'm part of a game I'm not aware of. Let's try to start again babe, but slowly.

Maria: I absolutely understand babe. But please riddle me this; have I lost your trust?

Kunle: Not yet. I don't have an objective reason to not trust you.

Maria: Okay babe, thank you.

Kunle: Yet! You're welcome (as he passionately kissed Maria, his lips lightly trembling). Plus falling in love with you again would be just so natural, warm, and so fast that I might miss when it's happened. Come, give me a tour (as he pinched Maria on the nose).

Maria gave Kunle a tour of her villa. It is a six bedroom villa, with nine bathrooms. Maria was very creative when she designed the villa. Lots of natural light, which Kunle couldn't immediately see, but he imagined. They ended up by the pool gazing at the stars on that cool Miami night. "Come, have a smoke and drink with me," Maria said to Kunle after the tour. She had a fully stocked electric humidor. She had real off brand and branded cigars from Cuban and Dominican farms along with a fine selection of rum and whiskey.

With a lit Cuban cigar and Havana Club in either hands, Kunle decided to attempt to get a better understanding of what had been happening in Maria's pretty little head the last few weeks. As they both looked up at the sky, Kunle started the conversation.

Kunle: So, how is therapy going?

Maria: It's going well, we only have three more sessions.

Kunle: Yea? Why is it timed?

Maria: Because I only signed up for therapy with my mom until dad's birthday.

Kunle: Oh right, how is that going?

Maria: The planning is going great! My dad is excited at the possibility of your attendance.

Kunle: Oh yea? Why?

Maria: Beats me, you've become like his favorite kid and you're not even his kid.

Kunle: Maybe he's doing it to signify to your mom that I'm important to you and ergo your happiness and well-being is important to him.

Maria: I actually haven't seen it that way!

Kunle: Don't let jealousy cloud your judgment!

Maria: Good point!

Kunle: Na, I'm fucking with you, that dude loves me (as he burst into a weird but cute laughter).

Maria: Shut up!

Kunle: I'm just saying!

Maria: So, how have you been? What have you been up to?

Kunle: You first, how's therapy?

Maria: Great! Mom revealed that the reason she was hesitant about giving us her blessing is because of her history! She also confessed that maybe there was a time she'd hoped I'd marry an American man.

Kunle: I'm not American enough? I'm as black as they come!

Maria: You know what I mean, a Black American man "With a strong name." Or maybe someone named Brad or fucking Kevin. Who knows?

Kunle: Oh, it's hard not to feel offended right now, but you're being vulnerable, so I'll shut up!

Maria: Thank you! But yea, it's been very good for us.

Kunle: That's awesome! How about you? Worked past any traumas?

Maria: Well, the therapist thinks I love you this much because I'm convinced that you'd provide me with the love and stability my dad has provided my mom.

Kunle: Oh, in other words, I'm like your father.

Maria: More or less, my mom liked that! One thing she loves about her marriage is the securities and love afforded to her by my dad.

Kunle: Yea, but I'm sure they built it together.

Maria: Him more than her!

Kunle: (Trying to do an impression of Jamie Fox on the "Gold Digger" track) "Oh she a gold digger..."

Maria: That's my Mother, KUNLE!.

Kunle: Sorry, it was an easy joke.

Maria: Yea, she definitely wanted his money and status thou, it seems!

They both laughed as Kunle took a drag from his fresh Cuban cigar and a sip from his Havana Club.

Kunle: Man, I just love your taste.

Maria: And I yours! Although, the cigar and booze choice were inspired by you.

Kunle: "Let me up grade you" (attempting to do a Jay-Z impression).

Maria: How have you been?

Kunle: I've been good! I'm a private pilot now!

Maria: Now way! Your plan is coming together!

Kunle: Yea, I actually flew myself here!

Maria: Wow, impressive! Make sure you tell my dad that! He'd love you even more!

Kunle: Yea? And I can probably sail his boat now too! Finished my classes on that; quite easy actually.

Maria: You've had a lot of time on your hands.

Kunle: Well, when you're single without kids and money is not your priority, you'd make time for what's really important. Also helps that I'm not working in public accounting and the hours anymore.

Maria: Dues paid?

Kunle: In full baby, in full!

Maria: That's awesome! Did you buy a plane yet?

Kunle: No, scrapped the private airline plan, but I'm going to go half with a friend.

Maria: Pilot friend?

Kunle: Yea, Met him in flight school! We play soccer together and occasionally hang out!

Maria: Oh shit, nice! Did you decide yet?

Kunle: No, but we know the specs we want. Gotta be able to make the journey to the Caribbean

Maria: How many aeronautical miles is that

Kunle: About 1,800. Oh and be able to sit six so we can do private flights.

Maria: So the airline bae plan is still in motion.

Kunle: Haha, sorta. If we decide to do it, we'd have to agree on terms.

Maria: This is so exciting, I'm proud of you babe.

Kunle; Thank you love.

Maria: Never had a doubt.

Kunle: What else have you've been up to?

Maria: I'm sorta retired now!

Kunle: Really? Nice! Cashed out?

Maria: Yea, a few more zeros than anticipated, so I'm living!

Kunle: AMAZING! Proud of you love.

Maria: Thank you! I followed your tax advice. My tax attorney was shocked at how knowledgeable I am about taxes and estate planning.

Kunle: Haha, happy to know I'm a value add.

Maria: More than you know. He said I "started the wheels of his mind," and he came up with a great plan. I think it was probably the same one you came up with.

Kunle: Yea? I don't remember, but I'm glad I can help.

Maria: You essentially taught me how to hide my money from you.

Kunle: Haha, what other way could I demonstrate to your parents that I don't want your money!

Maria: You helped me because of my parents?

Kunle: No, it was a joke.

Maria: Oh, haha.

Kunle: What was your walk away number?

Maria: 129.

Kunle: Pre or post tax?

Maria: Well, if certain precautions are taken and certain triggers are avoided, post tax.

Kunle: Damn girl! Where do I submit my sugar baby application?

Maria: You're already top of that line!

Kunle: That's what I like to hear.

Maria: Numero Uno.

Kunle: So where's your home base now, Miami?

Maria: Between Miami and DC.

Kunle: Wow, check you out! Why DC?

Maria: Connections. I hope you're not mad at me, but I sorta stole your idea.

Kunle: Which idea is that?

Maria: The one about helping make the dream of a journey to Africa a reality for those deserving.

Kunle: Yea, tell me more about that! I love it.

Maria: Yea! I started a non profit.

Kunle: Oh shit. 501(c)?

Maria: Hells yea, my boyfriend taught me a thing or two.

Kunle: Wow, I've created a monster.

Maria: A sexy one, with an irresistible tail.

Kunle: (Burst out laughing) A truly sexy monster. She makes my pants tingle.

Maria: As she should.

Kunle: So how's it going? Have you actually started operations?

Maria: Yes. Hired a staff of two and are trying to make connections in countries such as Ghana, Nigeria, Cameron, Uganda, and Tanzania.

Kunle: Nice! Did you start taking applications?

Maria: Not quite. Once everything is lined up, we will. Still need to convert the entity into a 501C.

Kunle: So walk me through it. Pitch me.

Maria: It's simple. The goal is to help people deserving of second chances get a second chance if they want one in Africa. Think people that are non criminal offenders with felonies. People who got locked up for petty theft, possession of marijuana below an ounce, trespassing, sending their kids to a school in a different zip code, etc.

Kunle: Yea, so are you paying me royalties or what?

Maria: We can use your help and connections. And since you already have networks in some of these countries, you'd be an asset.

Kunle: I usually don't work for free, but for access to you, I'll consider it.

Maria: Who said anything about free?

Kunle: I'm sorry sugar mama, I didn't mean to offend you. When do I start?

Maria: Haha, we'll talk about it later.

Kunle: Cool cool. Can I lay in your cabana over there?

Maria: Only if I can join you.

Kunle: Gazing at the stars is boring without you.

Maria: Good answer.

Kunle woke up to the sound of the gentle North Atlantic Ocean, blue skies with a few gentle birds doing a flyover in a beautiful pattern. "This is quite nice," he thought to himself. Maria was comfortably asleep on his chest under the cashmere blanket she went to grab, along with a pack of five pre-rolled joints shortly before they both fell asleep under the stars. They smoked half of one joint and enjoyed their night. Somehow he was comfortable as well. Usually his arm falls asleep after some time in this position, but somehow he's completely fine. "Maybe this is a sign we belong together." He reached for his phone and sent a message to his architect in Moshi, Tanzania.

Kunle: "Mambo vipi kaka!

Riziki: Salama! How are you?

Kunle: You know, chilling man. I'm in Miami and missing home.

Riziki: It's quite hard not to miss it.

Kunle: For sure. Listen, what are the odds of moving the delivery date up two months.

Riziki: Absolutely possible, but it'll cost a bit more due to your guidelines.

Kunle: Which one is that?

Riziki: The one requiring me to pay anyone of the people doing the heavy lifting who works more than six hours a day double.

Kunle: Ah, that one. Can you run the numbers and let me know how much extra it'll cost?

Riziki: I'm actually in front of my computer and was about to email you that we are going to come in under budget.

Kunle: My man!

Riziki: But with the new push, we're looking at an additional $6,000.

Kunle: Okay, let's get it done.

Riziki: Sawa (all right).

After his conversation with Riziki, he checked a few things; emails, the Morning Brief from New York Times, Instagram, work emails, and his WhatsApp. He puts his phone down and shortly after, Maria woke up.

Maria: I know you have to pee.

Kunle: Yea; been holding it for a few hours.

Maria: I bet (as she reached for a kiss). Morning gorgeous.

Kunle: Morning beautiful! How was your night?

Maria: Perfect, I've never passed the night out here.

Kunle: Yea?

Maria: Ever! How was yours and how's your morning going?

Kunle: Beautiful to both.

Maria: Awesome! Where's my phone?

Kunle: Probably next to you. Should I call it?

Maria: Got it.

Maria checked her messages and quickly sat up.

Maria: Oh shit.

Kunle: What?

Maria: Gina's connecting flight from Miami to Cartagena got canceled and she's rebooked on a flight for tomorrow night!

Kunle: Oh damn. Is she coming over?

Maria: Yea, I have to call her.

Kunle: Do that, I'll go to the bathroom. Which one has a spare toothbrush?

Maria: Follow me, the master has toiletry specifically chosen for you.

Kunle: I feel special.

Maria: That's just the tip of the iceberg. I even got your favorite milk, CBD.

Kunle: Okay! I forgot how detailed you are.

Maria: Anal.

Kunle: Not right now, I'm sure we both need to take a shit.

They both laughed as they walked by the infinity pool overlooking the blue ocean. Maria spoke to Gina on FaceTime while they both brush their teeth. Maria, still in the same outfit she had on the prior night; "looking like my true partner," Kunle thought to himself.

Maria: Yo, Gi. My bad, just seeing this.

Gina: Girl, I understand. Wasn't expecting you to be up right now.

Maria: You're on speaker, Kunle can hear you.

Gina: Hi Kunle, did you blow her back out?

Kunle: Hi Gina, miss you too.

Gina: Haha, funny. Girl, my flight got canceled due to a plane being taken off the fleet, but they got me on another one tomorrow night.

Maria: Oh okay. I'll come get you.

Gina: Thanks girl, I can also Uber.

Kunle: No, let's come get you, it'll be cute. Three black people cruising around Miami, Starbucks latte in the cup holders as we bump some gangsta music.

Gina: Temi, who invited you to the conversation? That does sound cute though.

Maria: Yea, I like that idea too. I'll bring the G.

Kunle: My idea Gina, my IDEA!!!

Gina: I can't lie, I do miss you and seeing Maria like this.

Maria: Girl, hang tight. I'll get you an oat milk latte.

Gina: Okay, I'll see you in a bit.

Kunle and Maria looked at each other and she observed that he looked rather dashing in his black button up shirt with the grand father collar, and all black jeans, with boots. And he had a morning glow to him that made him especially beautiful. His face was oily and his iris were white.

Kunle: Ready?

Maria: You're not going to wash your face?

Kunle: Do I need to?

Maria: I mean, no. I'm just shocked.

Kunle: Yea, it's easy being a man. But I see your shea butter, so I'll give my face rinse.

Maria: Then go have a glass of milk or something, after.

Kunle: Haha. I'll be in the kitchen, having a glass of milk if I feel like having a damn glass of milk.

Maria: Good boy.

Kunle: Ma'am.

Kunle said as he exited the generously detailed bathroom. There was a bath tub that also doubles as a hot tub, a walking shower with another bath tub in it, "I guess just in case you decide you want to take a bath instead." Kunle thought to himself.

Kunle was in the kitchen only for a few minutes before Maria joined him with a fresh face with only shae butter and natural sun screen on. Kunle was pleasantly surprised and was reminded of mornings with Maria. Like the time she woke him up in Cuba; as she was then, so she appeared now, absolutely stunning. Only thing missing is the flower in her hair, Kunle's bruised ego because he was fucked, well (though Maria felt the same way, but that's besides the point); and Cuba.

Maria: You look like you're looking at a ghost. Do I have too much sunscreen on?

Kunle: You have just the right amount on, babe.

Maria: Why are you looking at me like that then?

Kunle: You're just stunning and I'm taking it all in. Can I breathe?

Maria: Yes, breathe.

Kunle: I think you need a pacifier.

Maria: Fuck you. Let's go.

Kunle: You'd love that, wouldn't you?

Maria: Very much so. But right now, we have to pick up some coffee and Gina.

Kunle: Right. I'll drive.

Maria: Thank you kind sir.

She said as she moved closer to Kunle and leaned in for a kiss. "You're not so bad yourself." They both kissed passionately and Kunle grabbed Maria's but cheeks; one in each hand as he squeezed tighter. Maria was not expecting it, but she welcomed it and even verbally acknowledged Kunle's touch by moaning a bit.

Maria: Let's go, we'll be late.

Kunle: Right! You lead.

Maria and Kunle exited the house through the garage, but Kunle was able to fully observe the beauty in the architecture and especially loved the amount of natural light and the unobstructed view of the ocean.

Kunle: Damn girl, this is beautiful!

Maria: Thanks babe. I kept asking myself, what would Kunle appreciate?

Kunle: And?

Maria: I trusted that the outcome would be perfect.

Kunle: It absolutely is.

Maria tossed Kunle the keys to her Mercedes Benz G-Wagon, the AMG version that looks like it just wants trouble.

Kunle: Damn I love your taste.

Maria: And I yours.

Kunle: I'll be gentle. How much miles per gallon does this thing gets anyways?

Maria: I've only driven it twice but I've owned it for six months, so I don't know.

Kunle: Let's find out. Your tank is at 7/8, we should be good. Where to?

Maria: The address is programmed in the map, just start driving.

Kunle started the engine and they headed to pick up the coffees. After driving for about two miles and seeing the destination, Kunle realized they weren't going to Starbucks.

Kunle: No Starbucks?

Maria: This is better.

Kunle: Okay!

They picked up the coffee and headed to MIA to pick Gina up. They arrived about 5 minutes later than Maria had calculated, but Kunle was surprised at her accuracy. Gina emerged in her sweats and sneakers, with her Away branded luggage rolling behind her; one checked and one carry-on. She looked a bit tired, Maria thought to herself. Both Maria and Kunle exited the vehicle to welcome Gina and before Kunle could say hello, Gina interjected.

Gina: I love this, I love y'all like this.

Maria: Come here girl, oh my god. I miss you.

Gina: I miss you too. (They both hugged for ten seconds while Kunle loaded the luggage in the car).

Kunle: Hey Gina! How are you?

Gina: I'm well, give me a hug.

Kunle and Gina hugged and they all got back in the car, but not before one of the airport security guards gave Kunle the black nod. It was subtle, cool, and Gina saw it.

Gina: How'd you get so cool Kunle? (Gina said when they got back into the car).

Kunle: You know, do unto others and what not. That sort of thing.

Gina: That's why you gave that guy the nod?

Kunle: Yea, if I'm working in the hot Miami sun, I don't want no one just looking at me and shit, like I don't exist. Like I'm there like a pole haha. Acknowledge me or something!

Maria: Yea, that's Kunle for you.

Gina: Na, I fuck with it though.

The group let the airport and drove to Maria's house to freshen up and have breakfast.

CHAPTER 17

VIVIDLY

"Vividly!!!" Kunle responded to Maria's, "what do you remember" question. "I remember a lot of our moments vividly!" He said as he enjoys Maria's beautiful car. He looked into the sky because the top was down and it was a beautiful Miami night. In a deliberate attempt to not agitate Kunle, Maria was driving less erratic than usual. She was driving like a retired limousine driver, playing a playlist she specifically curated for Kunle. Poor guy didn't stand a chance. The playlist consisted of some of Kunle's favorite music, all of which she's grown to love because listening to music with Kunle was an experience. "You have to experience some songs, come let me show you." When Gyrate by Wizkid came on via Tidal, she remembered the first time Kunle played it for her, it was on their trip to Cuba. It was on the second day, Friday, and they were smoking on the rooftop of the amazingly modest and yet thoroughly perfect penthouse apartment Kunle booked on Airbnb. Kunle said he chose it because of the ocean view, which it didn't lack, and because it's probably the best spot to watch the amazing Havana sunsets. Kunle reminded Maria of the moment in Cuba when they danced to the song. "Remember that rooftop in Havana? I was like experience it with me." Maria recalled their conversation from that night:

Kunle: We should be dancing salsa or something, but I don't feel like that tonight (Kunle said as he takes a long and thoroughly satisfying pull from the weed they acquired from some dude who said he got it from some cop).

Maria: Yea? What do you feel like?

Kunle: Something silky smooth (he said as he felt his silk shirt graze his nipples as a result of the gentle breeze of the ocean). This (he said as he pressed play on Gyrate by Wizkid). But you have to experience it with me.

Maria: Experience it? This is already an experience. I'm wearing a silk pink Versace dress, sipping on Cuba Libre (rum and coke with lime garnish), listening to amazing music being played by the finest and most amazing lay of my life. This is an experience.

Kunle: Oh yea? Glad I'm useful for something. Your dress is beautiful babe!

Maria: Oh yea, and you're just so fucking amazing. Thank you.

Kunle: Let me show you how I feel about you. Dance with me.

Maria: Oooh, okay!

She recalled Kunle sitting up from the beach bed he laid on and hugging Maria from the back (as she stared into the deep blue ocean with the sunset behind her). He whispered in her ears "you're the most beautiful woman in the world." He loved her perfume, Lancome Le Vie Est Belle, and how she radiated beauty. She was still fully dressed from Lunch at Hotel Nacional because she wanted to take some photos and Kunle obliged. Her dress was pink with Medusa printed on it in strategic locations. It was beautiful and she perfectly complimented Kunle's royal blue Nigerian themed design and styled outfit. His hug was warm, a warm embrace she'll never re-live, but a moment she'll always experience on demand. She loved how she was able to feel his nipples through their silk outfit. They both danced slow and passionate. Randomly, Kunle would intentionally, but gently, graze her nipple. The marijuana is now kicking it and they both recalled how they bought it.

Kunle: Remember when Ronald told us he got the weed from a cop?

Maria: Yea, I was like what the fuck? I was low key scared.

Kunle: Haha, yea I understand. But you had nothing to be afraid of.

Maria: Yea, now I know. Why didn't you ask the street kid?

Kunle: Na, I always avoid that. Anywhere in the world I'm at, find the "white" people and you'll find the drugs, and if you're lucky that would lead you to weed.

Maria: Is that a stereotype? Never heard that before.

Kunle: Na, it's just an observation. Everywhere I've been on this earth, even in Africa, this has been true. Often time they don't have weed, but they'd know a reliable source.

Maria: HA! I guess it makes sense.

Kunle: I was low key scared that they might set us up like those kids, but I choose to trust them.

Watching them buy weed and then busting them right after.

Maria: Yea, plus not bringing the weed into the house, ha!

Kunle: Precautions, you know. (As they bought busted out in laughter).

Maria: Right, Mr. I trust them.

Kunle: But imagine those poor kids! Ronaldo said the cop, Ed, said the shock on their faces was priceless when they busted them as they watched the sunset.

Maria: That's fucked up.

Kunle: Yea, totally. But, karma would get them. It's only a matter of time.

Maria: You really believe in that shit.

Kunle: Not really, but it's my way of getting closure and leaving things behind.

Maria: I respect it.

Kunle: Yea, but it cost those poor kids two thousand dollars.

Maria: Yea, that can put a damp on your vacation.

Kunle: Yea, it can change the energy. Those "dumb Americans" should have know better than to buy that much weed, carry it on you while you smoke on the wall, (as he shook his head vigorously in disapproval). Does not mean those assholes should have laughed as much as they were laughing when he told the story.

Maria: Yea. Good thing they liked you. They could have been laughing at us.

Kunle: Yea. Worst case scenario, they probably needed a warrant or something to burst in here, so keeping the weed out was the smart play. Plus I made them take us somewhere we could relax as they rolled it, smoked with them, and got familiar fast with them. At this point, you'd not just be a dick, but a shitty person to still set us up after all that.

Maria: Us babe, I was there too. And I respected it and still do. It also probably helped that you tipped those guys well.

Kunle: Sorry babe and who knows, maybe. What a time we had!!!

Maria: Yea, remember that cigar factory tour? That was my favorite part.

Kunle: Yea, Pina Del Rio was a vibe. I enjoyed the caves better.

Maria: Right because you already did the cigar factory tour.

Kunle: Yea, though I wanted to stay lounger to learn their process, I feel like it was just too short.

Maria: I see, you were expecting too much. What do I always tell you about your expectations?

Kunle: Ha, good point. I imagined I'd be able to smoke a joint in that beautiful garden at Hotel Nacional, while I smoke a cigar as well.

Maria: But you still enjoyed it with just your cigar though, right?

Kunle: I enjoyed it more because you were there.

Maria: Aww, sweet.

Maria, now back to that beautiful Miami night after they had dropped Gina, she began to wonder how things were progressing. "Is he opening up?" Why is he bringing up memories? Kunle imagined what Maria was thinking about as they drove to have dinner at a seafood restaurant. Maria promised Kunle that the food would be 80% as tasty as what Kunle would get in little Haiti. He did mind, he wanted good service, candlelight, and jazz like music. However, to his surprise, the restaurant was owned by an Haitian woman. It was everything Kunle had imagined and then more. The service was spectacular, the ambiance gave Miami nights, catamarans, and blue skies as the sun dips over the Atlantic. The bread was warm, the linen tablecloths were clean, the candle was perfect, and the music was everything.

Maria: Is it up to your standards, Mr. Bougie?

Kunle: Oh, it's everything I needed. Especially the fact that it's black owned.

Maria: I knew you'd appreciate that.

Kunle: Yea. It's like someone was like this food is good, let's invest in it and elevate it.

Maria: Yea. Order something before you starve to cranky.

Kunle: Stop projecting.

Maria: You're right. I'm hungry though.

Kunle: The bread is on point, I told you.

Maria: Okay. When I get fat, you still going to love me?

Kunle: Even on the off-chance death did us part, I'd still love you after that continuously.

Maria: What happened to Mr. "don't make a promise you can't keep."

Kunle: He's making a promise he has every intention of keeping.

Maria: Okay babe.

The pair thoroughly enjoyed their dinner. Kunle had the lamb and Maria had the seafood boil. They both could not believe how enjoyable the experience was. They hung out for drinks as Kunle had bought a bottle of Macallan so they could both drink and talk their hearts out. Maria appreciated his presence and the time spent together. Truth of the matter is she had missed Kunle just as much as he had missed her. Other diners looked at them as a young couple, probably on their honeymoon, just enjoying their night. "Living their best lives." They looked so happy, in their synced outfits. Maria was wearing a lace dress that hugged her curves but is also loose and comfortable; a-lined. Kunle was wearing a watermelon-colored linen shirt, white linen shorts, and a navy-blue linen blazer, with a white handkerchief as the pocket square. They both looked dapper.

"How long have you both been together?" One of the diners, an older lady from Cuba, asked them at some point. After dessert, the pair relocated to the terrace of the restaurant, where they enjoyed the ocean breeze and amazing sunset as they smoked their Cuban cigars.

Kunle: Is it still an option to do this with you the rest of my life?

Maria: I'd rather have it no other way.

Kunle: Good (as he reached across the table for Maria's hand). I love you.

Maria: I love you too.

Maria began to wonder what happened and why is Kunle coming around? "How come he's more agreeable now? What's changed?" Kunle had been reflecting on their love story and realized that he needs to remove the stick up his ass and allow this woman to love him. Especially after his heart to heart with Gina at lunch when she was in Miami. He remembered Maria had gone to the bathroom when Gina broke the silence.

Gina: What did you do to my Maria?

Kunle: Huh? What do you mean?

Gina: It's like you broke her, you Yoruba Demon.

Kunle: Haha, nah my sister. I did no such thing. If anything, she broke me.

Gina: How so?

Kunle: Ever since she slid in my DMs, my life hasn't been the same, especially when she's not in it.

Gina: That's deep, but without me she wouldn't have slid in your DMs.

Kunle: What do you mean?

Gina: I mean I sent her your story the morning she slid in your DMs.

Kunle: Really? I guess we never had a reason to talk about it, so this is the first I'm hearing of it.

Gina: Yea! Aren't you glad I did that?

Kunle: I am, but why did you?

Gina: She was single, and you were her type, sophisticated. We were hanging out when she saw your profile for the first time. She was like, "he's fineeee."

Kunle: I'm flattered, I guess.

Gina: You should be. Do you know how many guy's profiles girls send to each other on Instagram?

Kunle: No?

Gina: Neither do I, so don't ask me.

Kunle: Okay. So what do you mean I broke her?

Gina: She's been a mess. I don't think she was ready to retire. I think she retired because she did not think she'd be able to focus as the C.O.O. for OTV (a unicorn tech company).

Kunle: OTV? She never mentioned that.

Gina: Off course she did not. I'm glad she did not accept the position though; I love the nonprofit for her.

Kunle: Yea, me too. So, she couldn't focus on work?

Gina: No, she could not focus on life. You were always on her mind.

Kunle: I see. Here she comes.

Maria: Talking about me?

Gina: Who else would we talk about?

Kunle: Yup.

Maria: Good.

Kunle imagined Gina had somehow influenced his decision to loosen up but wasn't sure to what degree. The three had a great day out in Miami that day, enjoying the life Maria had built for herself. After they picked Gina up from the airport, they headed to Maria's to freshen up and then to a brunch spot in South Beach. They ended up at a "bougie" soul food restaurant to accommodate Gina's strict dinning requirements. With Maria in the driver's seat, Gina in the passenger seat, and Kunle in the back seat behind Maria, and the sun on their faces as they exited the G-Wagen, they looked like a collection of rich kids who spends daddy's money recklessly. Only that they were adults, just looking to day drink while high as shit off edibles and Maria's THC pen.

They were well composed, especially being that they were only one of four parties currently dining at the establishment. The restaurant was well lit with abundance of natural light bursting through the huge windows, minimalist design with modern art hanging on the wall; the music being played was Motown and early sixties black pop music. Kunle liked the ambiance, but wished it was more relaxing and laid back. He would have preferred a darker room but did not mind where they ended up. The food was amazing and thoroughly enjoyed by all.

As they dined, Kunle processed his feeling and discovered that Maria felt like home. She felt like the piece of him that had been missing, but now feels even more complete than it previously was; home. He felt like she was the answer to all his questions, like his private artificial intelligence powered dictionary to help him understand life. He had missed how she solves problems, how she approaches situations, which is completely different from how he approaches things. He's missed how she balanced him out. Kunle continued to process his feelings as Gina and Maria became even more engulfed in their conversation, as he avoided reaching for his cell phone. The times Maria caught his Gaze, she wondered what he was thinking about, hoping they were pleasant thoughts. Kunle was impressed with Gina and Maria's friendship and how they both expressed their feelings towards each other. He could tell that they both genuinely miss and love one another. Kunle thought to himself, "this lady has something that you're not the only one missing, but she's still willing to give you a chance. You should probably take the opportunity."

After he left Miami, he knew what he had to do. Even though he still made Maria convince him that she'd "fight for his love," he knew he wanted her, so she did not have to fight that hard. When he left Miami and went back to Pittsburgh, he told Maria that he's going to clean out a room for her in his four bedroom townhouse, and also clean out a drawer for her in his bedroom and create a workspace for her in case she wants to come stay for as long as she needed. Though not surprised because she was used to Kunle's thoughtfulness, she was surprised at how quickly it was coming back.

Maria appreciated the fact that Kunle missed her more than he cared to admit, but she knew him enough to know that his actions told the full story. Seeing how open and how fast he seemed to want her back in his life, Maria was determined to do everything she could to deservingly charm her way back into Kunle's life, including bribing him. She bribed him once upon a time when they were both trying to figure out who's going to make the trip to see the other person?

Maria: Babe! Wait, can I call you babe?

Kunle: Sure, I see you've elevated your self-assigned a title I see.

Maria: What do you mean self-assigned? I've earned it, big head.

Kunle: Yes you have babe, yes you have. How are you.

Maria: I'm good. I miss you.

Kunle: I miss you more.

Maria: Do something about it.

Kunle: I am, just want to wrap up this European project.

Maria: Well, you better finish it because I'm booking us a trip to the Maldives.

Kunle: Oh you are? For when? Yes, I'll be there.

Maria: It is for a month from now.

Kunle: Oh, that's tight.

Maria: I have faith in you to make it work.

Kunle: I'll get to work. What do you want me to do and should I book the flight?

Maria: Work on that time off, two weeks off February 11 to March 3rd.

Though Kunle knew at the time that it'll be incredibly difficult to get the time off, he knew time spent with the love of his life was going to be boundaries he should start planning his work around. He recalled how the month leading up to the trip was filled with Maria shopping and obsessing over the details of the trip, but wouldn't include Kunle in the planning. She ordered them matching robes, mosquito repellent bands, sunscreen, various travel necessities. Kunle watched in amazement and often playfully teasing Maria. Kunle was able to deliver on his commitments a full week before he took off for the trip and was able to fully unplug and enjoy his time with Maria.

He remembered the trip being the trip to kickstart the next phase of their shared life adventure. Leading up to the trip, the pair spent time dating again, getting to know each other better. It was as if they were engaged in a game of who can outdo the next in terms of planning the most intimate and romantic date. Maria would never forget the time Kunle was able to get them passes to watch Alicia Keys do her sound check and floor seats to the actual concert. Or the sunset cruises Maria would invite Kunle to Miami for. They spent their limited time, the time spent in the same physical location, together or away from large crowds because they both wanted the intimacy they've been yearning for while they were separated.

CHAPTER 18

THE BIRTHDAY PARTY

It was a bit chaotic in the kitchen, Kunle observed, as Maria led him into the party through the least visible entry possible. He noticed the chefs; servers dressed in cocktail dresses; and the overpaid event planner in a body fitting black dress, high heels, and fake Hermes bag (Kunle knew because he recently got his mom one); all of them looking confused as to what Maria and Kunle were up to. They had just walked in after the planner, Stacy, knocked over a few champagne flutes that shattered.

Stacy: CLEAN THAT UP!!!!!! (she yells).

Kunle: Yes mommy (with his inside voice as Maria bursted into laughter).

Stacy: What's so funny?

Maria: Sorry, Kunle told me a joke outside that I just got.

Kunle: Ha, finally (as they both laughed out loud).

Maria: Just passing through, excuse us.

They went down a long hallway into a wonderfully decorated ball room. Kunle whispered to Maria,

Kunle: Who died?

Maria: Too much?

Kunle: Just the right amount of much, I love all the white, so simple, yet so much, and regal. Definitely regal.

Maria: Thanks love, exactly what I was going for!!! Ready to chill with my dad and his friends?

Kunle: You kidding? I was born to chill with the big boys, haha.

Maria: Good man (in a lowered voice audible to Kunle), kiss ass.

Kunle: I heard that.

Maria: I wanted you to.

They both emerged to a crowd occupied with various conversations filled with laughter and elegantly dressed folks. Kunle observed Maria's mom, Mercy, dressed in a red gown with details of gold.

Maria's dad spotted Kunle right away, with his "eighth sense" that seems to always call his attention to what he truly wants or needs to be doing. "That's my boy," he thought to himself; "don't move, don't show you're excited to see him; you already earned, his respect, don't lose it;" Dr. Martin Richards thought to himself, as the DJ, "an over paid piece of shit," spins the exotic sounds of Asa, a Nigerian Neo Soul Afrobeats artist. Kunle was extremely impressed as he began dancing like a homeless alcoholic that's currently high on marijuana, and it's a great high. It's a loving, silky smooth, lover man type of feeling. He noticed a cool, calm, collected, and classily man. "What a fucking man. Kunle was impressed because he saw traits of his father in Dr. Martin. He instantly nodded to his newly found idol. But his nod was smooth, measured, calm, collected, because he was doing it as he danced, no, glided down the red carpet in his smooth YSL loafer that only he knew what they were.

The shoes were smooth, a hazard if you don't know how to step in them, and they allowed him to glide down the red carpet, so it appeared. Maria's mother watched in amazement as each and everyone of her daughter in laws literally opened their mouth. They were all really shocked at the audacity, "the fucking audacity," of Kunle to be so captivating while "peacocking," and somehow made it all look so simple and elegant in his tailored outfit. It was a tuxedo, tailored by his tailor in Nigeria, with fabric Kunle picked up on his two day layover (to shop for this very fabric, but shh, he claimed he was linking up with an old colleague) in Prato Italy.

They watched in amazement as their husbands also smiled and nodded and all thought in their heads (various versions, mostly cooly vulgar), "that boy smooth." But then they caught themselves and looked over to their wives and noticed that they were watching in amazcment. And then the brothers all looked at each other across the room (14 feet triangle). Marcus nodded to each, signaling for them to meet him at the bar. They all understood the assignment and proceeded to the very kind barkeep, after notifying their wives. Kunle noticed, but headed to shake the celebrant's hand, even though he wanted to go and chill with the boys. He liked them, they were cool. This would be his first time hanging out with all of them. He always fantasized about inviting them out on his boat in Tanzania as he provides an atmosphere for some really fun times. He imagined he would have planned it with Maria, with mostly Maria doing the planning.

Kunle: The man of the hour (Kunle said, bowing slightly to Martin).

Martin: Well look who it is. I was starting to think you were a no show (as he smiled with his right hand stretched to greet Kunle, and his left hand holding a glass containing a generous pour of 30 year old Mccallan; from a bottle Kunle got him a months back when they first met).

Kunle: You know I have to make an entrance haha. I honestly thought no one would notice if I were late.

Martin: If a tree falls in the forest and no one hears it, did it really happen?

Kunle: It definitely happened, but what we'd miss is the beauty in the chaos of the fall, unless something got there to clean up the mess before everyone else, including replanting the fallen tree, then, your question stands.

Martin: Maria always bragged about how different you are and now our time in Zanzibar is coming to me.

Kunle: Haha! Happy birthday sir!

Martin: Hey fellas, this is Maria's boyfriend. Kunle, here's Zeus, Gandalf, IBK, and Charles.

Kunle: Gentle men, it's both a pleasure and a honor!

Gandalf: So you're Kunle. I've heard so much about you.

Kunle: They're all true.

IBK: You definitely look like a Kunle.

Kunle: (Bowing slightly) You already know sir.

Charles: So you're a Nigerian scammer?

Kunle: Yea, I had to somehow convince Maria that I'm worth the slight heart and headaches I'll probably cause her the rest of her life. And believe me, it's not easy.

Martin: Haha, y'all should go easy on him.

Charles: So what do you do?

Kunle: Well, I gave my two weeks notice yesterday at work. I'm the VP of international tax at Carks.

Charles: So you really are a scammer!

Kunle: Haha, you have to be a good one to take food from some attorney's mouth.
IBK: Are you an attorney?

Kunle: No, I did think about law school, but decided my future was in something and somewhere else.

Zeus: Like what?

Kunle: Well, not quite sure yet. I have six businesses I'm currently exploring, all based in Africa.

Martin: You ready?

Kunle: Maria convinced me...

Maria: Maria what?

Kunle: Is pregnant. Mind your business you beautiful creature.

Maria: That was a joke daddy. Kunle and his expensive jokes.

Martin: I know. You can relax fellas.

IBK: I was about to pull his ears to the side like a proper Nigerian uncle!

Kunle: Haha. Defense mechanism, I'm a little nervous. How's business uncle IBK?

Zeus: Uncle?

Maria: Temi is Nigerian too and a well mannered one at that.

IBK: Business is good, really good. I'm assuming Maria gave you the brief on all of us.

Kunle: She did and then I combined that with Google. You must be strategizing on expansion with the passage of the Tax Cut and Jobs Act!

IBK: I should be?

Kunle: Oh yea, there are various grants you can obtain from it.

Martin: Have you read it?

Kunle: Every single text. I've also been briefed by each one of the Big 4 firms.

Zeus: Oh corporate world, I miss those days.

IBK: I didn't know that Kunle, perhaps we should definitely talk more.

Martin: Are you coming golfing with us?

Maria: Dad, I thought that was just you and your boys.

Martin: Well, Kunle is one of the boys! We'll talk shop more.

Maria: Daddy, you did not invite any of your actual sons.

Kunle: On that note, I have to go say hello to Dr. Mercy, gentle men, please excuse me.

Martin: Because all your brothers would want to talk about is how to get me to part with all my money.

Maria: Kunle, aren't you forgetting something?

Kunle: Oh, yes. This is for you sir. I remember you liked the Cohibas in Dar, so I picked up two boxes for you. These were part of Castro's personal collection, so I got two boxes in case you feel like smoking one today.

Maria: Is that your way of asking for a cigar?

Kunle: You know me too well. I also got you this bottle of Macallan (as he reached into the gift bag to unveil the 50 year old Maccallan).

Martin: You are far too generous. This is a $200k bottle. My god, how rich are you?

Maria: Yes Kunle, damn. You've never gotten me such expensive gifts.

Kunle: I figured it's fair given all the knowledge you're going to impact on me. And (looking at Maria) I promise to do better when you turn 70.

Martin: Come here and shake me son.

Kunle: Before you shake my hands, I got these things from an estate auction of some guy in jail for financial fraud, so I got a deal.

IBK: What else did you buy?

Kunle: Some watches and parcels of land in South Africa. Gentlemen, I feel like I have to go say hello to Dr. Mercy.

Martin: I hope you got her something in that bag too.

Maria: Yea babe, I'm sure she's waiting in anticipation. She's been looking over here.

Kunle: Yup, gotta go.

Kunle excused himself and headed to Maria's mom, holding a box of Audemars he bought himself (but he decided he only need a couple of luxury watches). Upon approaching Dr. Mercy ("Mercy" for short), he prostrated fully (in part to make up for his tardiness, and to impress Mr. Maria's mother).

Kunle: Dr. Mercy, how are you? Apologies, my excuse is that the uncles kept me from coming to say hello earlier.

Mercy: Don't worry about them! How are you son? (As she reached for a hug).

Kunle: (Surprised at his new title) I'm well, better than ever now that my Maria is back in my life. How are you? I trust you have been good.

Mercy: I've been doing great; and thanks for embarrassing me in front of my friends. Thinking about the next time you're going to invite us to Tanzania.

Kunle: Haha, I'm sure they don't mind. Didn't Maria tell you you have an open invitation? I've finished construction of those villas and you're welcome to stay in the new hotel once it's completed.

Mercy: She did; you were such a gracious host the last time we visited.

Kunle: I'll be unemployed soon, so let me know when you start thinking about it. Also, I know it's not your birthday, but I got you a gift.

Mercy: You didn't have to.

Kunle: I understand, but Martin probably wouldn't be the man he is today without you. Happy birthday to you as well.

Mercy: Thank you so much son (as she gave him a really tight hug). This looks expensive.

Kunle: Nothing is too expensive for the lady that birthed Maria and afforded her all her privileges.

Mercy: Are you sure you're just 38 years old? You're so wise.

Kunle: Blame it on growing up in Nigeria with really wise parents.

Mercy: Well, thank them for me.

Kunle: I sure will.

Mercy: Come, come meet my friends.

Mercy introduced Kunle to some of her friends and they were all really impressed with him. They asked about his greeting of Maria's mom and he explained that's how he greets his parents and it felt appropriate. They all loved Mercy's watch and asked how much it costs. Kunle simply responded, "it'll be worth a lot more years from now." Kunle excused himself to go dance with his gorgeous date, who was occasionally looking over at him from the bar with her brothers. Kunle walked/danced over with a big smile, he was feeling himself because everyone was looking at him like he was the guest of honor (he felt so).

Kunle: Gentlemen!!! What's good?

Maria: I didn't realize I was growing a mustache.

Malcom: Haha, good luck getting out of that.

Marcus: Not much brother, how are you? Clean tux man.

Maria: Yes babe! Aren't you glad you listened to me?

Marvin: Hey man, want a drink?

Kunle: Yea, I'll take a Macallan, neat please.

Marvin: You've got it.

Kunle: Babe, turn around.

Maria: Why?

Malcom: Just do it.

Marvin: Like Nike!

Maria: Fine.

Kunle: Reaching in his pocket for a jewelry box.

Marcus: Uh Oh.

Maria: What? (As she was about to turn around)

Kunle: Hold that position (as he discretely spanked her butt, but only Maria's mom saw him do it). He revealed an emerald necklace and put it on Maria, after taking off her eight carat solitaire tanzanite necklace.

Maria: Babe! Oh my god this is huge.

Kunle: That's what she said. (Everyone burst into laughter). You like it?

Maria: Like it (as she took off her tanzanite necklace)? Babe, it's absolutely perfect, and it matches my outfit.

Kunle: I'm glad you like it!

Malcom: Maria didn't tell me you were loaded. That thing must have cost a small fortune.

Kunle: Ten years ago, maybe. It's an investment in the future of our kids if we have want them.

Maria: Good answer babe

Marvin: Here you go bro (handing Kunle the drink)!

Kunle: Much appreciated

Marvin: So you're the Kunle everyone has been talking about.

Maria: What do you mean?

Marvin: You don't know dad keeps tabs on him? You're his favorite and he wouldn't just let anyone come in here and whisk you away.

Kunle: Perfectly understandable!

Malcom: Haha, you're lucky he likes you. He once made my wife an offer to leave me.

Marcus: Well, she has an interesting past.

Maria: Stories for another day! Babe, how much did this run you?

Kunle: Well, I bought the stone in Colombia and the had it made into this in Dubai.

Malcom: Baller status.

Kunle: Hopefully I can keep it up (smiling/blushing).

Marcus: How do you mean

Maria: Kunle quit his job.

Kunle: Yup!!! Time to start living.

Marcus: What the fuck does that mean?

Martin: You'll understand one day Marc.

Maria: Hey daddy.

Martin: Hi angel.

Malcom: See? Dad's favorite.

Martin: You're all my favorite, but if that's how you feel, that's on you. Beautiful necklace Angel.

Maria: Thanks daddy, Kunle got it for me.

Marcus: From Dubai. No wonder it's shining. Is that 22 carats?

Maria: I'm not sure.

Kunle: The gold is 22 carats and the emerald is 43 carats.

Maria: HOLY SHIT (out loud).

Kunle: Language young lady.

Maria: Seriously? How much did this cost?

Kunle: The emerald was just shy of $15K.

Marcus: That's more than I paid for my wife's engagement ring.

Malcom: That's because not everyone is a cheapo like you.

Marcus: It's a waste if you ask me.

Maria: Well, no one did, Cheapo.

Marvin: How much did it cost to make?

Kunle: About $4,000.

Martin: Well worth it. And thank you for my wife's watch. She is busy showing it off.

Malcom: You got mom a watch? What kind of watch?

Martin: An Audemars. (All the boys said "DAMN" simultaneously).

Marvin: He's about to be mom's favorite.

Marcus: Feel threatened that your position is about to be taken?

Marvin: Ain't no one threatened. Which model?
Kunle: 11.59.

Maria: It's only 7 pm babe.

Marvin: No, that's the model number.

Malcom: Damn, that's heavy.

Martin: Yes, must have cost a pretty penny.

Kunle: Absolutely, but worth every single dime. Bought them from an estate auction, at deep discounts.

Marvin: Why not resell it and get her a Rolex or something

Martin: Because it's not about the money, but the intent of the gift.

Malcom: But still, I didn't know CPAs make that much money.

Kunle: Two friends decided to develop their own crypto currencies and asked me to do some consulting for them before they launched, so I told them to pay me in crypto.

Maria: That's my man!

Marvin: So, how much did you make when they hit.

Kunle: They are still about 98% away from their target fair market value, but I've realized about $40 million in profit already.

Marcus: Bro, that's what's up. Did you cash out?

Marvin: Yes, that's what "realized" (gesturing air quotes) mean genius.

Kunle: I understand his question though, you know finance jargons are tricky sometimes.

Martin: How much more are you still holding and which coins?

Kunle: I can't tell you because it can be argued that I'm giving you insider information, but I can tell you they're definitely not any of the big ones, but they both have been dominating headline news lately.

Marvin: Yup, we're all replaced as favorite son.

Martin: Insecure much?

Kunle: Ouch.

Maria: Ouch indeed! When is dinner? I can use a proper meal, and so can you Kunle.

Kunle: Nah, the food on the flight was pretty good.

Maria: I forgot you're not a picky anything.

Kunle: I'm a picky everything, that's why I'm loyal to some things.

Marcus: Dinner is supposed to be at 7. I see some movements, let's go get seated.

Maria: Common babe, let's get seated.

The group departed the bar area and headed to their assigned seats. Kunle couldn't help but hear various conversations happening in the background. "Man, that game 7 is one for the books," a man wearing a Tom Ford tuxedo said as he took a sip from his generously poured drink, which Kunle assumed was bourbon. "Fuck 'em, fuck 'em all; said the guy in salmon pink blazer and white pants.

Kunle: This is such a fashionable bunch.

Maria: Absolutely, they're fancy.

Kunle: You already know that dress has my mind in places it shouldn't be with your parents and us under the same roof.

Maria: Save that energy tiger, you're going to need it.

Kunle: What energy are you bringing? Normal hot girl energy? Or the lioness energy?

Maria: I'm thinking hot girl energy, but you never know. With you, I'm always on lioness energy.

Kunle: Haha. Facts though, but you know I got you no matter the energy.

Maria: One time, I just want you out of breath.

They both got to their seats, not too far from the DJ, who was playing Fela because it was dinner time. Dinner was served by the ushers dressed in white shirts and black pants and drinks were served by girls in cocktail dresses. When Maria was negotiating with the event company, she mentioned that she is not particularly interested in the girls in cocktail dresses because she assumed that it is "a bit ridiculous." However, the company mentioned that it is part of their branding and would rather have the "girls" wear them as that's when they've indicated that they're most comfortable. It didn't really matter to Maria, but she did not want to create a situation where some of the married men would get in trouble for staring at ladies in a cocktail dresses.

Kunle: Did you tell dude to play Fela? (Kunle said as he gestured to the DJ)

Maria: Nope! Just told him to play what felt good; after all, he's a professional.

Kunle: Nice! Dope choice!

Maria: Or maybe he's just trying to score brownie points with you.

Kunle: What do you mean?

Maria: You know what, never mind.

Kunle: Punk. I'd spank your butt, but you're lucky your brothers are here.

Maria: Pussy.

Kunle: You offering dessert already? Naughty Naughty.

Maria: Speaking of, dad wants you at the house, so come stay over.

Kunle: Really? What do you think?

Maria: I think that's the biggest invitation, to anyone, to join the family I've ever seen. And he kissed up to Marcus' wife's dad quite a bit.

Kunle: How so?

Maria: Was always showing off. Inviting him to places. You know he booked a private jet to fly him out to the Bahamas? Mom says it was their anniversary, but why was him and his wife, and another couple there with them?

Kunle: Bro code, they chipped in for the trip, I'd imagine. The other couples were probably in on it too.

Maria: Mm. I hate you. But love you too.

Kunle: Don't choke (as he leaned in for a kiss).

Maria: Don't make me.

Kunle: I love you.

The two passionately pecked, as noticed by Maria's parents as they enjoyed their seafood dinners; they were very classy, Kunle observed. Gold plated utensils, cotton napkins, and the meal was served by waitress dressed for the occasion. The bartenders were light skinned (and two of them had dreadlocks so it looks like they know what they're doing behind the bar), with broad chests. About thirty minutes after dinner was served, a live band played covers of various artists including; Marvin Gaye, Ottis Redding, Sam Cooke, Frank Sinatra, etc, etc.

Maria: I'm serious.

Kunle: So what do you think?

Maria: I'm not sure, but he sees something in you.

Kunle: Your happiness.

Maria: Yes, but there's more.

Kunle: I love that you think this way. It's such a satisfyingly relieving feeling.

Maria: That's why you can't do without me.

Kunle: This is true. And you can't live without me either. It's just that I'll cope better haha.

Maria: So don't ever leave me, dick.

Kunle: For life baby, that's my prediction. But we will fight and quarrel and disappoint each other.

Maria: Just always choose and put me first (as she stared Kunle dead in the eyes).

Kunle: Pinky swear (they both put their elbows on the table as Maria's cousin, Sean and his girlfriend Krista looked in amazement because they were seated on the other side across the circular table from each of Maria and Kunle). For life, I'll choose you as long as you don't shut me out for too long.

Maria: Deal (as she grabbed Kunle's head close and passionately kissed Kunle)!

They both realized they that had caught the gaze of about twenty five percent of the room, so they continued enjoying their dinner. Kunle had the steak because he felt like he'd need energy because he was hoping to bang Maria's brains out in his presidential suite that he used one of his ten upgrade nights for.

Kunle: So your dad's house? (As soon as he said that, the band started playing a cover of So Far So Good ("S.F.S.G."); a song by Phyno Phyno, a Nigerian Igbo artist Kunle introduced Maria's dad to when they were in Tanzania, one evening while watching the sunset, a ritual Kunle invited him to partake in. They listened to the song, played on Kunle's Bose portable speaker. They were both high on pot and they enjoyed a cigar as they sipped on fresh squeezed mango juice, blended with other fruits. He asked Kunle what the lyrics meant, but he didn't know. He was a bit disappointed, but he understood the struggle and focus of the younger man. The weight of his choices and vision. He cut him some slack and did his own research. He fell in love with the song and the artist. His one requirement in choosing a band, because he demanded a live band (he's a man of reach and taste), was that they can do a near perfect rendition of that song, and other classics.

Kunle watched him in amazement until the artist called Kunle by name "will Kunle and the boys join the dad on the dance floor?" He signaled to the boys and he reached in his gift basket and handed them all crisp two dollar bills. Two hundred dollars each and he instructed them to spray the money on their dad, in a rhythm that matches the music. They all followed his instructions as they formed a circle and created a mini blizzard around Maria's dad. Kunle gave them a moment as he came back to grab Maria to join them and he gave her crisp five dollar bills as he whispered "just to piss your brothers off, we'll tell them in 15 years why we did it." "Fucking troll," Maria whispered back as she slipped the stack of money Kunle was passing her under the table into her Hermes purse she purchased on a weekend get away to Paris. Funny thing is that the song S.F.S.G. was the theme of her France trip. She was coming out of her funk, getting herself ready to be back in Kunle's life because she realized earlier on that he was mostly attracted to her self confidence, at least she believed at the time.

They both joined in on the fun as Kunle tossed two whole stacks of two dollar bills (two hundred dollars) in the air as far up as he possibly could and it created a mini confetti of two dollar bills. The audience watched in amazement, some recording the moment. "What was the point of that?" Someone later asked Kunle, to which he responded, "why do we throw confettis?"

Kunle invited the guests to join in on the fun and the majority of the guests ended up throwing money in the air, for reasons unknown to them; they enjoyed it. After S.F.S.G, the band played a cover of Wonderful World by Sam Cooke, and then they instructed everyone to grab a partner for the next series of songs. Kunle whispered in Maria's ear:

Kunle: I'll go outside to smoke a cigar. Dance with your folks, I'll be there for like 30 minutes.

Maria: You don't want to dance with me?

Kunle: I want to, but we've already attracted everyone's attention.

Maria: Haha, thanks for thinking to limit the embarrassment.

Kunle headed outside and Maria started dancing with her little nephew, Antwan. The night was cool, and the band was playing a cover of Cruising by Smokey Robinson. Kunle gyrated as he lit his cigar with Joy. He wished he had a joint, and imagine if his cousins were here, someone would have some marijuana. While in the spirit, he texted; "babe, got anymore of that good smoke?" Maria did not respond as her phone was in her bag, which she sat down on the table.

Ten minutes had past and Kunle is still enjoying his cigar. Only a handful of people came outside and only two of those interacted with Kunle. One of them, Kingston, offered him a joint which he gladly accepted. The two talked for a few minutes and then Kingston returned to the party, "gotta get back to the wife, before she starts thinking I'm working or cheating." Kunle nodded as he took a long drag from the joint. "I hear that brother." As Kingston departed, Kunle heard the band start the cover of Before I Let Go, by Maze, Frankie Beverly; one of Kunle's favorite songs. At this point, people are starting to notice that Kunle was not in the room.

Feeling the gentle breeze of the perfect Atlanta summer night, Kunle started dancing with joy to the music. He was mid spin when he noticed Maria emerge from the door. The glorious sunset behind Kunle and Maria facing directly into the sun made her look like an angel, approaching Kunle in slow motion with her hair bouncy and gently blown by the light winds. She was wearing very minimal make up and Kunle could not hide his attraction for her because he used the tip of his left toe to stop the spin to avoid falling. Observing Kunle's sudden pause, Maria got a little self aware. She couldn't help to but notice Kunle's smile, strong jawline, sunglasses, and tailored tuxedo. She proceeded towards him and just when she opened her mouth to say something, she tripped on piece of cable. Luckily for Kunle, he was there to break her fall, just as Maria's parents emerged from the door and saw the whole thing.

Maria: Thanks angel.

Kunle: Dance with me.

Maria: There's nothing else in this world I'd rather do.

Kunle quickly glanced at his watch and noticed it was about 8:30. He wondered when the band would play his request. The two started dancing and Maria's dad pulled his wife and said "I love seeing her so happy. Let's give her some space."

Maria felt right in Kunle's arms, both to her and him. His perfume was just enough for her to literally get wet when she got closer to him as she laid her head on his shoulder. They both swayed until the end of the song and then continued swaying. The band announced that they are accepting five more requests as they started playing Feel Good by Beres Hammond, Kunle's request.

Kunle: Remember Barbados?

Maria: How can a girl forget? (She said as she removed Kunle's sunglasses and looked into his eyes).

The two dance passionately until the end of the song and Kunle resumed the conversation.

Kunle: I hope you'll have some more energy tonight (as Kunle grabbed Maria's butt cheek with his perfectly manicured hand, he felt the pure silk material of Maria's dress and he realized it's the one he got her a few months before she left him). I have some plans for you at the hotel tonight. I have to go there to grab a few things from my room if I'm staying over.

Maria: Okay, daddy!, I'll come with you.

Kunle: Sweet (as he leaned in to kiss her). When is this over and when do you have to be back home?

Maria: The band will stop at 9 and people should be out of here by 10, so about an hour left. We don't have to stay though.

Kunle: No, let's stay until your parents leave.

Maria: If I know my dad well, he's about ready to leave.

Kunle: It's his party.

Maria: I know, but he'll leave haha, but mom wouldn't let him.

Kunle: Let's go join them then.

The couple went back inside and walked in on a joyful Dr. Martin, who whispered to Kunle, yes, you can marry my daughter. Kunle was puzzled as to how he knew Kunle was going to ask. He already had a plan. He was going to kick his old ass in golf and then ask for his daughter's hand in marriage. He had imagined he'd have all the brothers presents as well. He spoke to Maria about his strategy and she bought into it. Maria's dad realized that he just messed up a potential surprise because he wasn't supposed to know. Maria told her mom, who in excitement told her husband, who couldn't contain himself and acknowledged his approval to Kunle without Kunle having to ask.

Kunle realizing what just happened tried not to gloat, but prostrated for Maria's Dad; a humbling sign to him to show his appreciation and utmost respect (even though he wanted to burst out laughing). Though Kunle thought he had a connection with Martin, he was nervous. A few stares, glares, and jaw droppings later, and Maria's parents are picking Kunle up from his prostration exactly how he imagined they would have. That was what he told Maria when he explained that her parents picking him up and hugging him after would signify full acceptance. "Look for the hug is what you're saying?" Maria asked as she made a playful mockery at what she assumed was Kunle's self perceived charm. She never imagined that he parent's reaction would be to hug him. She imagined her dad picking him up, leaning back, and then saying, "what the heck was that?"

However, as Kunle predicted, so it happened. To Maria's shock it was her mother's twenty-second hug that surprised her. The hug was so long that her dad had to join in the second time, and then invite her to come join them as the crowd looked on in confusion, "WTF! is happening?" Kunle would later imagine, as he drove Maria to the hotel.

Maria: I guess you were right (she broke the silence as they drove out of the parking lot of the birthday location. Waving to Maria's father who insisted on staying and was slightly disappointed that Kunle wasn't staying, but Kunle assured him in a calm reassuring voice, "I'll smoke as many cigars as you want with me this weekend! Or however long it takes for you to get tired of us.")! I honestly can't imagine a time when you planned something and were not right.

Kunle: That's because I'm always right. Even though I doubt myself sometimes.

Maria: I feel that!!

Kunle: I know you do, you're human! (Pausing for Maria's reaction, but she was silent, so he interrupted). Because you self assess your actions objectively, a rare trait that makes you so goddamn perfect and I can't wait to spend every living breath of my life with you.

Maria: I would love that very much you perfect man of mine! (She leans over to kiss Kunle as Kunle leaned in and gripped the wheels of the BMW i8 rental aka "BEAMER" [only green option available, he would have taken a Leaf]). I can't believe I'm this lucky.

Kunle: I can, we're good people. But I want to do really bad things to that ass tonight though.

Maria: Oh yea?

Kunle: Absolutely (as he reached over to reach for Maria's hands with his right hand, while placing his left comfortably on the steering).

Maria: Good thing I'm prepared because I've been looking forward to this.

Meanwhile back at the party that's now slowing down, Maria's parents are passionately dancing to Shaggy's Come Fly Wid Mi album that Kunle recommended when leaving them his Bose speakers because he realized that Maria's dad wanted to continue partying. Every song took Maria's parents down memory lane because the album is essentially a cover of classic songs from the West. Come Fly WIth Me is a song that has been covered by multitude of artists, over the decades, but this was one of the first reggae take that turned out close to perfect. Kunle imagined some of the songs would be better if they had vocals from some of Jamaica's leading vocal female reggae artist; the likes of Lela Ike, Savanna, Jaz Elise, Naomi Cowan, etcetera, came to mind. Maria's parents slowly danced as they waited for their Rolls Royce to pull up, and they continued dancing even after the driver came out to open the doors for them. It was a picturesque moment as the driver dressed in a top hat and a black tuxedo opened the door; little did they know they were about to go viral on Instagram.

They were dancing to Shaggy's cover of That's Life, a song that was originally recorded by Mario Montgomery in 1964. They were dancing so passionately and you can tell with the emotions invoked and displayed during their dance that they have a long and beautiful history.

Mean while, back at the hotel with Kunle and Maria, the car was with the valet and the couple waited for the elevator in the beautifully designed lobby of the W hotel in Buck-head. As soon as the elevator doors opened, they hopped in and were even more excited that they were the only people in the elevator. The couple had been fooling around in the car and Maria was all the way turned on. They started making out in the elevator and Kunle especially loved how Maria's silk outfit felt. He could see her nipples fully erect as he gently played with them on the short but eventful elevator ride (she took off her bra during the drive).

When they got into the room, Kunle turned on the complimentary Bose speaker and Maria requested to play the music, the first song she played was, Owner by the dancehall artist, Dexta Daps. Kunle, surprised and now even more eager for the journey he was about to embark on, knowing Maria understood the assignment. He sat down on the sofa with his jacket off, bow tie undone, shirt fully unbuttoned as he exposed his tiny 14k gold chain and shiny big chest, glass of eighteen years old Maccallan in one hand. Maria's lap dance was intense, as her silk dress moved with her. She twerked on Kunle, and literally with her ass bent over while she dragged his face into her ass as Fuck You Mean by Dexta Daps started playing. Kunle was shocked, but he enjoyed it a little too much, to Maria's surprise. He lifted her up as she continued dancing on him, fully trusting him to keep her secure in his big muscular arms. He could no longer take it, after watching Maria do the splits, twerk, gyrate, and some other acrobatics Kunle could not explain, to Nack, an Amapiano song by The Therapist. Shortly after, he slowly picked Maria up and lowered her as Jolene by Kes started to play on the speakers. They both danced passionately as Kunle stripped down to his boxers.

At this point, Maria's nipples were rock solid and Kunle couldn't resist putting the left one in his wet and buttery smooth lips. They had smoked a bit in the parking lot and they were both on the same wave length because Maria responded with a slight moan into Kunle ears as she pulled him a little closer, digging her perfectly manicured natural nails into Kunle's back. Kunle flipped her around and they both started to bump and grind. Kunle gently lifted Maria to the bed as Find Someone Like You by Snoh Allegra started playing. He lifted her dress and started to finger Maria to get a sense of how aroused she was. He continued kissing her passionately as he made his way down to her, still, fully erect nipples. He felt Maria tremble as she shivered from Kunle's gentle kisses while he played with her clitoris with his fingers. He then made his way down her clitoris as he began to flick it with his tongue. Maria grabbed his locks as she pulled his head in closer, signifying to Kunle that she's loving it but wants more tongue, "say less" Kunle thought to himself.

The sex that night was so intense that Maria upgraded Kunle from a sexual Knight to a sexual Demi God. She completely blacked out at some point and only snapped out of it when she started to "seriously" cramp on her left thigh. She felt how wet the bed was around her ass and it definitely wasn't from Kunle's sweat. Whenever she woke up throughout the night, she felt tremors from the sensation of the sex marathon they just had, meanwhile Kunle was mostly sound asleep. "We have to make it in time to help set up for breakfast," Kunle said to Maria as he kissed her on the forehead before passing out with her cheek on his chest.

By 8:30 the next morning, the couple were checked out of the W and were on their way to Maria's parent's.

Whenever Kunle reflected on the fourteen days he spent with Maria's family in Atlanta, he always smile when he remembers the moment he put the Beamer in park and pulled Maria so hard that she had to take off the seat belt and he kissed her so passionately that he had to fight back tears. He'd remember the sessions of golfing he played with Martin and his friends. How he met Ray, a very well connected Tanzanian Yemir who has connected Kunle with various key contacts, on one of those golf sessions.

CHAPTER 19

FAMILY AFFAIR

Kunle's Family dynamic is quite unique. Born and raised in Nigeria, West Africa, Kunle is one of two boys to his parents. His older brother, Mide, lives in Nigeria and helps run his father's architecture firm. Mide was married with three kids, against their mother's advice, he lived in Lagos City, Lagos, in a modern African castle as Maria called it. The house, dubbed "Afin," which means palace in Yoruba, has sixteen bedrooms, twenty- two bathrooms, a servant's quarters containing a three bedroom house with three bathrooms, a pool house, a stage, and a party room. The house was massive because, "why not?" Mide had designed the house, not only hoping to earn his father's respect, which he did, but to be his forever home in his favorite place in the world. Sitting on fourth acres, Mide's idea was to build a place that would be able to accommodate his immediate family for any occasion. The house was a true marvel.

Using pure wit, imagination, genii, and a very strong desire to earn the respect of his idol, Mide designed the house and sought to have the design copyrighted. As much as Mide's wife, Lola,' did not like having that much space, she was quite proud of her husband. It took Mide six months to put the house's design on paper but he had been designing it in his head since his senior year in college. Lola finds it incredibly impossible to forget how detailed her husband was, when he was describing the design when she met him in the library at University of Ibadan when they first met. They were both burning the midnight candle, studying hard for their last paper in what was one of the best schools in Africa the time.

Lola recalls looking up and noticing a very studious Mide buried in one of his architecture text books. He was quite focused, giving his full attention to his studies. Not once did he look up to catch her gaze as she would occasionally glance in his direction, hoping to catch his gaze. At the time in Yoruba culture, it was not common for a woman to approach a man, so many of them became quite skilled at getting men's attention. He finally looked up from the Architecture 403 text book he had been engulfed in, as he packed up his books to get some Suya as a late night snack so he could continue studying into the night. Coincidentally, Lola, was also getting ready to leave and wanted to go get some snack so she could also go continue studying at her dorm, at least the story went.

Luckily for Mide, he had been trained to focus on his studies by his "village." Before he departed for college, they told him several of the old, but tried and true, sayings such as; "remember the son of whom you are," or "face your studies, the girls, fame, and money would come, after". However, when he bumped into Lola, his dad, Segun, had began to change his tone around the subject of dating. On his visit home, Mide remembered their conversation:

Segun: So tell me about your girls, are they from good homes?

Mide: What girls dad?

Segun: Why do you think I was born yesterday? Don't you know I was you once?

Mide: I know dad, but you should know that means being studious and focused on the goal.

Segun: Yes my son, and I am incredibly proud of you for the man you're becoming. Now go and finish   accomplishing this goal, but have ten percent more fun than you did last year. It's your last   semester, live a little.

Mide: How dad? I have three really challenging classes and two arts classes you're making me take   because you said it'll make me a well rounded man.

Segun: I'm sure you can also take on entertaining a beautiful young lady.

Mide: I'm sure I can but I'm afraid my grades might suffer a bit.

Segun: And that's okay. If you can maintain a B average while entertaining a young lady, I'll give you   another gift upon graduation.

Mide: Dad, are you seriously telling me you'd reward me for being a B average student?

Segun: Only if you do it while exploring the dating life of young man in his youthful prime.

Mide: I wish there was a way I could capture this moment.

Segun: That's it, I'll buy you a camera.

Mide: Dad, are you serious?

Segun: Yes, just don't tell your mother.

Mide: You have my word dad, but I can't promise you I know how to "entertain a lady."

Segun: Don't worry, call me if you need advice.

Mide: Dad, women are different now, they have evolved.

Segun: Son, humans evolve, but we generally stay close to our true nature. It takes generations for man to change, remember that.

That faithful night Mide bumped into Lola, Mide had gone almost the full school term without meeting any lady of note. To be honest, he wasn't really looking. Between his African History, Theatre, Calculus, Architecture, and Physics classes, he also played soccer with his pals, and volunteered at a nearby clinic; he simply did not have the capacity for any woman. At least he thought, until he met Lola. The first thing he noticed was her beautiful skin, dimples as she blushed, while wearing a head wrap and a long sun dress. She was simply irresistible. He was shocked he did not freeze because he was taken by surprise.

Mide: After you (he said as he gestured towards the exit).

Lola: A true gentle man. My mother has warned me about your type.

Mide: What type is that? The book loving nerdy type?

Lola: The type that say that, and look like you.

Mide: What's wrong with my look.

Lola: Who said anything was wrong with your look?

The pair walked out of the library slowly, temporarily forgetting their ambition to study all night.

Mide: Where are you headed? I'm somehow feel the need to accompany you to your destination. You know, for security reasons.

Lola: Haha, security. That's the best you can do?

Mide: Seriously, the street cats are quite vicious as they try to get your attention at night, you know? Have you had dinner?

Lola: No, I've been in the library longer than you.

Mide: No way. When did you get there?

Lola: Around 8. I noticed you when you walked in, but I was sitting elsewhere.

Mide: Is that so?

Lola: Yes o.

Lola: Big man like you? Where are you going anyway?

Mide: I beg ò, I'm a small boy. But I wanted to get some Suya before heading back to my room to continue studying.

Lola: That sounds like a brilliant idea.

Mide: I'm something some would call a genius.

Lola: Sure.

Mide: I'll show you.

Lola: How? I don't even know your name, Mr. Gentle man.

Mide: My apologies, I'm Mide. And you are?

Lola: Temilola, but my friends call me Lola.

Mide: Nice to meet you Lola.

Lola: No, you can call me Temilola.

Mide: I can't be your friend?

Lola: Well, there's something special about you, so you are one of the privileged few that gets to call me   that.

Mide: A privilege I promise to try not to take for granted, ever.

Lola: Mr. Gentle man, making promises already.

Mide: Haha. Can I interest you in some Suya? Where are you heading by the way?

Lola: To get some suya with you, silly.

Mide: Okay then. But I have to ask you, you're not a Mami Wata (Marmaid), are you?

Lola: You don't actually believe in that, do you?

Mide: Well, there has been rumors of men going missing, and if you happen to be a Mami Wata, I can see   why they're all going missing (he said as he swallowed a nervous spit).

Lola: You can relax, I'll be your private Mami Wata. I promise to only kidnap you.

Mide: Don't play like that.

Lola: You started it.

Mide: Haha. I like you, you're quite funny.

Lola: Imagine how funnier I'd be after you've fed me (as they approached the Mallam (title for some men   from the Fulani tribe in Nigeria) selling the suya, a roast beef or lamb marinated in special sauces).

Mallam: Mide my guy, goody evening.

Mide: Musa, my guy. Well don sir.

Mallam: The usual?

Mide: The usual. Lola, do you know what you want?

Lola: (Speaking perfect Fulani to the Musa ordered herself a lamb Suya and also changed Kunle's order   without telling him). I ordered and told him to make your order special.

Mide: (Impressed with Lola's command of the language). You are an impressive woman.

Lola: I see someone maybe listens to Fela (she said as she watched Mide sway to Gentle that blasted from   the classic Mercedes Benz, "V-Boot," that drove by).

Mide: Yea, my dad loves him, so by extension.

Lola: This genius you're going to "show me," you're not doing a good job so far ò.

Mide: Haba, na fight? Maybe I should tell you about the house I plan to build in my 30s.

Lola: 30s? How old are you now?

Mide: I'm 20, you?

Lola: I'm also 20. But you stand so tall are so well mannered, like a 30 year old.

Lola remembers the passion in Mide's voice as he described what became Afin. Mide wanted to name it Temilola, but Lola told him to promise her that would be the name of their yacht before they knew they could afford one. "The house seems more like a palace. The boat seems more like me, floating through the universe." Maria listened to Lola's stories with delight by the fire in the backyard overlooking the infinity pool, which overlooked the ocean. Kunle, Mide, Lola, and Maria were all by the fire place as they smoked cigars, drank Macallan with fresh sweet orange squeezed in, and reminisced with Mide and Lola.

Maria: And I thought our story was cute.

Lola: It is really cute, in a modern way.

Maria: I'll take it. How come you never shared this beautiful story with me, Kunle.

Kunle: Because it's not my story to tell.

Mide: Probably because he didn't want to admit that his much older brother has more game than him.

Kunle: Had.

Lola: What game? Where? (As Maria and Lola bursted into laughter).

Mide: What seems to be the amusement? Just because I've suppressed it doesn't mean it isn't there.

Kunle: It definitely is not there. You that I called for dating advice once and you totally led me astray.

Mide: You know I don't know your game in America there.

Kunle: Like dad always say, (as Mide joined him) "humans are the same at their core, no matter the continent."

Maria: Sounds like a very wise man. When are they getting in again?

Mide: Those ones? Whenever the tide brings them.

Kunle: They're on the boat. Which one again?

Lola: The one and only Olakunle!!!

Maria: I still can't believe your parents named a boat after you.

Kunle: (As he slightly opened his mouth to slowly allow a mouth full of cigar smoke to escape) Because I'm   their favorite child.

Mide: Not because you bought it for them huh?

Kunle: Keep telling yourself that big bro. You know you're the prototype and I'm the perfect product.

Mide: I can't argue with you there.

Maria: What's the age gap again?

Kunle: Fifteen years.

Lola: Can you imagine?

Maria: Wow. Mama Kunle really wanted two huh?

Mide: She said that was the promise she made dad.

Kunle: Their compromise.

Lola: I love your parent's relationship. I hope you're planning to marry Kunle.

Kunle: Aunty Lola, haba (common on).

Lola: You better speak, see fine babe. Don't be like the men of these days, wandering around aimlessly.

Maria: Like sperms that should have been swallowed.

Kunle: WOAH. Language.

Lola: No, Maria is fine. I like her.

Kunle: Babe, here's where the cultural differences come in.

Maria: Ah, I see. Apologies didn't mean any disrespect.

Lola: You see, you already trying to limit our relationship. Don't you know I have to draw her in for us to   lure you back home?

Kunle: Y'all can come see me in TZ id you want.

Mide: Did your architect adopt the roof design?

Kunle: I hope he gets it right.

Mide: I told you, you should let me talk to him.

Kunle: Her. So you can be like, "I changed his diapers and designed his house for him."

Mide: First of all, I don't love you that much to change your diapers.

Kunle: You don't have to form (pretend like you are a big boy, larger in social status than you actually are)   here.

Mide: Second of all, I can still say I designed your house for you.

Kunle: Well, true, but no one would believe you. You have no proof.

Mide: You're sitting in my proof (as he got up to "turn the fire.")

Lola: He kinda does have a point.

Maria: Yea, you cannot say he does not have an influence.

Kunle: They've pulled you to their side already huh? Maybe you really are a mami wata, aunty Lola.

Mide: My Mami Wata.

Maria: (Amazed at the affection still between Mide and Lola) Wow. How long have you been together?

Lola: About thirteen years, married for twenty five.

Maria: Yea, I knew I was with the right guy. You cannot have your parent still married and your

older   brother married for twenty
five years with this level of affection and not be
serious about someone   you're planning a
future with.

Lola: That one? He's a lover boy. Did he tell you
about his first crush?

Kunle: Aunty.

Lola: I walked in on them kissing at 12, but acted
like I didn't see anything.

Kunle: She was like "small boy, your brother is
calling you."

Maria: HAHAHAHAHAHA. Did she really say
small boy?

Lola: Yup, I wanted to ridicule him so he could
remember he is a kid.

Kunle: Can't say it worked.

Lola: Do you know where princess is now?

Kunle: No clue. I tried looking her up ten years
ago, but nothing.

Maria: Yup, lover boy.

Mide: No game!

Kunle: At least I had a girlfriend at 12.

Mide: Here's your Pulitzer, bro (sarcasm).

Kunle: Haha.

Maria: Tell me about "Princess" (making air quotes).

Kunle: There is nothing to tell, I lost my virginity to her. We were children, playing kids play.

Maria: You lost your virginity at twelve?

Kunle: Thirteen, but let's switched topics.

Lola: Maria, how about your siblings? How many do you have?

Maria and Lola exchanged stories and they started to get to know each other better, while Kunle and Mide went for an evening stroll. Kunle told Mide about his plans to propose to Maria officially on their trip. Mide was happy for his little brother. Not only because Maria is perfect, but also because he's proud of the man he had become. Mide remembers visiting Kunle while he was getting his Master's degree, heartbroken and on a noodle diet. He was so lost that he tossed himself into his books and swore off women, at twenty-two.

Mide: I'm proud of you bro.

Kunle: Because I'm getting married? I guess that makes me a man in these parts.

Mide: Look at you, "these parts" (saying it in a funny accent meant to mimic Kunle's western influenced   accent). Talking like you have forgotten where you came from. Does the burger change your voice   there? I know it takes away your manhood with all that synthetic shit.

Kunle: Organic only bro, we're privileged over here.

Mide: It's all fake. Come back home for everything real.

Kunle: Tanzania is close enough.

Mide: Did you tell dad that's your plan? To move to Tanzania and not Nigeria?

Kunle: I told mom and I'm sure she's told dad.

Mide: Naturally.

Kunle: Yea, she didn't take it well, but she understood.

Mide: I imagine how dad took it.

Kunle: We may never know.

Mide: Like so many other things about that man.

Kunle: Don't worry, I'll gaslight him into telling me all his secrets.

Mide: Good luck.

Kunle: You just watch.

Mide: Let's go get ready to go to the Shrine (referring to Fela's Shrine in Lagos on the main land).

Kunle: The parents are not coming here directly right?

Mide: They are, but they know their way around, they have their own wing in the house, remember?

Kunle: Right. You really did it, huh?

Mide: Did what?

Kunle: Built the family house you always dreamt of.

Mide: Yea, hard not to growing up on various sites with dad.

Kunle: Yea, definitely proud of you for this.

Mide: Just this.

Kunle: Amongst other things, you know.

Mide: You better give me my roses now ò, this one that you're not moving back to Nigeria.

Kunle: I never said that ò, I just said the next decade of my life is in Tanzania.

Mide: Anyways, I found you that land in Kwara state.

Kunle: Ése (thank you, as they approached Lola and Maria that are a little tipsy from the champagne).

Mide: You ladies ready? What's so funny?

Lola: I'm telling some old stories of Kunle.

Maria: With pictures.

Kunle: Lawd.

Maria: It's cute. You were such a cute kid. Is it true you used to help mom around the house?

Kunle: We have to go, we're going to Fela Shrine.

Maria: Yay!!! This has been on my bucket list for some time. Ever since I saw that play on Broadway.

Mide: Gawd.

Lola: I didn't mind it.

Mide: Because you just wanted to see the story on Broadway.

Lola: Spoken like a true Fela fan.

Kunle: Big bro, you get rizzla?

Lola: (Bursting out laughing) this one?

Mide: I do actually.

Lola: You do? Since when?

Mide: Since I knew my weed head little bro was coming home from yankee.

Kunle: See Maria? This is my influence.

Mide: Look at how you turned out.

They all went in to get dressed and came out looking very modest but quite sophisticated as they headed out to two identical Mercedes Benz G-Wagons because they were being driven. The ladies were in one car (Lola's) and the boys were in the other (Mide's). Their drivers drove into the beautiful December night.

CHAPTER 20

THE RITUAL

The next morning, when Kunle woke up from one of his most peaceful sleep in recent memory, he noticed the room was completely dark but comfortable with the sounds of Asa playing on very low volume, Maria's way of waking Kunle up after their epic night at The Shrine. He appreciated the gesture as he woke up from his deep sleep. Slightly unease because the love of his life wasn't by his side. He sat up and drank the cup of water Maria had placed next him to with a note reading "out doing yoga and enjoying your amazing country," before leaving the room. He smiled, like a the grateful fiancé he truly was, knowing well that Maria is out there charming the socks off his pops. He thought to himself, "shit, I should be making the introductions.

He got up and opened the blackout blinds to observe Maria doing Yoga with Lola while his mom, dad, and Mide were getting ready to have coffee as Bimpe, the live in assistant wheeled out a cart. Kunle went to brush his teeth, washed his face and lathered on some shea butter on his freshly washed face. He briefly examined himself as he headed downstairs with a bag of treats he brought for his parents. Rocking his polarized sunglasses while still rocking his PJs made of sateen (borderline silk), his mother was so proud to lay eyes on him as she smiles joyfully and uncontrollably as his dad said "that's my boy." Setting his speaker along with the goody bag down on the table, Kunle prostrated for his parents as Maria and Lola approached. Maria, recorded the moment as they walked towards the group.

Kunle: Eku ile ma, eku ile sir (a salutation you extend when you go to someone's house in Yoruba).

Yemi: My son, ka bọ (welcome). How was your journey.

Kola: Omo mi atata, lati ijo yi (my lovely son, it's been a while).

Kunle: I know daddy, I've been away too long.

Mide: You said it.

Kunle: (Slightly prostrating for his older brother) Sup bro, how far?

Mide: I dey ó, I see you don't do this often.

Kunle: What, go out and stay out till 2 am?

Kola: He's forgotten how to live haha.

Yemi: Ignore them, they're bad influences.

Kunle: I know mom. I trust you've met my beautiful bride to be in flesh.

Kola: Not yet, actually. We woke up not too long ago too.

Yemi: Speak for yourself.

Kunle: Why didn't you join them for yoga?

Yemi: I wanted Lola and Maria to bond, to have their moment.

Lola: Good morning mommy! You should have joined us.

Maria: Good morning mom (kneeing down on both knees as Kunle had coached her to. "My mom picking you up is a sign of acceptance, I think," she remembered Kunle telling her).

Yemi: (Looking down at Maria and walking close to her) Come, let me have a look at you my daughter. You truly are a marvel. I can see why Kunle has stayed away for so long now.

Kunle: Mommy, it's not her fault. I just want to be able to come and spend an extended period of time with you guys.

Yemi: Who said anything about it being her fault, Mr. Woke.

Kola: You are here now and we could not be happier to see you both.

Yemi: Get up my child, (as she picked her up from the ground and wrapped her in a tight and very warm embrace that lasted for a minute as everyone looked in amazement and Kunle's mom prayed for Maria; "you will for ever be the head and not the tail, you will be a great mother, leader, partner, and wife, etc.").

Kola: Can I meet Maria too?

Yemi: Jealous man.

Kola: The one you married huh?

Maria: (Kneeling down for Kola who immediately picked her up) Good morning Maria, and welcome home my daughter.

Kunle: Group hug (as Maria, Kola, Lola, and Kunle's mom hurdled together and hugged Maria, like it was some kind of a ritual).

Mide: He's the sensitive one.

Lola: (Coughing in a slight mockery of Mide) mm.

Mide: Mind your business (as the group broke their embrace).

Kunle: I got you your favorite Dad, Maccallan 25.

Kola: That's my boy! Bimpe, get some glasses.

Maria: Isn't it early (she whispered to Kunle).

Kola: It's never too early for this (as he pointed the top of the bottle to Yemi, who double tapped it and then to Mide, Kola, Lola, Kunle, and then Maria, as they all followed Yemi's lead).

Kola poured some of the drinks on the ground to complete the ritual, and poured the drinks in cups and individually handed to everyone.

Kola: May your bond be strong, may your union be generational, may your marriage be peaceful and filled with happiness, love, patience, understanding, knowledge, and may your marriage be fruitful. This I command.

Kunle: (Along with everyone except Maria echoing) Áse (so shall it be).

Maria: (Tearfully and late) Ase!

Everyone took their a sip the fine whiskey from their glasses.

Maria: I don't know what to say, but my heart is heavy. Kunle did not prepare me for this part.

Lola: That's because you're the first woman he's ever brought home and he's probably unaware of the custom.

Kunle: This is true.

Maria: I wish my parents were here to witness that.

Kunle: You can fill them in.

Mide: I think Taju (his driver/security/bodyguard/henchman, etc) might have captured it.

Kunle: Where is he?

Mide: Look up (pointing to a drone flying hundred feet above).

Kunle: Okay then, I thought you well.

Kola: Kids.

Maria: Haha, boys and their toys.

Yemi: Right, toys. Let's sit.

Maria could not stop admiring the grey haired Yemi as Kunle opened a brand-new box of Cohiba Maduro Chocolate for the group to smoke. He cut the cigars and handed them out as Bimpe serve them hot coffee and the breeze cooled the cloudy morning.

Bimpe: I brought some ice incase anyone wants it.

Kunle: Thank you Bimpe. How are you?

Bimpe: I'm okay ó oga (boss).

Kunle: How are your kids?

Bimpe: They're fine sir.

Kunle: Is Kunle almost done with university?

Bimpe: Yes sir, he works with Oga sir.

Kunle: (Looking over at Mide) really?

Mide: Yup, a prodigy.

Bimpe: Thank you sir.

Kunle: Please, grab a chair, join us.

Kola: Speaking of parents, when are yours getting in?

Kunle: Tomorrow sir, they should be here between 10 and 12.

Lola: Oh, they're flying private!

Kunle: Yea, wanted them to come here in comfort.

Lola: Ah, rich people.

Kola: That's my son.

Maria: Can I please get something off my chest?

Mide: Uh oh.

Kola: Ah, egba mi (save me). What have you done Kunle.

Maria: I promise it's nothing bad, I think. It's just that ever since our first date that I asked Kunle about you Mrs. Olu.

Yemi: Call me mom or Aunty Yemi, please. I understand your culture is different.

Maria: Mom, they way he described you, I thought to myself "I hope such a phenomenal woman would permit me to marry her son."

Yemi: You have my blessing my daughter.

Maria: Thank you ma. I'm just touched that the moment is here and you're not hesitating to accept me with open arms, literally.

Kola: (Blowing out a huge smoke from his Cigar) I love this cigar.

Yemi: Ignore him.

Kola: Please do at your own peril. But what exactly did he say (as everyone bursted out laughing)?

Yemi: You are welcome my dear. Also, I am very happy he's not gay or bringing someone evil home.

Mide: You can say white mom.

Yemi: I actually don't care if he marries a white woman, as long as she's not the type that think their race is superior because of their skin tone. I was starting to wonder if he was gay sha.

Lola: "Are you a gay?" (a common amongst Nigerians from a meme)

Kunle: Okay, enough racist chat.

The family spent the day smoking and drinking and having a grand old time catching up. Everyone was interested in Maria's background, and she did not hold anything back as she briefed them on her family history, family tree, and about her parents and siblings. Maria was truly happy that her parents would meet their equals in Kunle's parents.

Coffee time lasted about two hours and the group went inside to go get ready for a wedding Kunle's parents were guests of honor at. They extended an invitation to Kunle and Maria who did not turn it down. After they were fully dressed, the group reemerged in African attire, including Maria, wearing a dress Kunle had designed and had made for her. It fit her perfectly and she couldn't get enough of it.

Kunle: Dad, is it okay if I smoke some igbo (weed)?

Kola: Only if you're sharing. Also, do you have some eyedrops?

Yemi: You this boy.

Mide: Imagine, wayward child.

Lola: Look who's talking.

Kunle lit up a joint and passed another to Maria to light.

Maria: (Whispering in Kunle's ears) Should we be doing this in front of your parents?

Kunle: Babe, it's okay. I told you my parents are very liberal.

Maria: Okay, okay, okay (tilting her head in approval with a smile).

The group finished a joint and half of the other, as the drivers pulled the two G-wagons around. The all got into the cars, but not before Kunle took some stunning pictures of Maria. "You look lovely, babe," he whispered in her ears as he showed her some of the frames.

Lola: Must be nice to have a boyfriend who sees you.

Yemi: Kola sees me all the time, I must say it's nice.

Mide: Apple doesn't fall far from the tree, they say.

Kunle: That's right; only that you're not an apple.

Maria: What is he then? Take a picture of Lola and me, please.

Kunle: With pleasure.

Maria: Mm, you said that a little too enthusiastically.

Kunle: No, no, no. We're not doing this. Not going to have you in here ganging up with them against me.

Lola: You know I've always been on your side.

Mide: Welcome to the partnered side brother, good to have you here.

Kunle: Aunty Lola, exactly my point. I could always count on you to be in my corner, now it looks like that's changing.

Maria: You have to tell me about his little girlfriends.

Kunle: I'm sure we can track them down.

Mide: Except for Phillip's daughter, Chidinma.

Kola: How dare you invoke that name?

Kunle: It's healthy to talk about these things dad. Family picture time.

Yemi: Yes love, our son has a point.

Kola: Taju, I beg, come help me take some dope photos.

Taju: Yes sir. Una (you guys are) too fine sha.

Kunle: Ose (Thanks).

The group departed for the party that turned out to be one for the books. They all had so much fun that no a single one of them woke up before 9:30 am the next morning.

CHAPTER 21

THE
PROPOSAL

After a successful introduction of the parents, Kunle and Maria stopped over in Italy for a couple of weeks on their way back to the US. Kunle had been secretly planning aspects of the trip for some time, though Maria was fully aware of the plan to visit her favorite city, Venice, Italy. Maria had no idea what Kunle had up his sleeves, but she knew he was up to something. Kunle wanted to propose to Maria in Venice, so he had to make some plans in secrete. Upon their arrival at the Marco Polo airport in Venice, Maria was already excited as Kunle had planned for them to be chauffeured to a boat that brought them to the magnificent villa Kunle booked.

The Chauffeur pulled up to the hanger as soon as their plane's door opened and the first crew members descended. It was a Rolls Royce Phantom and the Chauffeur had assistance from what can only be described as a flower man; someone he hired to set a trail of roses to capture each and every one of Maria's steps when appropriate. As they disembark from the jet, Maria was shocked at the reception. She was already suspicious of Kunle after he insisted that they fly private to Venice, and now this.

Maria: Dude, are you trying to go broke impressing me?

Kunle: It's impossible with you by my side babe, just indulge me these next few weeks and you'll have an authoritative say in how I spend my money.

Maria: What's special about the next few weeks?

Kunle: Well, I don't have any other vacations planned, yet.

Maria: Ah, your money bro! Let's blow it.

Kunle: Common, that's the spirit (reaching out for Maria's hand).

As Maria took the first steps out of the jet, she had to find her footing as her an Kunle had been enjoying a trip to the mile high club during descend. Kunle observing her slight tremble which let to the slight fumble, he smiled and they both heard the band Kunle had hired start playing a cover of Love in Portofino by Andrea Bocelli. Maria took a sharp look back at Kunle, who attempted to gesture innocence and responded:

Kunle: Came with the package.

Maria: Yea, okay.

The couple made their way down to the car as their small bags were traded for Dom Pérignon P2 Plénitude Brut Champagne as the chauffeur placed their luggages in the car. Maria was hiding her amazement, pretty well too as she toasted with Kunle while the band played the music in lowered tone, giving the violinist a solo secession. Kunle made a toast:

"To the love of my life, my forever girlfriend
To the woman whom has loved and inspired me beyond comprehension
To the love of my life and the source of inspiration unlike any other
To my perfect woman, with the perfect heart, and perfect everything I can and cannot see but can feel

To my forever love, my one and only, my chance encounter
I promise to always remember that fate united us because we were destined to be
To my eternal love, I will always choose you and forever serve you and you only
Cheers babe!

Maria: (In tears as she realized the band had started playing Love Me Tender by Andrea Bocelli). That's so sweet babe. I promise to always serve you and never fail to be by your side; in this life and the ones to come. You have captured my heart in a way I did not know was possible and cannot describe.

Kunle: Dance with me?

Maria: Yes babe, my forever dance partner.

The couple started to dance as the flight crew, chauffeur and flower man, watched on. The band got a bit more excited as the harp and violin played, moving Maria to uncontrollable tears, and Kunle's heart got heavy. When the band began to conclude their rendition of Love Me Tender, Kunle thanked them and nodded to the Chauffeur, a signal it was time to begin their adventure. The Chauffeur nodded back and proceeded open the car doors for the couple whom had been dancing on a popup red carpet that was specially set up for them. Kunle stopped swaying and the music came to a complete stop. Maria looking up at Kunle as the onlookers clapped for the couple.

Maria: What are you up to Lover?

Kunle: It's your dream trip, ain't it?

Maria: Is that why it took you so long to bring me to Venice?

Kunle: I wanted it to be a trip you deserve, and you deserve the world babe. Sorry it took me this long.

Maria: Don't set expectations you can't meet.

Kunle: I may have one or two more tricks under my sleeves.

Kunle kissed Maria again, with more passion and more determination this time grabbing her beautiful butt. One of the flight crew member, Sophia, whispered to the pilot, Chris, "I will have that." Their welcoming party at the hanger lasted about fifteen minutes and Kunle led Maria into the car with the Chauffeur, Roberto, holding the door for the couple.

On their drive to the boat, Kunle instructed Roberto to make a stop somewhere and gave him the address. "Where's that?" Maria asked and Kunle responded, "a tailor's shop." Unbeknownst to Maria, Kunle had been scouting for tailors to design his perfect Italian suit. Additionally, the tailor was instructed to take Maria's measurements because Kunle want to memorialize their trip with the perfect outfits.

They arrived at the tailor's shop and Maria's first impression was that this is not your average Italian tailor. They were welcomed by a secretary/assistant wearing Christian Louboutin shoes, a really tight fitting skirt suit, and a really nice shirt that Maria instantaneously said, "I need that shirt."

Christina: We should have one in your size.

Maria: You heard that?

Christina: I hear a lot of things.

Kunle: Not creepy at all Christina.

Christina: Welcome Mr. Olu.

Maria: Y'all know each other?

Kunle: Yea, we go wayyyy back.

Christina: Yes, Mr. Olu and I have been corresponding (speaking with a sexy Italian accent that's deliberately sexy by accentuating certain sounds).

Kunle: Yea, it's by appointment only, but I wasn't expecting her to recognize me.

Christina: It's my job to recognize every one of our clients.

Maria: Talk about customer service.

Christina: Can I offer you something to drink?

Maria: Got any champagne?

Kunle: That's how you're feeling huh?

Maria: Not my fault, you started it Lover.

Christina: Coming right up. I'll tell Enzo you're here. He's excited to meet you both.

Kunle: Thanks Christina and please call me Olu.

Christina: Yes sir.

Maria: What kind of tailor shop is this?

Kunle: The kind that makes a suit that cost fifty-thousand euros.

Maria: Uh oh, please don't' say that.

Christina reemerged with a chilled bottle of Dom, two champagne flutes, and a man dressed in what looked to Kunle like the perfectly fitted suit.

Kunle: You're not joining us?

Enzo: You must be Mr. Olu and the lovely Ms. Maria. I've heard so much about you.

Kunle: You must be Mr. Enzo.

Enzo: That I am (as he reached out for a handshake).

Kunle: Well, very nice to meet you.

Enzo: Likewise. Please call me Enzo (as he pops the champagne)

Kunle: You've got it.

Enzo: Christina, perhaps we can join the happy couple in a toast. Let's make an exception and have a sip with our new clients.

Kunle: Please, we already finished a bottle and we've been in the country less than 2 hours.

Enzo: Haha! Benvenuto in Italia1

Maria: Aye! Sounds like you're complaining about that, Kunle. Grazie!

The crew had a toast "to connections," Enzo said with Kunle following up with "and chance encounters." All echoed cheers.

Christina: I think you guys are my favorite clients so far.

Maria: Hopefully my Lovers' perfectionistic tendencies does not ruin that.

Kunle: Perfectionistic huh?

Maria: I said what I said.

Enzo: Right this way (he said as he gestured towards a beautiful fitting room where a few suits and dresses were hung neatly).

Maria: I love that dress.

Christina: Leave the bottle, I'll put it in the ice bucket so you don't get your hands wet.

Enzo: Good, because it's yours. Let's see how it fits.

Maria: (looking back at Kunle) Lover, what have you done?

Kunle: Nothing you wouldn't.

Enzo: How are you feeling about that beige suit Mr. Olu?

Kunle: I love it.

Enzo: Please try it on in that room, both of you.

The couple disappeared into the inner dressing room. Maria and Kunle reemerged two minutes later, Kunle in a beige suite and Maria in a black perfectly fitting 100% mulberry silk evening gown that fitted her like it was made for the red carpet.

Maria: I am never taking this thing off.

Kunle: Don't make promises you can't keep. You'd have to shower at some point (he said with a smile).

Maria: Oh, it'll not leave my sight when that happens.

Kunle: You look incredible babe.

Maria: Can you make two more of these?

Enzo: I think you may have a few more outfits. Let's see those first.

Christina: Oh my my. Good thing I did not steal that outfit. I don't think I posses the right features to bring it to life like you are.

Kunle: Haha thank you for not doing that.

Maria: Yes, thank you for not stealing it. I would have tracked you down.

Kunle: Can we take these today?

Enzo: Yes, but I need to take Maria's measurement for one more dress.

Kunle: Please, have at it.

Maria: How many outfits are you making me?

Enzo: Please try on the blue, green and white dresses.

Maria: These are all mine?

Christina: And then some. You seem to have a great boyfriend(?) in your hands.

Maria: You heard that lover? Great boyfriend (as she flashed her left ring finger at him).

Kunle: Right, I should put a ring on that finger before you loose it to sharia law.

Maria: Right, or before Enzo attempt to steal me away with these dresses.

When they were done trying on the dresses, Kunle asked if they could keep the bottle and Christina obliged.

Christina: With the amounts of money you're spending? We have a few more bottles for you if you'd like.

Kunle: We'll take that too.

Maria: Speaking of money, how much are these because I seriously want a few more.

Kunle: Only eight thousand euros.

Christina: Speaking of, can I chat with you outside Kunle?

Kunle: Sure.

Maria: Don't steal him away now.

Christina: I'll try not to haha.

Kunle left to settle the tab, which he opted to pay in Bitcoin because Christina told him they'd wave the VAT taxes that way. Maria and Kunle left Enzo boutique with two shopping bags filled with four dresses and two suits. Maria could not believe Kunle has now commissioned a total of twenty five outfits tailored for her on this trip. "I guess we're starting our lives together with a whole new wardrobe huh?" Maria said on their short drive to the doc, where Maria observed a sixty foot yacht dubbed The Maria and wondered, "are we going on that thing?"

Roberto: Give me two minutes sir, let me get everything ready (as he turned the music up, from a playlist curated by Kunle. At this point, When I fall in Love by Michael Buble was playing).

Maria: Lover, what are you up to?

Kunle: I'd have to say I love it when you call me "Lover," babe.

Maria: Lover, answer the question.

Kunle: Hoping to win your heart in Venice. Hoping to spoil you to the point that you cannot think about Venice without thinking about being here with me.

Maria: No pressure.

Kunle: Not at all.

A few minutes later, Roberto opened the door. When the couple exited the car, they were greeted by a staff of four, with another bottle of Dom, two Monte Christo cigars, and Stephanie served them in Versace champagne flutes.

Maria: Now you're just showing off.

Kunle: My imagination is showing off.

Maria: Isn't that the lady that was playing the harp?

Kunle: Where? There was a harp somewhere?

Maria: Shut up.

Lorenzo: Hello beautiful, I'm captain Lorenzo, but please call me Lorenzo (as he placed his white captain hat on Maria's head) and I'll call you Captain.

Maria: Oh, you're bestowing your powers on me?

Band Leader: Ah one, two, (and the music started playing, a cover of I Only Have Eyes for You).

Maria: (whispering in Kunle's ears who reacted with a blush) Oh, you're definitely getting some extra love tonight. You might want to cut down on the champagne Lover, but that has never been a problem for you.

Lorenzo: Nice to meet you Mr. Olu, right this way.

The couple followed the captain onto The Maria as the flower man decorated Maria's path onto the boat. Kunle, with a wide smile on his face as he observes Maria joyfully and almost with an abandoned twirl in her step, followed Lorenzo onto the boat. At this point, Kunle had requested an Afro beats playlist with the band playing a cover of "Ye" by Burna Boy. Kunle imagined himself on the top deck raining down crisp one hundred dollar bills on Maria, Like Leonardo DiCaprio in Wolf of Wall Street saying "fun coupon" as he tosses her money. This time however, the band had an Afro Beats saxophonist which Kunle requested because "it'll add life" to the music. He was right, he had unlocked the vibes as Maria started to bop her head, pour champagne in her glass (after grabbing it for it from the lady carrying it behind her), puffing her cigar, and listening to Afro Beats. "The vibe was vybing," like Kunle would say.

They set Sail for the villa Kunle had reserved for the couple for their four days stay in Venice before they'd go to Rome for another four days, and Lake Cuomo for another 4 days, before returning to Florida.

Maria: I can definitely use a lazy night.

Kunle: Yea? What've you got in mind?

Maria: Are we staying on the boat? How long do we have the boat for?

Kunle: During our stay here and in Lake Cuomo. It's a friend's boat and he's not in the country.

Maria: Fucking Nigerians man!

Kunle: (As he took a long drag from his cigar, and the breeze blowing his tailored cotton shirt) You know we're lit.

Maria: I love it though, I love you.

Kunle: We also have a villa somewhere, with the boat docked in front.

Maria: Also a friend's?

Kunle: No, but I'm paying my friend for his boat, no special treatments.

Maria: Would you charge your friends money to use our boats and say in our villas?

Kunle: With our combined financial situation? No, no need. We don't have to work if we choose not to.

Maria: Good answer.

Kunle: So a chill night in or on a boat? I can make that happen.

Maria: Love the sound of that.

Kunle: We do have a lunch reservation at this fancy spot on the Grand Canal for 4, that's what one of those dresses or any other fancy dress you might have brought is meant for.

Maria: Oh, I'm definitely rocking the white lace. It'll pop with my hair and red lipstick.

Kunle: Which lace is that?

Maria: The dry lace you said was your favorite from Nigeria.

Kunle: Oh, I love that dress. I'm wearing the blue tuxedo Enzo made.

Maria: Seriously, how much is that suit? It's giving I don't let "peasants" touch me vibes.

Kunle: Fifty thousand euros.

Maria: Oh fuck out of here.

Kunle: I'm serious.

Maria: No occasion is worth that much, and besides, that's not who you are.

Kunle: To you, it's not worth that much, but you'll see.

Maria: Either way, it's beautiful and I trust your judgment babe.

Kunle: Now dance with me (as the band switched to Essence by Wizkid and Tems).

The couple danced as the boat gently sailed the Venetian Lagoon to the villa so the couple could go get ready for their "fancy" early dinner/late lunch. They enjoyed a few more Afro Beats rendition by the band and the Saxophonist standing in as the vocalist. When Kunle watched the band's videos on YouTube before reaching out, he realized that individually, each one of the members had been experimenting with Afro Beats, so he just played band coordinator and found them the musical notes to the songs, they practiced and voila! Maria would call Kunle a dork, and Kunle knows she says it as a compliment because he sees things like these.

When they arrived at the villa, it was everything you'd expect. Ancient Italian design with art installations (sculptures, etc.) in the front yard, and all over the garden overlooking the lagoon. Maria was impressed, but wasn't surprised because she adjusted her expectations based on Kunle's spending patterns. They both took a quick thirty minutes bath accompanied with a quickie in the magnificent bathroom that a feels more like a bedroom with the giant four person soak in tub in the middle standing in as the bed. A standing shower with windows looking into the lagoon and a balcony. It's a dream bathroom.

When the pair emerged from the villa to head to dinner, the band was outside awaiting them, along with a camera crew, a new addition Maria thought, as she noticed the blue skies, the sun beaming on the water in front of her, and an assortment of flowers now decorating the villa. The band started to play one of Maria's favorite song, a cover of Cruising by Smokey Robinson.

Maria: This is too perfect Lover, I love it. I love it all. I love you for making this happen.

Kunle: Anything for you Love.

Maria: You know, I don't know what I did to deserve you, but I promise not to change my ways.

Kunle: No need, you're already truly perfect.

Maria: Come on, let's enjoy these expensive photographers you've hired to take photos of us.

Kunle: They really are; notice the drone?

Maria: I trust you to satisfy your thirst for birds eye view of everything.

Kunle: You know me too well.

Kunle picked a red rose from one of the arrangements, shortened the stem, and placed it on Maria's left ear, making sure to not block "her good side." They posed for a series of pictures and the band got set up on the boat as they started to play a cover of I want you Around by Snoh Aalegra, this time with vocals and saxophone as backup. As soon as they stepped on the boat at 3:30 pm, the boat began to sail gently as the couple danced in their fine linen and beautifully perfumed and oiled bodies. The photographing crew came with them on the boat and kept taking pictures of the couple. Maria did not question it as she didn't mind having coverage of her ultra luxurious dream trip sponsored by her Nigerian boyfriend, who isn't a scammer.

When they got to dinner, Maria realized that Kunle had reserved the whole restaurants for their meal; he claimed he did so because he wanted to connect with the inner child so that he could understand why Maria chose Venice as her favorite city. The smaller boat docked right in front of the restaurant.

Kunle: How do you like the restaurant?

Maria: It's perfect, oh my god. You've outdone yourself.

Kunle: Just trying to be your last and most memorable boyfriend.

Maria: You already are Lover, even before this trip.

Kunle: You spoil me with your modesty. I appreciate that about you.

Tommaso: Welcome Mr. Olu and Ms. Maria. Thank you for choosing to dine with us tonight. I hope everything is to your liking.

Kunle: Thank you for having us.

Maria: Absolutely, this is a fine establishment. I'll have to comeback.

Tommaso: I'm sure we will be glad to have you back. Right this way.

Kunle had asked to be seated inside for appetizers to give their bodies time to regulate from the shower and lagoon breeze. The band went outside to get set up as Kunle and Maria sat down inside watching them joke with each other through the windows as Kunle enjoyed his Autumn Fritto Mistos and Maria her Marinated Olives. They paired it with a bottle of fine white Italian wine.

Kunle: What made you decide that Venice was your favorite city?

Maria: As a kid, from reading and watching romantic content. I'd dream and fantasize about vacationing here with a guy, like you, which became later became Idris Elba in college. It was my favorite fantasy in high school. I guess it must have been the new hormones or something.

Kunle: What about as an adult?

Maria: I now know there are more romantic destinations on this planet alone that are more beautiful and sophisticated even. But I'm still incredibly grateful for this fantasy, especially now that's its being fulfilled.

Kunle: (Placing his right hand on Maria's left) I'm glad I'm the man of your dreams.

Maria: Shut up silly (playfully).

Kunle: Common, eat up. You really are beautiful, you know that?

Maria: Thanks babe. Music to my ears.

Kunle: Haha. I might actually write you a song titled beautiful and have it played during our wedding.

Maria: Oh my god. Funny thing is I believe you, dork.

Kunle: Keep calling me dork and watch me embarrass you.

Maria: Can I tell you a secrete?

Kunle: Anytime babe.

Maria: I love it when you embarrass me.

The couple finished their appetizers and migrated to the terrace overlooking the water with boats passing by. Maria made a remark to "where's Waldo" after they've watched like the 50th gondola pass by.

Kunle: We should take a gondola back after our walk. I hope your shoes are comfortable.

Maria: Absolutely babe, you know me too well.

Kunle: Cool.

The couple enjoyed their dinner with the band playing various Italian and American classic romantic Motown hits. After dinner and on their walk, Kunle stopped to reserve a gondola. After their hour leisurely stroll through one of Venice' shopping centers, they returned to their appointment spot. Kunle saw a guy playing the guitar, so and he offered him one thousand euros for his guitar, which he agreed. Kunle settled him and they got on the gondola. Maria watched, wandering what Kunle was up to.

Kunle: How long is the ride?

Andrea: As long as you want, Senior.

Kunle: Sweet. Put us down for one hour. Is it okay if we lay down right?

Andrea: Yes sir.

Maria: Who's sleeping?

Kunle: That steak did it's thing on me haha. I have the itis.

Maria: Haha. I know what you mean.

About twenty minutes into their ride, Kunle grabbed the bottle of fifty year old Maccallan and proposed a toast. He simply toasted to "the rest of our lives." After enjoying his drink and about thirty minutes into their ride, he cleared his throat and began to tune the guitar. Andrea and Maria watched on in amazement as Kunle broke into a song, Marry You by Bruno Mars. Adjusting his position to look Maria dead in the eyes, he broke the silence.

Kunle: This is dedicated to you love, my ride or die.

It's a beautiful night, we're looking for something dumb to do,
hey baby I think I wanna marry you.
It's a beautiful night, we're looking for something dumb to do.

Hey baby, I think I wanna marry you. (Clearing his throat) here we go.

From the top now;

It's a beautiful night, we're looking for something dumb to do,

hey baby I think I wanna marry you.

Is it the look in your eyes or is it this dancing juice?

Who cares, baby, I think I wanna marry you

Well, I know this little chapel on the boulevard we can go

No one will know, oh, come on girl

Who cares if we're trashed, got a pocket full of cash we can blow

Shots of patron and it's on, girl

Don't say no, no, no, no, no

Just say yeah, yeah, yeah, yeah, yeah

And we'll go, go, go, go, go

If you're ready, like I'm ready

'Cause it's a beautiful night, we're looking for something dumb to do Hey baby, I think I wanna marry you

Is it the look in your eyes or is it this dancing juice?

Who cares, baby, I think I wanna marry you, oh

Realizing what was happening when she saw the drone flying and the flower man throwing flowers onto the water from a bridge as the gondola passed by with the sun setting behind them. Maria said "YES!" Kunle, realizing that Maria had caught on, did not stop singing as Maria Yelled yes as she stood up on the boat and leaned into Kunle for a passionate kiss, completely disrupting his performance. He reached into his pocket for a blue box containing an eight carat AAA grade tanzanite ring in 18K white gold that he had designed for Maria.

Maria: OH MY GOD THAT THING IS GORG.

Kunle: (Placing the ring on Maria's ring finger). Perfect fit.

Maria: Yes baby, I see why now. This trip is perfect.

Kunle: Now you know why we're here.

The band started playing as they pulled up to the villa which has been decorated with flowers and set up for an evening dinner with candle light. Maria walked up to the band; can I make a request?

Luna: Si

Maria: Do for love by Snoh Aalegra, with the saxophone, please.

They obliged as Maria retuned to Kunle who poured her a glass of Dom with fresh strawberries and later lit a cigar and a joint. "Let me guess, your friend hooked you up." "No, Christina did," Kunle responded.

The couple enjoyed their champagne as they enjoyed what's left of the sunset and listened to beautiful music and ended up cuddled up in a hammock in the courtyard overlooking the lagoon with Snoh Aalegra playing on the Bose speakers once the band departed after sunset. That night, the couple made passion-filled love, with Maria moaning in tones Kunle had never heard. They also fucked all over the villa because Kunle had expelled the staff of six till the morning, after Maria had warned him to get rid of them. She intended to be "wild and loud" and she did not disappoint. The next morning over coffee and the sound of Snoh Aalegra, Maria reminded Kunle of how lucky she was to be with him.

Maria: You really are perfect, Lover, you know that? I'm really a lucky girl.
Kunle: You inspire me to be perfect Love. And you're saying it like you're making a discovery.
Maria: It's just nice that you never seize to remind me daily how perfect you are and we are together. I'll forever choose you babe.

The rest of the trip was memorable and she loved the sound of people addressing her as Mrs. Olu, at this point she did not bother correcting them.

CHAPTER 22

A STORIED LIFE

On their run on Paje beach that beautiful September morning, Kunle's QC Earbuds helped him zone out, but into his thoughts by minimizing all the background noise, but his mind filled the background noise with the sounds of crashing waves as he's come accustomed to; he felt the waves on his foot that's thoroughly enjoying the feel of the ultra fine!, white!, beautiful!, sand of the great Indian Ocean on Paje Beach!!!; while Roller Coaster by Burna Boy featuring J Balvin played in the background, Kunle reflected on his deep love for Maria still, after ten years of being Married, after that awful phase of the Ex's drama. They had moved to Tanzania together and created a space they both built together; Kunle describes it in conversations with Maria saying "it's like we went on 'God mode' in this game of life" and they got to design their perfect life. They had two charming, cultured, well mannered, strong, caring, resilient, compassionate, empathetic, and advocative daughters; they are a relatively healthy family with resources to live in the highest echelons of any society in the world, and they were happily and madly in love with one another.

Running 100 yards behind him was Maria, who's equally as zoned the fuck out, but on some gangster shit. She also loves the QC Earbuds, so much that she preorders them each time a new set drops. "You're gonna make the kids def babe," Kunle would say, because Maria wanted to give the kids the hand me downs. "They're gonna be fine babe," Maria would say. "Like you always say, 'by the time I go def, they'd have a cure for loss of hearing." They did reach a compromise, which was that the kids will get the Over the ear noice canceling headphones and the ear muffs has to "perfectly fit;" one of Kunle's requirement. Once a new version of all the QC ear and headphones were available, they give the older version to a deserving kid they tutor (employees' kids, farmers' kids, neighborhood kids. Kunle bought them iPads and they use it to tutor).

She was listening to Skeleton Cartier as she imagines how she plans to fuck the shit out of Kunle that night, but mostly after appreciating their unplanned growth together (financial). She imagined that there is a human side to "Capital" that her MBA did not quite cover because it's hard to quantify or teach but something that came naturally to Kunle and translates to their entire little perfect family unit. She always appreciated the amazing dad Kunle is. Despite not wanting children, he agreed to "compromise" and have two. Ever since Maria first informed him that she was pregnant, it as as if Kunle had training as a Midwife/Doula. He became the most loving and caring husband anyone could wish for. Maria never felt so safe, cared for, loved, and worshiped. Maria once asked how come he's such a perfect husband when she's pregnant when he did not want children? Kunle responded and said "the kid is important to you and you're important to me. If your happiness and safety is my priority in life, I have to give you all the support you need in this journey. Additionally, we can afford to hire whatever help or assistance we might need with the kids when it becomes overwhelming."

Not only was Kunle helpful with Maria's daily needs in being a mother, you know, a father and true partner, he was also incredibly prepared for the future. They had set up multiple trusts for the kids in addition to their own separate trusts, something Kunle made sure Maria hired a third party attorney to review, approve, and issue an opinion memo that if their marriage was to dissolve, Maria would not loose what she brought into the marriage, and the kids' trust would be left intact. She appreciated how Kunle never cheats anyone and always made sure that everyone involved in a deal understands the potential upside and downside and understand the risks and rewards because he realizes (mansplain anyone?) they may not understand. She especially appreciated how Kunle had set up an exit strategy "because we live in Africa!" Kunle would always say in his fake thick Nigerian accent to make sure Maria get the message that it might get politically unstable at any point. "This man is a genius," she recalls telling her dad as they played golf in Switzerland on a father daughter vacation Kunle organized for them. She was explaining the corporate structure Kunle put in place to repatriate their earnings.

She changed the song on her smart watch to Everybody Mad by O.T. Genesis, something she heard Kunle listening to while planning their extended trip back to the United States. She recalled the conversation;

Maria: That's odd, why that track?

Kunle: You're dragging me back to some not so familiar places.

Maria: The States?

Kunle: And Nigeria.

Maria: But you're Nigerian.

Kunle: Exactly! I think everyone thinks we're smart and the secrete is we're mostly prepared and always have a plan. So I'm preparing.

Maria: I'll give you that, but can't say for every single Nigerian.

Kunle: Ture, but I appreciate your opinion.

Maria: (She secretly loves how humble Kunle is about accepting compliments) What about England?

Kunle: We're only going for a month and its very familia because it's unfamiliar, and I have a lot of cousins I don't know there, so it's all love.

Maria: What the fuck do you mean?

Kunle: Rephrase the question.

Maria: I mean, what do you mean by it's familiar because it's unfamiliar and all love?

Kunle: Oh because we can play the rich uncle's family card to get away with ignorant shit because we're unfamiliar with their culture and we're tourists.

Maria: Interesting!

Kunle: I know you think it's crazy.

Maria: I see the logic in it, that's all.

"I digress," Maria thought to herself as she also was trying out Kunle's method of preparation and she now realizes that listening to songs from her past seems to help her recall "the character of a place," as Kunle had said. The ocean breeze brought a less gentle wave that caught her attention as she realized that Kunle had stopped at the coffee shop, aka "the fueling station." She appreciated they had both grown healthy and gorgeous and still attracted to each other. She never had a doubt that she'll end up here, she just couldn't put the dream together herself. Their tenth anniversary was that day, and they had a big dinner planned. What was supposed to be an intimate family affair became a get together of "who's who" in their community, as Kunle came to understand when Richard, the Pretentious neighbor everyone knows is not "real," explained to him. Kunle wanted to surprise Maria with a small barbecue sunset dinner at their villa in

Michamvi, Zanzibar, so he sought to engage the head chef, Richard, at their boutique hotel. He did not anticipate Richard telling his wife, who is friends with "some important people."

Kunle recalls his phone call with a minister he was lobbying to fight for a line item in the national budget for youth sports development. "I'm disappointed you did not invite me to your dinner party, it's quite the talk of the town." Kingston said to Kunle.

Kunle: Wait oh!, what is that? What dinner again?

Kingston: I heard you're having a surprise anniversary dinner for the Mrs.

Kunle: Oh yea, it's our 10 year anniversary so I wanted to have something intimate with her and the kids. Her parents would be in town, hell, they live thirty minutes from us, so them too.

Kingston: (Sensing the resentment in his tone, at least Kunle assumed) That's not what I heard at all. All I know is that my wife was shocked that she wasn't picking out a dress for a dinner at your estate.

Kunle: Perhaps we can have a dinner party to celebrate the anniversary of our relocation into your beautiful country.

Kingston: What anniversary? Are you not going to leave us soon?

Kunle: But until then, we can celebrate the mile stone. It would also be a time to publicly appreciate our amazing team.

Kingston: You and Maria really do have something special. The way Lucy is always so happy when she talks about Maria just amazes me. She said she talks like you both have a true partnership.

Kunle: Well, what do you say to her?

Kingston: I ignore her of course, and act like I'm not thinking about it.

Kunle: Haha. Yea, Maria is something. I never thought I'd love being married, but she is just perfect for me. I should write that down for my speech to her.

Kingston: Are you sure you don't want people present? It sounds like you have something up your sleeves.

Kunle: Haha. Yea, I'm sure. But I'll talk to babe about having a dinner party to appreciate Tanzania. I'll tie it to the harvest party. But instead of giving 40% to the community, I'll only sell enough to fulfill deliveries I cannot cancel, and give all the rest to the community? If we do not deliver watermelons, cabbage, etc to Europe, it should not result in a shortage of produce in the European market (he was wrong).

Kingston: I cannot let you leave us. You are exactly the kind of foreign investors we need. You must invite the president.

Kunle: Only if Maria is fine with it. It would be a swell event!

As Kunle recalls, while checking his watch and stopped at their coffee spot. He stared longingly at Maria in her ultra comfortable sports clothes that she somehow cannot get people to stop appreciating with unsolicited stares, even though Kunle always told her that it's the punishment of being gorgeous.

Maria: Babe, I love you.

Kunle: I love you more babe (as he looks at the waiter and ordered two goat milk lattes and toasted croissants). I can't stop thinking about this dinner (they're both seated and facing the beautiful Indian Ocean, with its crystal turquoise water).

Maria: What about it?

Kunle: I don't know, it's not me.

Maria: Yes it is. Just don't think of it as a "big dinner."

Kunle: But it is. Everyone is going to be there. It's really got me reflecting on how I met everyone and what I loved about them.

Maria: Loved?

Kunle: Yea, loved. You know I have to love someone to a certain degree to trust them to work with me, at least at the top levels.

Maria: Yea, I see what you mean. Well, let's go over the guest list on the flight to Moshi and I'll quiz you.

Kunle: Deal!

Their intimate dinner was that night. Kunle managed to maneuver the secrete being out in the open by saying it's the dinner idea he wanted to talk to Maria about. She bought it, and he did not have to lie. "Change the narrative." That was always Kunle's recommendation whenever public figures came to him for consultation on strategy. "Change the narrative as you implement your changes. Don't focus on the praise, it'll come later." It always worked.

To Maria, it was just a regular day. She got Kunle a very nice gift; Kunle had told her he made reservations at one of their favorite restaurants, which, to Maria meant that he has reserved a very huge portion of the restaurant, probably the whole place. Little did she know that a feast was being made, bags being packed for her, and a home spa, including a massage, mud bath, cocktails, is prepared all for them. Best part is the kids are involved up until the massage when they get to go away to the park with the nannies and drivers, who would bring them to Michamvi beach in Zanzibar later the next morning.

Maria: Come back, where did you go?

Kunle: I have something to say to you.

Maria: Please don't ruin my coffee.

Kunle: Wow, that's the first thing you think of? It's our 10 years anniversary and you still think I'll not   know how to deliver news to you?

Maria: Well, yea. So don't ruin my coffee.

Kunle: Wow. Now i just lost my train of thought. I was about to freestyle my appreciation speech to you,   now I wouldn't because I can't.

Maria: So sensitive.

Kunle: And you're such a bully.

Maria: I still find it incredibly difficult that anyone is afraid of you.

Kunle: I don't operate based on fear. I lead by vision and communication.

Maria: I know babe, that's why I love you.

Kunle: Ever since that faithful morning that you slid in my DMs, I knew that you were going to alter the very balance and trajectory of my life, and I allowed it to happen. Somehow I knew that you were my perfect person. Not like you were made for me in some supernatural way, but more like you get me and I get you; we understand each other. There hasn't been a day in the last decade that you ever let me down. I don't know how you managed that. Thank you for always listening to me. You really are my rock and because of that, I make you the choice of my life, daily. And I try my best to show up for us and our dreams and collective ambitions. I especially appreciate how you kept it together when the kids came. A mother like you I never knew I needed, I knew you'd be a perfect life companion. Baby, I don't know what life would be like without you and I don't ever want to find out because I'm sure it'll be dull and full of resentment.

With you baby, my choice is clear. My heart is full and my soul is satisfied. You fill my home with warmth, my boats with your amazingness that money cannot buy. My perfect baby mother, life partner, roommate, wife, friend, and partner. To the woman of my life, the mother of my children, joy of my soul, and the biggest reason I'm able to maintain my peace, thank you for choosing to go at it with me baby!!

Maria was speechless for some time as her eyes got teary; she then grabbed Kunle's hand.

Maria: Baby, no. Thank you. Every day you have managed to show me love so pure and vulnerable that I didn't know was possible. You run every decision by me, even the ones you've already decided. In you I have a true partner. You hide nothing from me, love me, protect and provide for me, and somehow manage to make me feel like the only woman that matters. I don't think you understand that I chose you for reasons unknown to me, but somehow understood by me. You have attended to my every needs, even the ones that made no sense. Like agreeing to have Temi in France.

Kunle: The million dollar baby.

Maria: Our million dollar baby.

Kunle: (Under his breath) Your million dollar baby.

Maria: And how you stepped up to be the best father and husband a woman can ever ask for, even though you didn't want children. (Maria said as she removed some of her big and naturally lusciously curly hair from her face to sip some of her latte on the beautiful blue and white sand beach of Paje) Baby, I'm the lucky one. You always tell and show me your appreciation for me. Most importantly, your trust. I wouldn't chose to do this life with anyone else but you baby. My sugar baby.

Kunle: I love it when you say that. Does that mean I get to suck on your nipples when we get home?

Maria: Shh, we're in public.

Kunle: (Observing Rafiki clearing his throat) So what? Are you not my wife (as he sips from his latte). What's up Rafiki, how are you?

Rafiki: Mambo vipi kaka (What's up brother?)?

Kunle: Fresh (Cool)! Vipi?

Rafiki: Fresh! I saw my brother having coffee with his beautiful wife, so i came to say hello. You guys really   inspire us here kaka.

Kunle: Asante sana kaka. (Thank you brother). It's our 10th year wedding anniversary today, so we're   just having a conversation, reflecting.

Maria: Mambo vipi Rafiki.

Rafiki: Fresh! Mambo vipi dada, and congratulations!!! You guys enjoy your morning.

Kunle: Asante sana!

As Rafiki walked away in his tailored African print fabric, Kunle said "Hey Siri, play She's Royal by Taurus Riley."

Maria: That's how you're feeling?

Kunle: Yes baby, you truly are. And I love you.

Maria: I love you more.

The pair kissed passionately and one of the local kids made a "eww, get a room" comment.

Maria: Let's do it baby, long day ahead.

Kunle: You're right.

The pair put on their ear phones and held each other's hands as they walked bare foot on the beautiful Indian Ocean beach back to their villa.

Later that night, the pair were refreshed, dressed in silk clothes and on their private plane, headed for Moshi, where Kunle had planned an intimate sunset dinner for the family. He had employed the head chef at their lodge in Moshi to prepare a roast lamb dinner with the lamb made in different varieties. Roasted, smoked, fried, etc., etc. And he wanted desserts made out of whatever fruits was in season, with the dinner set on the roof top of their mini mansion that has Mt. Kilimanjaro and the sun sets behind it, as the back drop. Candle light, local Chaga (a tribe in Tanzania) band playing, a fire pit, champagne flowing, lamb eating, edibles consumed, and clothes tailored for the occasion, sweats made from cashmere that Kunle bought the fabric on his trip to India.

Temi: I love you mommy. I love you daddy. (Says Temi, their 5 year old daughter, as she chews with her   mouth full with roasted lamb).

Whitney: I love you too daddy, I love you mommy. (Says Whitney, their 7 year old daughter, who's agreeing with her sister).

Kunle: We love you too, but remember.

Temi: Don't chew with your mouth open.

The dinner was simply delicious. Tranquil, on a clear cool night with a full moon. Kunle had requested that two extra security men, in addition to the four that usually guard the estate. They also brought their Grey Hound (Skip) and German Sheppard (Pit) with them on the trip because the kids insisted, but promise not to bring them on the safari. He wanted the family to enjoy the night sky together as he told stories to the kids around the gas fire pit on the rooftop. Whitney and Temi adores their parents, Kunle and Maria. Their curly hair came from Maria, definitely. Kunle imagines he'd never get that image of Maria fixing their hair while they're both seated on the bathroom counter with the beautiful Indian Ocean as their backdrop. "Y'all look like you should be on a cereal box, you're all so gorgeous," Kunle recalls saying as he went in for a kiss from Maria, rubbing the kids' heads, but they wanted kisscs too.

Though he did not want kids, because he was right, they're a lot of work and frankly still not really worth the sacrifice, he however appreciated Maria for understanding his views and position, and understanding when he needs to just go to their other beach house next door to just "kick it" away from the kids, often times, she joins him. Or when he asks that they sneak a romantic evening on the boat, or out partying with Maria while the nannies watch and care for the princesses.

Kunle: How am I doing?

Maria: How do you mean?

Kunle: You don't have to answer now, but as a husband, how am I doing?

Maria: Okay, I'll tell you later, but I was expecting that question.

Kunle: I love that I'm predictable.

Maria: Me too, no surprises because you always include me in everything. I appreciate you baby.

Kunle: And I adore you baby.

Whitney: You're going to miss it!!! (In the sweetest voice)!

Temi: No, they're experiencing it, right daddy?

Kunle: Yes sweetie, put on your shades.

Whitley: Yes, Temi, put on your shades. You'll see better that way.

Temi: Okay! (In an angelic voice that Kunle knew, and guessed right, would bring Maria to tears).

The whole scenery was amazing as Kunle observed Robert flying the drone over them. He's seen the house from a bird's eye view many times over. The design of the house is quite impressive. It sat on forty four acres of land with perfect landscaping, a soccer field, outdoor basket ball and tennis courts, mini golfing for the girls, and a gym/play area. The main dwelling has eighteen bedrooms with twenty four bathrooms. Maria is glad that she allowed Kunle to design the house, though she is yet to admit it to Kunle; she never thought she'd agree that he has a better way of envisioning things, which translate to amazing designs. The house was designed in such a way that it's hard to miss Kilimanjaro, from every angle in every room. The eco friendly design was one of Kunle's dream houses. Observing the drone, Kunle imagined he had been reflecting on his life from a bird's eyes view. He proceeded to further express his gratitude to Maria.

Kunle: I'm glad you're my partner in all of this.

Maria: How do you mean?

Kunle: I mean, my partner in life. I cannot imagine doing it with anyone else.

Maria: Not without lack of trying either.

Kunle: Whatever, it was a crazy ex.

Whitney: What's an Ex?

Kunle: Usually an old friend.

Whitney: Does their name become "Ex?"

Maria: No honey, you just say that to avoid saying their name.

Temi: I get it, like bingo was an ex pet.

Kunle: Exactly like that sweetie. But you only call someone that you don't want to talk to anymore an ex.

The family finished dinner and danced all night long, and slept under the stars inside a glass auxiliary dwelling unit Kunle installed specifically for nights like these. He was convinced it was a magical night for all the girls, especially when the band started playing classic Berres Hammond and Kunle asked Maria to dance. Skin to skin (as the girls mimic their parents), the cashmere felt oh so soft on their skins. Kunle also had a gift of picking the lightest and softest possible fabric required for comfort for any occasion, a "fringe benefit" Maria would say. Kunle and Maria rotated dancing with the girls under the stars. Kunle did not want the night to end because he always recalls the memory of his own dad dancing with him under the stars on one of the rooftops of the many buildings he grew up in, each always had a rooftop.

The next morning, Kunle had arranged for the girls to be picked up for a safari and insisted that they wore face masks because of the dust. Meanwhile, back at the estate, daddy and mommy were doing daddy and mommy business. Running a mock in the house having wild rabid sex like they were doing it out of spite; on the marble kitchen counter, on the edge of the couch in the living room, the mahogany dinning table, in the bathroom, the 2nd living room, the office, and then they ended up making passionate love and passing out for hours, to the point that they had to rush to have a late lunch with the kids, sweaty, but they smelt amazing because Maria made sure they had the top tier perfumes.

Kunle recalled all of this as he tried to think about his speech for the their dinner with the dignitaries. The President of Tanzania and Zanzibar both accepted their invitation even though he tries to stay out of politics. The dinner was filled with who's whom of their society. Kunle persuaded the top artist in the country to perform a few songs, and then invited a top Nigerian artist to close out the show. All in all, everyone had a blast. Kunle was glad.

His speech was both unnerving, moving, passionate, and appreciative.

"Thank you! I know I say that so much that I think some of you might think I don't mean it or make fun of me for it. But each single time I say it, I mean it. I wish I could accelerate my plans so my dreams and our individual, but connected, visions can be brought to life. It breaks my heart seeing the roads in other communities outside our little bubble all messed up with rain flooding the roads, and people living in buildings that are not finished. With all the money we make in this community, the least we can do is give a little back. This community has been nothing but amazing to me. This country that I fell in love with has accepted me and I'm sorry if I'm speaking out of place, but I promise that if you don't quit me, I'll see to it that we empower those communities like we have empowered and continue empowering the ones we have businesses in. To my amazing staff! Please don't stand up, but I just want to say thank you so so so so so s so so so so so so so much for all you do. I have watched you gone out of your way to assure that our guests and customers get the best experiences. Thank you! Though most of you say it's because of the, bring your family to work day (a perk where each employe gets to bring their family to experience a resort as a high rolling guest, all expenses paid by the company. Kunle imagined if the people providing the goods and services experience the transaction from the side of the customer and imagined they're paying all that money for the experience, they'd go the extra mile when they're serving others; he was right)."

You are nothing but amazing! To the Minsters of Tourism, Agriculture, and Town Planning, thank you for believing in our visions and grand designs. To my top Partners, thank you for all you do to ensure our lives are smooth and efficient. You're simply amazing. And to my most important partner, the equity and blood partner, my amazing wife, Thank you babe, you're my rock!!! To my beautiful daughters, thank you so much! And from us to you, our community partners, thank you!!!

Immediately after his speech, the band started playing a Tanzanian song saying thank you, a special request from Kunle. As The two top artist performed together and close the night out, Kunle was glad that the music distracted everyone because they were all drunk and having an amazing time! Kunle spent the time only focusing on Maria, something Maria always enjoys and Kunle was always happy to do. "She is priority number 1!!!" Kunle will always say it like he's reminding whoever is listening. The pair are great dancers for their demographic, to the point that some people actually enjoy watching them dance, which was odd to the pair, but did not "question the admiration." It was an amazing night, but Kunle warned Maria that he'd probably have to give the presidents a tour of the villages he alluded to in his speech. She was okay with it, she appreciates the fact that Kunle had noble intentions.

The night was full of elegance as people assembled outside Kunle's Masawe resort in Zanzibar. The resort is seven star by all standards, but Kunle priced the rooms as a 3 star hotel (he was making a killing on volume) and paid his staff double the salary of his competitors, and gave them great benefits. So they were always happy to serve and were always pleasant. Often times, guests were surprised by how elegant the resort was; it was beautifully decorated, mostly, by Maria. It has 150 room resort with seven pools and 18 fire pits all on the beautiful Indian Ocean and a gorgeous beach. However, the clear night sky and full moon graced the night with the perfect back drop as the moon was directly above the Indian Ocean, something the guests could see as they pull up to the complementary valet. That night, Kunle was dressed in a silk outfit that he had made and so was Maria. The elegantly designed dress hugged her curvaceous body, a sight to see! Kunle's shoes were designed by a local Italian designer he discovered while shopping during one of his business trips to the country. They were elongated, slightly, giving Kunle the executive look, but his silk outfit that highlights his chest and the fact that he exercised made him look so relaxed and relatable.

That evening, the pair drove to the venue on the road they had helped pave, in their convertible Rolls Royce with the top down and the speed not exceeding 30 miles per hour because Maria insisted that her hair could handle it. She trusted her products (she operates an organic hairline that Kunle supplies the raw materials for and she oversees the production and logistics to distribute/sell in the western markets. She generates hundreds of millions in revenue). Kunle was glad because he wanted to enjoy the drive as the sun prepares to set. Kunle had invited the presidents and a few of the gusts to come watch the sunset from one of the rooftops (Kunle explained to other guests that felt left out that he wanted to play it safe and not exceed the capacity and risk the building collapsing. He set up an equally equipped rooftop on the vertical building in the compound for the remaining gusts. A total of three roof top barbecue was simultaneously happening and Kunle and Maria rotated taking turns to spend time at each.

When Kunle pulled up to the Venue, the girls were being driven behind them in a Mercedes Benz G-Wagon as they watched animal documentaries on the screens. The plan was that the kids would be taken back home after the ceremony and the couple would spend the evening at the resort and stay at their other villa. Kunle in his all black silk outfit, red Nigerian hat (round with no brim), and his fine Italian shoes steps out and waited for Maria as the driver opens the car for her. The pair then proceeded to get the kids out of the car as Kunle holds Temi's hand in her bright multicolored Ankara ("African print") outfit with a ribbon and a flower that Kunle gave her and her sister, in her hair. Whitney's outfit matched her sister's as Maria waited for Kunle and Temi to join them, extending her hand so they can walk into the venue. The family looked classy, stressless, and regal, as they walked the red carpet. One of the staff started to clap as everyone around joins in on the adoration, though to the Olu's surprise. The daughters wave as they ran to go hug Stephanie, their parents most trusted partner (employee). The presidents were observing from their suites because they were staying at the resort.

When the party was over, shortly after nine pm, the couple wanted to take a walk on the ocean, so they decide to drive back home to Paje and walk there.

The drive was simply breathtaking and just as Kunle had imagined and told the story to Maria twelve years earlier when she asked Kunle to tell her a story. The night was filled with stars and which caused Kunle to switch off the headlight at some point so the couple could take it in; Kunle drove home that night relying heavily on the car's sensors. Upon getting to their simple modern villa (which Kunle refuses to call a mansion, thought it had eight bedrooms and sixteen bathrooms), the two took off their shoes and tossed it into the Rolls (as Kazi, their security guard watched and smiled) and immediately raced each other to the beach like two adults in love. The couple ran through the garden, boycotting the house entirely, to get to the beach. Their walk that night was magical with the full strength of the moon felt by both, that special night; Kunle couldn't shut up about it.

Their walk was cute; the water was warm, the sand was soft, the breeze was gentle. The pair enjoyed each other's company as they strolled down the beach in silence, listening to just the sound of the beach. Kunle finally broke the silence.

Kunle: Ever wondered what lies out there in the deep deep ends?

Maria: I know you do, hence you wouldn't be learning to dive.

Kunle: Haha, true.

Maria: I don't want to know though, sometimes ignorance is bliss.

Kunle: That I agree with.

Maria: I do know for sure though, that you'll protect me and that in itself is worth the price of admission.

Kunle: Into the ocean?

Maria: No, into our partnership.

Kunle: Ah, so true. I OFTEN, (stressing the often) feel like I'm living everyone's dream and not their reality.

Maria: How so, sugar?

Kunle: Let's get some BBQ goat meat, I'll tell you more on our walk back.

The couple ordered barbecue from a fantastic local food restaurant to snack on on the roof top of their beach front villa. Kunle felt especially content that night, and so was Maria. She thanked Kunle for seeing that she would be happy here and she recalled seeing her parents amazed the entire night. "I think they had a blast," Maria said to Kunle as she squeeze his hand. The night was simply amazing and Kunle was glad everything was to Maria's satisfaction.

Kunle: What I was trying to say earlier was that I feel like we live a fairytale life; the kind everyone desires, but are not fortunate enough to attain.

Maria: I can see how you'd think that! I want you to know that I'll say yes to you, over and over and over. Sometimes I watch you and just wondered what I ever did to deserve you because I don't think I do.

Kunle: Nah, babe. We deserve each other. We both try and excel at being decent humans and treat everyone like the universe is a rational ex lover with god complex.

Maria: Not the god complex.

Kunle: Yup, I said it.

Maria: You've been hanging with Isaiah too much haha.

Kunle: Nah, but it did say god complex yesterday.

Maria: Don't let Temi hear you call it, "it."

Kunle: Haha, it's a robot. I'll never let her forget how her first crush was a fucking robot.

Maria: At least its not one of the 14 MEN that takes care of us.

Kunle: Or her nanny.

Maria: That too.

Kunle reflected on his life and thought to himself, "It's a sweet life! Thank the younger me for choosing the best partner possible!"

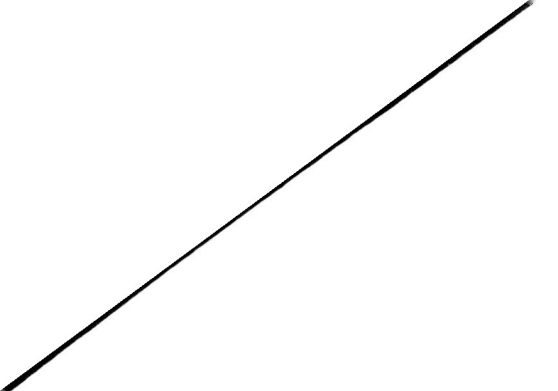

www.ingramcontent.com/pod-product-compliance
Lightning Source LLC
Chambersburg PA
CBHW030755260626
47169CB00001B/65